Sharon Gosling is the international bestselling author of multiple middle-grade historical adventure books for children, including *The Diamond Thief*, *The Golden Butterfly*, *The House of Hidden Wonders* and *The Extraordinary Voyage of Katy Willacott*. She is also the author of YA Scandi horror *FIR* as well as adult fiction including *The House Beneath the Cliffs* and *The Lighthouse Bookshop*. Having started her career as an entertainment journalist, she still also occasionally writes non-fiction making-of books about television and film. Titles include *Tomb Raider: The Art and Making of the Film*, *The Art and Making of Penny Dreadful* and *Wonder Woman: The Art and Making of the Film*.

Sharon lives with her husband in a very small village on the side of a fell in the far north of Cumbria.

Also by Sharon Gosling

The House Beneath the Cliffs
The Lighthouse Bookshop
The Forgotten Garden
The Secret Orchard
The Forest Hideaway

SHARON GOSLING

The Hidden Library

SIMON & SCHUSTER

London · New York · Amsterdam/Antwerp · Sydney/Melbourne · Toronto · New Delhi

First published in Great Britain by Simon & Schuster UK Ltd, 2026

1 3 5 7 9 10 8 6 4 2

Simon & Schuster UK Ltd, 7th Floor,
199 Bishopsgate, London, EC2M 3TY

Simon & Schuster Australia, Sydney
Simon & Schuster India, New Delhi

www.simonandschuster.co.uk
www.simonandschuster.com.au
www.simonandschuster.co.in

The authorised representative in the EEA is Simon & Schuster Netherlands BV, Herculesplein 96, 3584 AA Utrecht, Netherlands. info@simonandschuster.nl

A CIP catalogue record for this book is available from the British Library

Paperback ISBN: 978-1-3985-3891-7
eBook ISBN: 978-1-3985-3892-4
Audio ISBN: 978-1-3985-3893-1

Typeset in Bembo by M Rules
Printed and Bound in the UK using 100% Renewable Electricity at CPI Group (UK) Ltd

For Clare, Louise and Sara-Jade. Thank you.

'For neither good nor evil can last for ever,
and so it follows that as evil has lasted a long time,
good must now be close at hand.'

— MIGUEL DE CERVANTES

Sigh no more, ladies, sigh no more.
Men were deceivers ever,
One foot in sea, and one on shore,
To one thing constant never.

— WILLIAM SHAKESPEARE

Prologue

The wind ripped the breath from her lungs as she tried to turn into it. Across the water Helen saw the two figures struggling in the darkness. The night was so deep and so wild that they were indistinguishable from one another. From this distance they looked like one diabolical creature, limbs writhing as the motorboat lifted and fell, lifted and fell on the riot of waves. It was only when a flash of moonlight broke through the clouds that she saw their two faces, angry mouths stretched wide in shouts that were drowned out by the roar of the storm. A second later, all was darkness again.

A wave struck her own boat and nearly knocked her off her feet, the deck bucking skyward. She clutched at the lifeless instrument panel, feet slipping, knuckles white beneath the driving rain. She could barely see, her hair plastered against her head, teeth crashing together as she shivered in the blasting wind. What could she do? The two boats were being driven apart, each rolling wave pushing them further away from each other. She reached for the radio, but it was dead.

A roaring shout split the air, audible even over the storm, followed by a dull crack and a sharp splash. Then, in another slash of moonlight, the motorboat was visible again.

There was only one figure left standing on its deck. It was impossible to tell who it was.

The moonlight disappeared. The other boat was swallowed once more by darkness.

Time slowed.

The storm raged on.

Chapter One

There was a tiny pink rhinestone glittering on the floor of their plum velvet booth, the kind that probably came from a painted nail. The club was that kind of place: glitzy, over-the-top. Melanie had booked it.

Leave it to me, she'd said, her sing-song voice high and happy when she'd called Helen after seeing the press announcement. *If this isn't a reason to winkle out the whole gang for a night on the town, then what is?*

It had been a while since Helen had been out like this – with the closest of her girlfriends, drinking elaborate cocktails and laughing together. They were all older now, in their thirties. Most of them had families, none of them had much time. The last event she'd seen Mel, Rachel and Jo all at as a group was probably the book launch, almost a year ago now. After uni their meetups had reduced year by year, until mostly confined to weddings and 'big' birthdays, communication in between taking place via WhatsApp group and Instagram update, or quickly snatched coffees one-on-one. But they'd all made time for this.

Her big moment.

Helen smiled at the chatter around her and took another sip of her Old Fashioned – it really was very good, but then so it should be considering what it cost. Melanie made a show of clinking her plastic stirrer against her daiquiri glass as if it were a spoon.

'A toast!' declared Melanie, the friend she had known since they were both only just old enough to walk. The mêlée hushed a little. 'To Helen. We're all *so* proud of you. Your book has already taken over the world, obviously, so a film version of it is just the icing on the cake – but here's to you conquering Hollywood too!'

A familiar trace of electricity skittered across Helen's shoulders. The movie deal had been in the ether for months – before *All of the Above* had even been published, long before it hit multiple bestseller lists around the world. The idea of it had risen like a myth, a rumour, something dreamed up and talked about but forever ephemeral and definitely not real, *never* real. But now, impossibly, it was. Her novel was going to be made into a film by—

'. . . by Perle Anders, no less,' Jo added, her glass held high. 'The greatest film actress of our age has chosen an adaptation of your book as her directorial debut. I don't know how you're keeping your head,' she added. 'I would have exploded the minute I found out!'

Helen laughed, because *yes*. It really *was* utterly surreal.

'It's crazy, isn't it?' she said. 'I keep thinking I'm going to wake up and someone will tell me it was all just a joke.'

Melanie reached out and pulled her into a hug, the daiquiri sloshing with dangerous momentum. 'You deserve it,' she said, her chin squashed against Helen's shoulder. 'You, more than anyone, deserve all the good things.'

'Well, *that*'s not true,' Helen said, hugging back. 'But thank you all so much for being here to celebrate with me. I love that we've all managed to stay in touch, despite everything. Despite *life*.'

'Hey,' Rachel said. 'We're women supporting women. That's what it's all about, isn't it? Just like you wrote about. In your book . . . *and* in this film.'

The assembly cheered, glasses were raised and emptied, and their waitress for the night reappeared to take another very expensive order.

'Will you get to be on set while they're filming?' Melanie asked later, as she reapplied her mascara in front of one of several huge gilt-framed mirrors that took up the whole wall. 'Oh my God – will you actually get to *meet* Perle?'

The ladies' bathroom was another lush expanse of velvet, though teal-coloured this time. It was large enough to have a powder room with actual thrones beside floor-to-ceiling mirrors and ceramic sinks as well as cubicles. Helen sat, angling herself so that she didn't have to look at her own reflection. The atmospheric lighting only highlighted her imperfections: that awful, unnatural kink in her nose. As with so many things in life, it was best not to look.

'I already have met her, actually,' Helen said. 'Well, sort of. We had a meeting over Zoom.'

'*What?*' Her friend turned to look at her, agog. 'How did I not know about that the *second* it happened?'

Helen spread her hands. 'I couldn't tell you. NDA. Wasn't allowed to say anything to anyone until the deal was signed. It wouldn't have happened otherwise. Even now there's tons of stuff I can't talk about.'

'Well,' Melanie said, 'as long as they're not changing a single thing about the story. *All of the Above* is the new feminist bible for a reason.'

'Don't call it that,' Helen said, with a grimace. 'It's just setting me up for a fall. It's just a book, that's all. Just a story.'

'*I* didn't call it that,' her friend pointed out. 'That was the *Guardian*. Anyway, what have you got to be worried about? No one's had a bad word to say about it since it came out.'

Helen shifted in her seat. A throne wasn't made for comfort. 'There'll be someone out there wanting to take me down a peg or two. There always is.' There was a brief silence, and Helen looked up to find Melanie watching her. 'What?'

Her friend shook her head. 'You're the author of a runaway worldwide bestseller and you still can't be confident enough to hold your head up. I hate that. I mean, I know *why*. But I hate it.'

'It's not that I'm not confident in myself,' Helen said, as

her phone bleeped in her clutch. 'I just don't have much faith in other people.'

She pulled out her phone. The bleep had been a text. The number wasn't in her phone, but it only took her a second to realize who it was from. She stared in shock as Melanie said something, but Helen had been consumed by a horror so cold and expansive that she didn't hear anything beyond a distant mumble from very far away.

'Helen? What is it?'

When Helen didn't answer, Melanie moved closer, taking the phone from her hand.

Darling, the text read. *What news. So happy for you. Looking forward to seeing what you've got for me on the film. Calling in my marker, lol. Let's chat soon? It's been too long. I've missed you. B xxx*

Melanie read it with a frown on her face. She looked up, about to ask a question, but something in Helen's expression meant she didn't need to.

'No way,' Melanie said. 'No, it can't be. It's not . . . that's not from *him*?'

'It is,' Helen whispered.

'You're not still talking to him?'

'No,' Helen said, hoarsely. 'I'm not, I haven't, not – not in for ever. It must be ten years! More.'

Melanie shook the phone. 'How is he not blocked?'

'He is,' Helen said, faintly. 'That's not . . . it's a new number.'

'And what the hell does he mean, he's "calling in his

marker"?' her friend demanded. 'He – what? Wants a part on the film? Is that it? Is he that delusional? Is he . . . is this *blackmail*? Does he really think—'

Helen's head spun. All those very expensive whisky cocktails were not playing well with the sudden tumult in her gut. She pushed herself up, stumbled to the nearest toilet, and threw up, noisily.

'Oh, screw this,' she heard Melanie say behind her. 'He's not doing this to you, not again. I'm going to answer, all right?'

Helen tried to say no, but her body was too focused on rejecting everything inside her. By the time she'd emptied her stomach, it was too late. She knelt on the floor, trembling.

'There,' Melanie said, triumphant. She pushed her way into the cubicle beside Helen and held out the phone so that Helen could see the screen. Melanie swayed a little in her drunken state. 'That's what I've said. Read it, and then block the bastard.'

I DON'T OWE YOU A THING, YOU WASHED-UP OLD CREEP, the text read. *CONTACT ME AGAIN AND I'LL TELL YOUR WIFE, LOSER.*

Helen stared at the screen, sweating, blurred at her edges, a storm at her centre. 'You didn't . . . you didn't really send that?'

'I did.'

Helen's heart died a little more. 'But he'll think I wrote it!'

'That's the whole point,' Melanie said. 'Right, I'm blocking him now.'

'Wait—'

Helen grabbed for the phone, but Melanie held it out of reach. Her face was set hard. 'If you apologize to him, I will never forgive you,' she said. 'I am not doing this again. *You* are not doing this again. Do you remember what this leech did to you?'

Helen swallowed. 'Yes,' she said. *Except*, said that accusatory whisper, *what had he done, really, besides take what she'd offered him?*

'Good,' Melanie said. She pressed a button on the phone screen, waited for a second, then handed it back to Helen. 'Then you'll thank me in the morning. Come on. We both need another drink. And then another after that. And then a whole load more after that. You're celebrating, remember? We're celebrating *you*.'

Helen hoisted herself up from the floor. Her phone screen informed her that the number had been blocked.

'Come on,' Melanie shouted, over her shoulder. She'd opened the door to the bar, and the sound of people partying on into the night flooded past her into the quiet of the bathroom. From a distance, Helen heard a collective cheer from Rachel and Jo at Melanie's reappearance. 'Let's chase that monster out of your mind. We did it once. We can do it again.'

There was a loud, incessant and extremely unpleasant cacophony echoing somewhere far too near her ear. It stopped and started a few times before Helen surfaced enough to realize that it was a phone ringing. *Her* phone. Her mobile.

Where was it? She tried to move her head, but discovered that someone had hammered a whole box of razor-sharp nails into her skull while she was passed out. She was tangled in sheets – Helen opened her eyes enough to work out that she was at home, at least, in her own bed, fully clothed and alone – and had the worst hangover she'd had in years, the malevolent sort that crawls right into your psyche and presides over your dying soul. She lay there, trying to work out how she'd got into this state. She rarely drank much, but they had been celebrating, hadn't they? Yes. That was it. Whisky cocktails. The carpet bomb of drinks. Had she somehow forgotten that she was no longer in her twenties?

The phone rang again. Helen scrabbled to find it without opening her eyes, levering herself up amid her pillows. The screen was a floodlight, so bright she couldn't look at it. She tried to stop it ringing but ended up answering it instead. She knew she'd done this because she could hear a strident American accent barking at her from the other side of the planet.

'Helen? Are you there?'

She belatedly identified the voice as belonging to Claude Ripley, one of the executive producers she'd been working with as part of the film deal. A perma-tanned thirty-something Californian with teeth whiter than the ceramic of her kitchen sink, he'd immediately reminded Helen of Rob Lowe: definitely from the same gene pool. Claude described himself as 'the money wrangler'. They were about the same age, but he always made her feel like a clueless teen. Conspicuous success oozed like aftershave from his every pore.

'Claude?' She angled herself up more, gingerly winching the phone to her ear.

'Helen? I've been calling you for hours.'

'S-sorry,' she muttered, rubbing one hand over her eyes. They were gritty. Had she taken off her make-up before bed? Unlikely. The pain got worse as she tried to lift her head. She felt sick. 'I've been . . . I'm not—'

'Did I *wake* you?' Claude asked, incredulous.

'I . . . What time is it?'

'It's after eleven there,' Claude said. 'Were you seriously sleeping in? We need to talk. This is a disaster. Is it true?'

'What?' Helen asked, utterly confused. 'Is what true?'

There was a pause on the other end of the line. 'Get it together. I'm sending you a conferencing link now. Be online in twenty. Got it?'

'Okay,' she managed. 'Got it.'

He rang off and Helen dropped her phone, sinking back amid the debris of her bed. A second later a piercing *ping* announced the arrival of the promised link. They wanted her to have a meeting, now? There hadn't been one scheduled, she knew that much – not that she'd intended to have a hangover this bad, or at all, but she wasn't a complete idiot. She'd never have agreed to a night out if she'd known she had to be on top of her game the next day. Anyway, wasn't it the middle of the night over there? And wasn't it Saturday? She was pretty sure it was Saturday, unless she'd somehow lost an entire weekend and this was now Monday morning, which she did not think was the case because she could hear her downstairs neighbours moving about and Helen only ever had proof anyone actually lived there at the weekend. If it were 11am on a Monday morning, they would be at work. And what was with Claude's attitude? She'd got used to the weirdly abrupt West Coast manner, but he'd been downright rude on that call. What was all that about a disaster? Was there some problem with the film deal? If there was, it wouldn't be her issue to sort out, surely? Should she call her agent? Probably.

Helen went to pick up the phone again but raising her head made it spin like that scene from *The Exorcist*. Bile rose in her throat. Also like that scene from *The Exorcist*, actually, and she definitely didn't want to think about that at this moment. Bad idea. All bad.

Get in the shower, she told herself. *Casino Royale it. That'll help.*

She crawled out of bed and made it to the bathroom. There was no chance of her standing up, so Helen sat in the shower tray and let the water cascade over her hot skin. It helped, a bit. Enough to clear her thoughts a little, anyway. What the hell was going on? Helen never drank this much. She tried to remember the night before as she levered herself to her feet to turn off the shower, but being upright just made her hopelessly dizzy. Helen realized she really was going to be sick, made it to the toilet just in time, and it was as she was dragging her hair back from her face that she had a flashback.

She'd done this last night, hadn't she? She'd been sick and Melanie had been there—

It's not . . . that's not from him*?*

I'm going to answer . . .

Helen coughed and gasped, and as she sat back on the cold tiles of her bathroom floor, she heard her phone ringing again. Icy fear crawled up her spine as her recall returned. The name of a man she hadn't seen for years popping up on her phone. Her reaction. *Melanie*'s reaction.

Oh no.

Her phone had stopped ringing again by the time she got to it. There was a string of missed calls and unopened text messages. The last one was still previewed on her screen. It was from Melanie.

I'm so, so sorry, it said. *This is my fault. Should I come round?*

Helen pulled on a pair of jeans and a white shirt, dragged a comb through her hair and scooped it back into a ponytail, only towel-dry because she couldn't face drying it and anyway, she didn't have time. She went into the kitchen and drank a pint of water standing by the sink, then swallowed paracetamol and ibuprofen even though she knew it was bad to take both at once. Helen had a feeling her life was already over, so what was the point in suffering more than necessary on her way down? She poured herself another pint of water and got out her laptop, standing it on the kitchen counter. She didn't want to sit; her nerves were raw, she was stripped to the bone. She couldn't touch anything, couldn't settle.

'Jeez,' Claude said, the minute his face coalesced on her screen. 'You look like shit.'

'I'm sorry about earlier,' Helen said, voice hoarse. 'I had a few too many drinks last night. We were celebrating.'

'Celebrating. Right,' he said. His face was stony, his tone sardonic.

'I haven't . . . I don't know what's going on,' Helen said, weakly. She could guess. The gist of it, anyway. That text from Melanie. *Both* texts from Melanie, the one she'd sent to *him* and the one this morning. *I'm so, so sorry*. But she didn't *know*.

'Does that mean you haven't been online today?'

Helen shook her head, immediately regretted it, and squeezed her eyes shut against the pain. The shame. This was surreal. She'd spent so long expecting this to happen, and yet now that it had, she couldn't quite grasp it. 'I was . . . asleep until I answered your call.'

'Right,' Claude said again. 'Well then, let me ask you straight. Because maybe, just maybe, we can make all of this go away. As long as you can give the right answer to this question. Okay?'

'Okay,' Helen said, faintly.

'Here we go then,' said Claude. 'Have you, Helen Thorne, at any point engaged in an affair with actor and married father of two, Brett Pottinger, husband to beloved British actress Alice Marsh?'

'Yes,' Helen said. 'But—'

On the screen, Claude held up a hand to stop her. 'Thank you,' he said. 'That's all Ms Anders will need to know.'

Chapter Two

Helen would have turned off her phone and shut her laptop, but between the calls and emails from muckrakers and journalists were others from her agent that she needed to answer. From her publisher, too. They had been about to launch pre-sales of her second book, to make the most of the film announcement, but now they were 'holding back while Marketing and Sales looked at a few things.' By that evening, it was clear that Helen's career – such as it had been – was over.

'Is there a Me Too element here?' was what her agent, Katy, wanted to know. 'Because you know, if there is—'

'There isn't,' Helen said, even though she could imagine what Melanie would be screaming into her ear if she could hear this conversation. '*Tell them! Tell them what happened! Tell them everything, right now!*'

'You just – chose to sleep with a married man? A man with a family? A man married to an actress universally beloved by the British public?'

It wasn't like that, Helen almost said. But what was the point? She'd dug this hole for herself, hadn't she? And he'd warned her, that first time she'd told him she didn't want to see him again. He'd warned her that if it ever came out, all the British press would care about was that she'd made a mockery of poor, plucky underdog Alice Marsh. She could still see his face as he'd said it. Grinning, because he was 'joking', but really because he knew he'd already won a war she hadn't even known she'd been in until that very moment.

'Yes,' Helen said instead, because she was having trouble forming words of more than one syllable.

'Well,' Katy said, heavily. 'I'll do what I can. But I have to tell you that this has caused havoc with the Americans. They want out. They're bellowing about the disrepute clause in the contract. Disrepute! As if they hadn't all gladly taken Weinstein's dollar back then. It's all tosh, of course it is, but I don't have to tell you they have more lawyers than we'll ever be able to muster. It wouldn't be quite so bad if you hadn't *embarrassed* them all so, Helen. That goes for the Americans *and* the critics on both sides of the pond. They've all been banging on about how you're the voice of the modern self-made woman and now it turns out you were knobbing another self-made woman's husband for quite a long time. She was raised in foster care, Helen. She was a homeless addict between the ages of eighteen and twenty-one. The term "to pull yourself up by the bootstraps" could have been coined for her. One can see their point.'

'Yes,' Helen said, again, too defeated to say anything else.

What would be the use? There was no defence. She'd done it, after all.

'Anyway, I don't want to pile on,' Katy said. 'I'll do my best. It'd probably be a good idea for you to lie low for a while.'

'Yes,' Helen said a final time, and hung up the phone, which immediately rang again. She glanced at the screen to see that it was Melanie, but that was another conversation she couldn't handle right then, so she cut it off and called her mother instead.

'I've been getting messages from all and sundry all day,' said Irene Thorne, when she answered. 'I didn't want to believe it. Brett Pottinger? Mind you, I always thought that sounded like a made-up name. Like it should be on a champagne label instead of a person.'

'It's not real,' Helen confirmed. 'His actual name is Bertie Piggle. He changed it.'

'Well, yes, you would, wouldn't you?' said her mother, and sighed. 'Oh, Helen. I thought we'd raised you better than that.'

Helen's eyes filled with tears. It wasn't worth trying to explain, she knew that. There was no good in feeling sorry for herself: she'd got herself into this situation, after all. But she hated that she'd let her mother down. Again. The film was something she could have been proud of, and now—

'I'm sorry,' she said. There was a brief silence in which Helen thought they were probably both thinking about her father, long gone (a relief, given these circumstances) but such a hard-working, upstanding man. 'Mum, I've got to get away. Can I come there? Can I come to Spain?'

Her mother was speaking to her from the holiday villa she'd bought on the Costa del Sol after Helen's father had died. Brexit had been a nightmare, but Irene was a solicitor and tenacious by nature. She loved the place, had kept it despite all the red tape, and 'popped out' as often as she could, renting it to holiday makers the rest of the time unless Helen wanted it herself. It was spacious enough for them both to be there, gleaming and white-washed, with a small outdoor pool and a balcony overlooking the blue, blue sea: lemon trees in the garden, fresh fish at the restaurants down by the marina.

'I'm not sure that's a good idea, darling, is it?' her mother asked. 'It wouldn't take much to find you here – it's the summer holidays; there are a lot of Brits about, you know – and I can't imagine photos of you lounging by a pool beneath the Spanish sun with a glass of Fino in your hand would make the best impression right now.'

Helen squeezed her eyes shut. Her mother was right, of course. She very often was.

'But listen,' her mother said. 'If you really want to get away from it all, I've got another idea. How about an island off the coast of Northumberland?'

'A what? Where?'

There was a rustling on the other end of the phone, as if her mother was wrestling with something. Her voice was muffled for a moment, and then cleared again. 'Just getting the details up on the iPad,' she said. 'We've been trying to work out how to deal with it. The firm's got this client who died. Cyril Gissing, his name was. He owned an island off the coast of Northumberland.'

'He owned an *island*?'

'Just a small one,' her mother said, as if this somehow made it less extraordinary. 'Rathbrooke, it's called. Technically it's a Farne Island, but unlike the others, it's not owned by the National Trust. Anyway, long story short, he's died with no obvious heirs – he certainly doesn't have any direct family, which is a problem as we don't have a will on file. He'd asked us to get rid of the old one because he was in the process of updating it to reflect some sort of change in circumstances, but that was several years ago. We should have followed up, but he was Jared's client. Gissing stayed with the firm when he moved on and with one thing and another it slipped through the cracks. Gissing was a very quiet client, we rarely had contact with him, and it doesn't look as if he ever supplied us with the new one. We're the executors, so we need someone to go up there, find the will if there is one, and also deal with the house. He was a bit of a collector – he's got all sorts of antiques and books, I think. It needs cataloguing and such, so that we can begin to sort out probate. No one in the office really wants to deal with it. It's a long way to go and it sounds pretty primitive, even though it's Grade I listed. As you might expect, it being an island you can only get there by boat and there's no phone or internet signal in the house, either. Which for most people would be a pain in the arse, obviously, but might be perfect for you at the moment. And what with that Master's you did, I know you could handle it.'

Helen winced at this further reminder of a painful period in her past. When her acting career had fallen apart, she'd turned, as always, to books. Specifically, she'd hidden away doing a postgrad degree at Edinburgh University, studying for an MSc in Book History and Material Culture, spending as much time as she could amid their immense library of rare volumes. Helen had half thought that she might become a librarian: closet herself away in a dusty private collection or museum somewhere, with only old books for company.

Helen stared blearily around her small living room. It was lined with books, which were still her insulation from the world. The only patch of wall without bookshelves was the one her writing desk was set against. On the wall over it she had proudly hung a framed poster of *All of the Above*. It had seemed like such an achievement, to publish a book. A door of her own making, that she could open and step through into a new world: a solid, level ground she'd been trying to reach for years after tumbling to the bottom of a ravine that had once seemed impossible to escape. How she wished now that she'd stuck to her original plan: to look after the books of others instead of writing her own. If she'd known what a stir *All of the Above* would cause, she might not have even tried to publish. She'd known, however, what many readers don't: how few books hit the kind of numbers hers had accomplished. How many books – and authors – vanish into obscurity after publication. This truth had made her feel that she would always remain in safe anonymity. It hadn't even occurred to her to use a pen name. Her initial panic at its success had subsided over time, when there had been no sign of the kind of blowback she'd been bracing for since she'd finally torn herself away from Brett's influence. But now . . .

'Okay,' she said. 'I'll do it. I can leave tomorrow. Can you send me the details?'

'Will do,' said her mother, juggling again. 'That's great, actually, truly, because my junior Mick was beginning to think I might send him, and he seems to have some sort of visceral fear of anything further north than the Watford Gap.'

Helen packed that night. Her mother emailed her a slew of instructions and a legal agreement for her to sign digitally that made her an official agent of the firm, with a modest temporary salary. She read the contract and signed. What else was she going to do? The phone hadn't stopped ringing. If they didn't already know where she lived, they'd find out soon enough. She imagined Brett and Alice were having a tougher time of it, being the more glamorous end of the story (and, yes, she did feel guilty about Alice, of course she did, she always had, even when . . .), but *she* was the Scarlet Woman. Someone somewhere would be itching for a photograph of her. The more she thought about it, the more Helen was glad her mother had pointed out the folly that would have been her dashing off to Spain. If anyone did get a snap of her, she needed to at least look as if she were in sackcloth and ashes; as if everything in her life had burned to the ground.

Which it had.

The only person Helen told about her plan to go north was Melanie, and that was because she needed to borrow her friend's car. She was afraid that if she took her own and drove straight from the flat it would be too easy to follow her, island or no island. Perhaps that was paranoid. Perhaps not.

'I'm so sorry,' Melanie said, as soon as she picked up the phone. Her voice sounded hoarse, as if she'd been sobbing. 'This is all my fault, I should never have—'

'None of that matters now,' Helen said, cutting her off. 'Really. It doesn't. What's done is done, okay? It was going to come out sooner or later anyway, wasn't it? It was insane of me to think it wouldn't.'

'But how *did* it come out?' Melanie asked, still sobbing. 'We were on our own in that bathroom. And we didn't even say his name. If you look online, there's so much *detail*.'

'It was him,' Helen said, tiredly. 'Brett. He used to say it all the time: *Better be nice to me, Helen. You wouldn't want us to be splashed all over the tabloids, would you?* He'd say it like he was joking. After a while I realized he wasn't, not really. It was a warning.'

'But – why?' Melanie asked, still crying. 'When he was in it too?'

'Because he wanted me to be scared of what would happen,' Helen said. 'It worked. He always said I'd be the one they came after if it came out. That text you sent probably pushed him over the edge because he thought I wasn't scared any more. And, look – he was right, wasn't he? I *am* the one they've come after.'

'Only because they haven't heard the other side of the story,' Melanie argued. 'Helen, you've got to fight back. I know you blame yourself for all of it, but you need to tell them what happened when—'

'I don't,' Helen said, refusing to listen. 'It won't help. None of it. It'll only make it worse. We had an affair. He didn't force me into it.'

'He lied though, didn't he? That they weren't together anymore. And you were so young—'

'I was old enough to pick up a phone,' Helen said. 'I was old enough to find out for myself. I wanted it to be true, so I went along with it. And then it was too late. That's on me. That'll always be on me, Mel. Anyway, that's not why I'm calling. I need your help.'

Melanie was more than happy to put Helen on her insurance. They worked out a way of thwarting any potential tails that made Helen feel as if she were an extra in an episode of *Slow Horses*. It involved an early-morning exchange of cars at the Bluewater shopping centre. Helen hoped that the general chaos that was forever the Dartford Crossing combined with a different vehicle would thwart any followers. And if anyone followed Helen's car, they'd find Melanie driving it.

When they met the next morning, Melanie gave her a fierce hug and tried to apologize again.

'This isn't fair,' she said. 'You know that, don't you? This *isn't* your fault. It never was.'

Helen would never believe it, and she didn't want to have that conversation. Not again. She wondered if she'd ever feel anything other than utterly exhausted ever again.

'I've got to go,' she said, pulling away from her friend after one final squeeze, unfamiliar car keys in hand. 'Thanks for the car. I'll be in touch. Please don't tell anyone that you've seen me.'

Chapter Three

Helen's journey to Northumberland took her up the A1 motorway, splicing England from south to north as she by-passed (among others) Cambridge, Leeds, Darlington and Newcastle. She would travel further and further north until, a few miles short of the Scottish border, she reached the small coastal town of Seahouses, where her mother had arranged for Helen to meet someone named Rufus at a pub called the Schooner Inn. It was Rufus who would take her by boat to Rathbrooke Island.

It did not occur to her to ask exactly who Rufus was, but she assumed he ran some sort of water taxi service. She also hadn't looked up the Farne Islands. She had vaguely heard of them (hadn't there been a famous folk group called Lindisfarne back in the day? And wasn't that where they'd filmed *28 Years Later*?), but since Irene had been so nonchalant about the fact that a) her firm had a client that owned 'just a small one' and b) it seemed an easy proposition to hop to it from the mainland, in Helen's mind it had become one of several that the locals zipped between, probably all day and as easily as she popped to Tesco's for milk. She hadn't researched it on Google because the idea of going online at all filled her with a deep, existential dread.

With a seven-hour drive, however – she couldn't put the radio on in case a news bulletin reminded her of what was on her heels – Helen thought it would probably be a good idea to find out where exactly she had committed to going.

'Siri,' she said to her phone, which was mounted onto her dashboard so that it could provide her with directions. 'Tell me about Rathbrooke Island in Northumberland.'

There was a sliver of a pause while Siri thought about it, and then a disembodied voice announced that this was what it had found on Wikipedia.

'Rathbrooke Island is a landmass in private possession situated in the North Sea, due south of the Farne Islands in Northumberland, England. Just over a mile off the coast, it is the closest of this small island chain to the mainland and the only landmass in the archipelago not administered by the National Trust. The island covers an area of approximately ten hectares. The largest structure on the island is Rathbrooke Hall, which has been the seat of the Gissing family since 1604, when the island was gifted to Stanhope Gissing, the then Duke of Northumberland. The stately home is notable for having been constructed around a peel tower that had been erected in the previous century.'

That seemed to be all the information that Siri could glean. It seemed extraordinary to Helen that a great house standing since 1604 could have had so little written about it, but she supposed that if it were still in the same family – or at least it had been until the death of its most recent occupant – a private island could be very private indeed. She really had nothing to go on, except . . .

'Siri,' Helen asked the air, again. 'What's a peel tower?'

This time the answer was swifter, but just as concise.

'Peel towers were fortified buildings, often square keep-like structures of several storeys, which were constructed along the borderlands of Northern England and the Scottish Marches during the fourteenth and fifteenth centuries. Their primary purpose was defence, and as such they were generally constructed with very thick stone walls and narrow slit windows. They were used as places of refuge for both people and animals during times of unrest, when whole communities would shelter within their walls until danger had passed.'

Despite Wikipedia's description of Rathbrooke Hall as a 'stately home', the image instantly conjured in Helen's mind by this explanation was less Pemberley and more decaying Gormenghast. A square, windowless keep with a mass of terrified people and farm animals crammed into it sounded to her like the precis of a horror film.

The idea of an isolated island had seemed like the perfect situation yesterday. Now, with the image of a thick-walled, dank and gloomy hovel looming in Helen's head, especially one recently abandoned by an old man so isolated he'd had no family, she was having second thoughts.

She only noticed the weather changing when she had to

put the windscreen wipers on as the first drops of rain hit the glass. It was then that she saw the darkening sky, the thick, gathering clouds lit an ominous deep grey-blue by the afternoon light. By the time she was finally bypassing Newcastle, at least an hour late thanks to an accident near Scotch Corner, she could feel the wind pushing against the car and the rain was lashing her windows. It wasn't yet 5pm but night had decided to come early.

She was still on the A1, but it was smaller now, edged by a different landscape. The North Sea was close, not that she could see it in the state that was beyond her windscreen. The wipers were doing overtime to bat away the driving rain, but even in the short seconds that they were able to clear her view, all she could see beyond was a lurking mist that shrouded blank fields and stands of trees huddling together like cliques of muttering gossips. Everything was grey, lost in itself. She drove on, wishing she'd stopped at the motel she'd seen across the forecourt of the last service station she passed. This thought was compounded when Siri announced that she had a message, which turned out to be from her mother.

Just seen the news about the storm, Siri relayed. *Hope you're not driving into it.*

Helen, hunched over the steering wheel, swore. Should she turn back? She was moments away from doing just that when she saw the exit for Seahouses, which was now only seven miles away. She could make that.

She could barely see Seahouses as she drove into it, but got the impression of yellow sandstone, and was just able to make out a small high street lined with smaller shops, a mid-sized Co-op, an amusement arcade, fish-and-chip restaurants and takeaways – all closed now, though she had no idea whether this was because of the weather or the fact that it was a Sunday. There was no one on the streets, though that wasn't surprising given that the rain and wind hadn't lessened. The roads grew narrower as she followed the directions to the Schooner Inn. She crawled along, peering through the windshield. Through the sheets of rain she saw lit windows and drawn curtains. Almost every windowsill had either a model sailing boat or a lighthouse in it. Every house had a name too, instead of just a number, most neatly carved on slate and mounted beside a key safe. Holiday lets, all of them.

The pub came into view on a corner, beyond which she could see a slope leading down to the darkened harbour and beyond it the North Sea, bucking like a live thing. Helen looked for a parking space and pulled into a small gap that had no yellow lines. The road was really too narrow for even Melanie's little car, but still, Helen had no idea where else she was supposed to park. She could move when she knew more. She leaned on the steering wheel for a moment, relief flooding through her. She'd made it this far, at least. The rain hammered over her head, deafening. The wind was howling down the narrow street. What would they do now? Surely no one would go out in a boat in a storm like this? Rufus would want to go home, no doubt. She'd have to find somewhere to stay. She hadn't passed any big hotels, just street after street of

Airbnbs. She took her phone from its dashboard cradle and sent her mum a quick text: *Storm here but so am I. Just going to meet Rufus.*

Helen pushed open the car door, battling the wind. Leaving her case in the car, she ran across the narrow street to the pub, soaked even by that small journey through the rain. She pushed open the door and went inside. Wiping the rain from her face, she was about to ask if anyone knew Rufus when a figure heaved himself up from a stool beside the bar. Though stooping slightly with age, he was tall and broad-shouldered, with white hair and a face hewn of angles that made him look like the sort of sculpture of a fisherman that would stand in the window of one of the holiday cottages up the road. He was in an old and oft repaired navy wool sweater that looked handmade, layered over other sweaters that were equally well worn. His hands bore no wedding ring and were even more weathered than his clothing.

'Helen Thorne, is it?' he said, bluntly.

'Rufus?'

'Aye. You should have been here ages ago. I've been waiting.'

'I'm sorry,' Helen said, although she thought it was only just over an hour later than the ETA she'd given. She wondered if there had been some miscommunication on her mother's part. 'There was an accident.'

The old man wasn't listening. Instead he downed his half-finished pint in one final draught and shrugged on a shapeless wax jacket. 'Let's get going.'

'Wait,' Helen said, not sure what he meant. 'Get going where?'

He stared at her. 'Rathbrooke, of course.'

'The . . . the *island*? You want to leave *now*? In *this*?' Helen asked, incredulous. The wind outside was howling loud enough to be heard over the muted hubbub in the pub.

Rufus frowned. 'You think we should wait a few more hours, until the weather's even worse? Until it's properly dark, mebbe?'

'No, but—' Helen looked pointedly out of the window just as a crisp packet vaulted past, buffeted by the gusting wind. 'Shouldn't we stay here until it passes?'

The old man's frown grew deeper. 'I can't do that.'

'It's fine,' she said. 'You go home and I'll get a hotel for the night. We can go over to Rathbrooke once the storm's blown out.'

'I live on the island.'

'I– Oh.' Helen hadn't known this. She hadn't thought to ask. She hadn't asked much of anything, not in her rush to get out of London. 'I'm sorry. I didn't know that.'

Helen became aware that most of the other patrons were listening to their conversation while studiously pretending their attention was elsewhere. One of them had taken out his phone and was studying it. He kept flicking his gaze up to look at her. Fresh anxiety twisted in Helen's gut. Had he taken a picture of her face and searched for it? If he had, what had he found? An old screenshot of her, maybe? Some lurid details about her regrettable past? A gutter press blog appealing for information about her whereabouts – or even better, a new photograph?

'I've got to get back,' Rufus was saying. 'They need me there. Anyway, it's not a storm, not yet. Right now it's nowt but a squall. I've seen worse upsets in my pint glass. So—'

'Fine,' Helen said, abruptly. 'Come on, then. Let's go.'

She caught the flicker of surprise that passed across the old man's face.

'Like you said, you've been waiting long enough,' Helen said, heading for the door.

Chapter Four

Outside, the rain slatted against her face in a sharp torrent that definitely felt more than a 'squall' to Helen, but she'd lost any desire to stay put. A gale of laughter erupted inside the pub as she dragged her case from the boot of Melanie's car. She winced. Was she being paranoid to think that was about her? Probably not, even if they hadn't realized who she was. Her suspicion was confirmed a second later when Rufus appeared behind her, wrenching the pub's door open to emit a gust of warm, beery air and the last wisps of laughter. Clearly his mates had given him a few parting shots as he'd followed in her wake.

'Come on, then,' he said, hitching his collar up around his ears and taking off down the sloping wind-blown street towards the harbour. 'Let's get on with it.'

Helen battled with her bag as she tried to keep up with him, fighting against the strong gusts of wind that whipped it back against her legs with every step. Helen raised her face, gasping as she struggled to draw breath. Rufus strode on ahead, down a narrow road that channelled them between a line of lock-ups with their backs to the water and a row of newer, taller buildings that looked like flats created as yet more holiday lets. Overhead, the last light of the day was lingering in an inky, clouded sky, the faintest tint of blue fighting a losing battle against the true dark of night. The storm got worse as they reached the harbour proper, a series of concrete walls sheltering a number of small boats in their lee. She could make out a few fishing boats and a handful of pleasure craft. There were larger vessels, too, catamarans designed to carry multiple passengers – tour boats, Helen guessed. They were all bobbing wildly on the tide despite the shelter of the high harbour walls. None of them, not even the largest of the tour boats, seemed big enough to take on the waves she could see rolling out in the open water of the North Sea.

Rufus led her onto one of the harbour's wings. The concrete was slippery, and Helen had to watch her step. Rufus shimmied down a steep ladder to a small motorboat, as if he was about to embark on a pleasant summer's day cruise instead of facing the worst maelstrom Helen had ever experienced. Painted in curling script along the side of the boat was a name: *Lady Jane*.

'Wait,' she shouted, reaching the steps but not clambering down them – unsure of how she'd even manage such a task with her case. Her face was already numb from the lash of the cold wind and rain. 'This can't be safe. How long will it take to get to the island?'

Rufus looked up at her from the little boat's deck, rain spattering his forbidding face, his white beard only partially hiding a clenched jaw. 'I can get you there in twenty minutes. Are you coming or not? Because if you're not, you'll need somewhere to stay for two nights. I'm not coming back over again until Wednesday. Maybe Friday if there's no other reason to make the trip. I'll have work to do.'

'Alright, alright,' she said, and hefted her case, trying to ease it down the steps in front of her, convinced she would lose her balance and plunge head-first onto the boat's deck below. Rufus must have thought this too, because he moved closer, reaching up to grasp it, taking it from her hand and hoisting it down onto the deck and then beneath the small roof of the boat's half-open cabin. Helen clambered after it, landing on the heaving deck with legs that already felt like jelly.

'Strap in,' the old man yelled to her, waving her into the seat beside his pilot's chair as he battened down her case. 'Might be a bumpy ride.'

This was an understatement of ludicrous proportions. Helen shut her eyes, gripped her small plastic seat, and prayed to a god she had never really believed in as they left the relative shelter of Seahouses harbour to head out into open water. It was like being in an aircraft in heavy turbulence, but a hundred times worse. She was soaked before they'd been underway for five minutes, repeatedly doused in icy North Sea spray. The sound of the storm was immense, ripping and roaring around them like a wild animal, obscuring even the thrum of the engine, and she couldn't understand how the little boat could keep afloat, much less cut a watery path through the writhing sea. It rose and fell, rose and fell, sometimes riding the waves, sometimes losing synchronicity and smashing down hard enough to rattle her frozen bones. Helen started out trying to count minutes, but soon gave up. Time stretched into an eternity in which there was only the storm and her being tossed around with an ancient madman on top of it.

She only opened her eyes when there was a sudden drop in engine power. Helen felt rather than heard it, the shifting down of a gear as the boat lost speed. At first, she assumed the engine had given up and they were about to capsize, then she saw a shape looming ahead of them out of the darkness. Through the murk she caught sight of lights, pendulous and golden. She couldn't work out what they were, or, more importantly, *where* they were. They seemed to be suspended in mid-air at regular intervals, perhaps four or five metres apart, stretching in a line for some distance before curving out of sight in both directions.

'What are they?' she shouted to Rufus.

'What are what?' he yelled back, his gnarled hands working the boat's wheel.

'Those lights – look!' she pointed, and he glanced along the line she was indicating.

'That's the island wall.'

Helen wasn't sure she'd heard him properly. 'The what?'

'You'll see soon enough,' he replied, before falling silent, a look of concentration on his face.

Helen left him to navigate. They sailed ever closer to the lights, until she was near enough to see that they were indeed pinioned to a wall – behind the swell of their illumination she could make out the hewn edges of sandstone blocks, stretching as far as she could see along the top of a sheer cliff of dark, cragged rock high above them. The lights were fixed in a line two-thirds of the way up this barrier. Wiping rain from her eyes, she counted twenty before they vanished as the wall curved out of view, presumably following the line of the island's edge. Did it go right the way around the circumference of the landmass? There was a watchtower, too, or something like it – a square turret with a flat roof sitting proud at one end of the wall. Her stomach, already a mess of nerves and nausea thanks to the journey from Seahouses harbour, now clenched anew. This looked like a prison. That wall had to be to keep something in, because surely the huge cliff, not to mention the sea itself, would have no problem keeping anything unwanted out.

The engine sped up again and with a jolt Helen realized that Rufus was heading straight for the cliff. For a confused, terrified moment she thought that he was going to ram them straight into it, but then she saw that what looked like solid rock in the darkness was actually hiding an inlet. Rufus navigated into a narrow channel, immediately jinking hard to port on the storm tide so that they were flanked on one side by a high harbour wall that had a walkway halfway down it, and on the other by the even higher cliff, topped by the island wall. The wind immediately dropped, the little channel of water and the tiny harbour to which it led well protected from the full force of the storm. The only other boat sheltering from the wild waters outside was an even smaller wooden sailing dingy with an outboard motor. Squinting through the rain, Helen was just able to make out the name, painted in white on the side: this, apparently, was the *Quick But Dirty*. Rufus pulled the motorboat in beside it and tied up, leaping onto the walkway with an agility that belied his years.

Helen's teeth were chattering as she hauled her luggage up to the boat's rail, but was too exhausted to lift it. Rufus leaned down to take it from her, dumping it onto the wet walkway before leaning back down to offer her his arm. Helen took it and he pulled her up and over onto the stone path, which was slippery with sea water and rain despite the shelter of the harbour wall.

'Watch your step,' he said, gruffly, and she saw that his beard was beaded with spray. 'I'll take your bag now.'

She followed, head bowed against the rain. The wind still roared and whined, but it was a battle they were no longer part of. Incessant rain and the occasional errant gust aside, they were out of the worst.

Rufus led her up a narrow flight of stone steps, and the noise of the wind rose in her ears again. At the top he passed through a metal gate, pulling a small torch from his pocket to light their way. They went on down a pale pebble path that appeared out of the darkness like a winding trickle of tarnished silver. Helen could hear, though not see, foliage whipping back and forth on her periphery, as if they were making their way through a forest. She could feel the spray of rain thrown from wind-blown leaves, but all she could make out were indistinct black shapes, blasted by the gale. She kept her head down and tried not to stumble on her cold feet.

She became aware of something large and darker even than the surrounding night looming before them, a structure blocking out the clouds overhead. Beneath her feet the pebbles turned into the uneven slabs of a stone courtyard. The wind dropped even more as they moved towards the house. All was darkness aside from Rufus's torch, but then, as she searched the void ahead of them, Helen spotted another light. This one was smaller, yellow and flickering, and finally the old man lifted the torch to show French doors, their glass wet with rain. Through them she could see a woman holding a small torch in front of her so that it uplit her face in a way that made it impossible to see her features with any clarity, except that she was scowling almost as hard as Rufus.

As they reached the door, the woman opened it for them and held her torch away as they entered.

'Electricity's out,' she said, shortly, to Rufus. 'We'll need the generator. And the sheep are still out – the wind got under the barn door again. I can't gather them on my own.'

The old man cursed. 'This is Helen Thorne.'

Helen looked at the woman, expecting her to introduce herself, but instead she frowned harder and turned away, took two paces and then looked back. In the shadows, Helen couldn't work out how old she was. Forty? Older? Younger?

'I'll show you where you can sleep but then I've got to get the generator running,' she said.

Helen followed but Rufus didn't. The woman led her through another door, taking her deeper into the house, and Helen would have given anything for a torch at that moment. Beyond the door through which they passed was a silence that made Helen's ears buzz. It felt unnatural after the rage of the storm. She found herself in a corridor – or, at least, she thought it was a corridor, the candle showing her even less than Rufus's torch had as her guide hurried her along. They reached a wide staircase of dark, polished wood with a very old and threadbare woven carpet cascading down its centre. Up they went, Helen keenly aware of the cavernous space that reached above them, unseen. On the wall beside them she caught glimpses of wallpaper that seemed to flicker gold as they passed. There were paintings, too, set in huge, gilded frames that glowed in the torchlight but were otherwise indistinct. The stairs creaked beneath their feet, and then curved in a hairpin beside an immense window that reflected the light from a multitude of segmented panes – small, uneven diamonds as faceted as any elaborate cut stone. Cold seeped from the window, the glass rattling with every step they took. After another flight of stairs, they reached a landing. The woman crossed it without pause, sure-footed despite the lack of light, as if she knew every inch of this place better than the lines of her own palm.

Helen's guide pushed open another door and beyond was recognizably a sitting room, though what Helen was most grateful to see was the fierce fire burning in the stone hearth. The room was warm and small enough to feel cosy, but with enough space to house a sofa and two armchairs positioned around the fire. On a low table in front of the sofa, Helen saw that someone had laid out a tray that bore a bowl of something hot and steaming, as well as a plate of thickly sliced bread. There was even another plate with a slice of cake on it, and a glass of red wine. Sitting beside this feast was, to Helen's intense relief, a battery-operated storm lamp.

'The pub called to let me know Rufus had left. I thought you'd probably be hungry,' the woman said, as she bustled to another door beside the hearth and pushed it open, gesturing vaguely inside. 'Bedroom's in there.' She pointed to a door on the other side of the hearth. 'Bathroom's there, although there won't be hot water until I can get the generator going and even then, I wouldn't recommend a shower until we're back on the mains as the blasted thing is very temperamental. All right? Got everything you need? Good,' she said, before Helen could answer. 'I'll see you in the morning.'

'Wait,' Helen said, as the woman headed for the door. 'I don't . . . I'm sorry, but who are you?'

'Sorry. I'm Martha Darling, Mr Gissing's housekeeper. Do eat that before it gets cold,' the woman said, nodding at the bowl on the table. She headed for the door.

'Wait,' Helen called after her, head spinning with so many questions. The one that surfaced first was: 'I thought there was no phone on the island?'

The housekeeper looked back at her from the door, her

hand gripping the handle as she paused. 'There's one in the cottage,' she said. 'Mr Gissing just didn't want one in the house. I've got to go. I'll see you in the morning.'

With that she disappeared, pulling the door shut behind her. Her footsteps echoed on the floorboards outside before being swallowed by silence.

Helen stood for a moment, frozen to the spot. The fire crackled in the grate and the wind niggled at the windows, pushing its cold fingers against more uneven diamonds of old glass. The curtains – heavy swathes of mustard-coloured velvet – had not been drawn against the night. Helen flicked on the storm lamp before going to the window. She could see nothing aside from her own distorted reflection in the glass. Then, from below, there came the sound of a door slamming and she saw two circles of light: Rufus and Martha, leaving. She watched them go, aware that the interior of the house was silent in the wake of their exit. A huge hulk of a place, ancient and empty apart from her.

The light of the torches they carried faded away, leaving the storm outside in darkness and her alone in the void. Helen shivered and turned away from the window. She went to the bedroom and stood on the threshold, holding the storm lamp aloft. Inside the room the air was cool, still and dead. She could just make out an immense four-poster bed, neatly made, and portrait-bedecked walls that were painted a deep rust red. Surely this hadn't been Cyril Gissing's room? They wouldn't have put her, a total stranger, in his room, would they?

Still, Helen wasn't going to take the chance. Either way,

the decor made her think of Jane Eyre's terrifying sojourn in the Red Room. The sitting room was warmer anyway and she was still soaked. She ducked into the room long enough to drag a quilt and a pillow from the bed, dumping it on the sofa facing the fireplace. She went into the bathroom – dated, cold, but clean – and grabbed towels. Back in front of the fire, she opened her case, relieved to find that everything inside was still dry. She changed quickly and spread her wet clothes out on the hearth before collapsing on the sofa. The bowl on the table held stew, which was still steaming slightly. She ate quickly, the meal delicious. The meat was lamb, which made her think of what Martha had said in greeting to Rufus, about the sheep being out. She wondered if the two of them were trying to gather the animals now.

The wind was still blowing outside, and in fact she thought it might have worsened since she'd arrived. The shadows around her moved as if they were alive. Twice she turned, thinking that someone had crept into the room, but it was just the bulk of a crowded bookcase animated by the flickering flames. Not knowing the dimensions of the house unsettled Helen in the extreme. She was on the second floor, she knew, but there had been other stairs leading up beyond the flight they had climbed, so there was at least one more floor above her too, and above that perhaps another, or at the very least an attic. Was she really the only person in this huge house right now? Her mum had said nothing about Martha. Perhaps there were other staff that Helen didn't know about either.

As she pondered this, the quilt tugged around her shoulders, Helen heard the sound of footsteps somewhere close by. They were quick, like a child running, as if by thinking of the idea of kids living here Helen had somehow conjured them into being. She froze, but the sound had already gone. Had that been outside the door, or was there another bedroom directly above her?

She listened for more sounds but heard none and so reached for the cake, which was apple and some sort of berry – blackberry, maybe? – sweet and moist. Outside, the storm raged on.

Finishing the cake, she pushed away the plate and was reaching for the wine again when from somewhere distant came a crash. It hadn't been outside, in the storm, but inside, in the house, she was sure of it. Heart thumping, Helen got up and went to the door. She paused for a moment, listening, and then opened it a crack. Outside, the cold air of the house was a solid thing, pressing in against her face. She couldn't see anything. There was just a black void. Another crash – this one sounded nearer – had her slamming the door shut again, pressing hard against it. She felt something jamming into her thigh beneath the door handle and looked down to see an ancient black key sticking out of a lock. She turned it.

Helen stepped back from the door, waiting to hear more, but all was silent apart from the storm and the crackling fire. She went back to the sofa and huddled on it again, drawing the quilt around her. After slugging the last of the wine, wishing there was more, she squashed a pillow behind her.

In the morning, or at least the minute the storm blew itself out, Helen decided that she'd use the phone in the cottage – wherever that was – to call her mother and tell her that she couldn't do this job after all. It didn't matter what was waiting for her at home – this entire, weird place and everyone in it was a giant red flag. There was no way she was staying. One sleepless night would be more than enough.

*

Cyril, my dear, dear friend:

I know, I know, I know – this letter is late, unconscionably so. Forgive me! I have been on an adventure of which I believe you will approve, especially since it was you who sent me on it in the first place. Do you remember, some months back now – or perhaps even years; time passes at such a pace – you mentioned that in your researches you believed you had located the possible resting place of a forgotten first edition of Spinoza's Ethics*? Well, you were right – or at least, you were in the vicinity of being right. It was not in the great house of the town, as you surmised, because that had been split into apartments in the 80s, and no longer held any of its old treasures. At first I thought its library had vanished to the winds, and indeed much of it had, but in fact some of those seeds had not carried so far after all. I found poor unfortunate Baruch languishing in a local school, which was too small to even have a library or a librarian, and what books they have are poorly organized. Spinoza lay forgotten in a box that had yet to be unpacked despite sitting there in* *a cupboard for years. Without your leads and my visit, he probably would have remained there for decades longer still, until he mouldered into dust.*

In any case, the journey was a long and arduous one – the nearest port was miles from the town and from there I had to make my way into the mountains. There is no public transport, and I could not find someone to sell me a car. I did not want to employ a driver, for obvious reasons – my arrival in port had caused interest enough – and so most of the way I traversed on foot. And you know, Cyril, you know how shaped for the sea my legs are: if we were meant to walk everywhere, God would not have covered most of the Earth with water that we cannot drink, only sail upon.

Anyway, here is the volume. I hope you will agree that it was worth my efforts and also my absence from our letters to locate it and deliver it to you. Is it not beautiful? I know you will find the right home for it, one that will make the necessary restorations and ensure it will survive in a better state than it has been kept these past centuries. I compensated the school as best I could, though I dare say not quite what the box I took away with me was worth. I know you will want to send them more, so here is the address.

I must go now. I look forward to your next letter and promise that I will not be so tardy with my reply for my next turn. Send me another quest, my friend, perhaps one far, far away. The dear Alejandra and I are pining for the highest of seas. Madrid makes me so restless and mournful. Would that

I could live upon the sea, but then where would I keep my books?

I am, as always, your faithful friend and dedicated servant,

Thiago Montera

Chapter Five

Helen woke with a jolt. The fire had burned to ash and the storm lamp was out. For a moment she thought it was still night, but then gradually she became aware of a faint glow – daylight, filtering in around the edges of the curtains. She levered herself up from beneath the cocoon of the quilt, surprised that she had slept at all. Around her the house was silent, inside and out.

She went to the window and parted one of the curtains. Bright sunlight made her squint for a moment until her eyes adjusted. Below her was the courtyard; half was terrace, the other a perfectly kept lawn. The grass was laid in a square, with flagged stone paths cutting evenly through it. A stone fountain in the shape of a series of leaping dolphins stood at its centre. The water wasn't running, but Helen thought it must look spectacular when it was.

At the rear of the lawn was a high red-brick wall with an arch in it, through which Helen could see the beginnings of the winding path she had followed Rufus along the night before. Looking left and right out of the window, she could also see a little more of the house. It had three wings built around three sides of the courtyard that enclosed the terrace and the lawn. Helen was in the central section. The impression she'd had last night was that the room she'd slept in was right in the middle of the building, but now she could see that she was further to the right, close to the wing that abutted that side of the house. The sun was just hitting her side of the house and half of the terrace, suggesting that she was facing south, so north would be behind her, and the wing to which she was closest stood to the west. She could see three floors of windows, all made of the same tiny panes of glass as the one through which she peered.

Leaning back to study the window in front of her, Helen saw that the tiny diamond panes were set in lead. They must be the originals, never replaced, which meant she was looking through glass that had been fitted four hundred years ago. She'd assumed that the strange, uneven effect was deliberate – a weird quirk requested by the owner, but no. It was just age. The lead had buckled over centuries of changing temperatures, but still held glass that must have been handmade with great care and at massive expense. Helen laid her fingertips against the window, a little overwhelmed by the history beneath her hand.

A movement towards the rear of the garden caught her eye. Someone had walked past the archway in the wall – Rufus, she thought, hunched over a wheelbarrow, his crown of white hair crammed under a flat cap. He was on the path beyond the enclosed lawn. Helen looked at her watch and saw that it was barely 8am.

Suddenly restless for fresh air, she decided she would shower later. Trying the light switch – a strange, ornate brass affair that would bear closer scrutiny another time – the overhead light flickered on, so perhaps there would be at least a splash of hot water. After pulling on her jeans and changing the T-shirt she had slept in, she was relieved to find that the jumper and coat she'd been wearing the day before had dried overnight thanks to the fire.

At the door, she hesitated for a second before turning the key, remembering the footsteps and strange sounds she'd heard the night before. But stepping through it again revealed not the narrow, poky corridor she'd expected, but a wide landing opening out from the stairs Martha had brought her up when she'd arrived. Off this landing – sizeable enough that it would have fitted most of her London flat within its confines – led more doors, all closed. Beneath her feet were planks of stripped wood, oiled dark and worn smooth by the passage of countless footsteps. The walls were covered in elaborate paper, peeling and damaged in places but still showing a vibrant pattern of large vines and other foliage, amid which perched colourful exotic birds from all over the world – golden pheasants and birds of paradise, scarlet macaws, green parakeets – all set against a gold background formed by tiny, interlocking triangles. Amid this richly feathered menagerie were mounted more paintings – a few dramatic land- and seascapes, but mostly staid portraits of stern-faced forebears, connections long gone and forgotten, forever incongruous against the riot of bird life. Narrow tables of age-pocked dark wood with exquisitely carved barley-twist legs housed dusty leather-bound books and other knickknacks, while long-stopped clocks and framed sepia-toned photographs lurked beside mementos of more uncertain purpose.

The landing must traverse the whole width of Rathbrooke Hall, for opposite her Helen could see another window, cut of the same small, warped diamond panes. She went to it, and was gifted a view of the cold, grey-green expanse of the North Sea, the ragged shore of the mainland straggling into the distance to the west, the smudged shadows of the other Farne Islands ahead of her to the north. She looked down but could see no sign of the island wall, only a stretch of rough grass that led to the cliff and the water far below. Its proximity made her shudder. How long would it be before this entire edifice crumbled into the sea?

There came the sudden sound of footsteps echoing somewhere behind her, the same swift, truncated patter she'd heard the night before. Helen turned, sharply, but there was no one there.

'Hello?'

There was no answer. At the other end of the landing, beside the staircase up which she'd followed Martha and that continued on to the floor above, was a set of large double doors. They were ornately studded with iron rivets and carved with a crude motif of roses – the entrance to the west wing, as ancient as the windows. Maybe this was where Martha lived? Perhaps she was younger than Helen had thought and had a young family living here with her, toddlers charging about within. Helen went to the door and tried the handle, but it was locked. She knocked, and though there was no answer, she thought she heard another skittering of footsteps – and was she imagining it, or was that a laugh echoing in the distance?

Helen retreated from the door and went down the stairs, quickly retracing the steps she had taken the night before. Wanting more than anything to be outside, she didn't linger on the lower floor. For a moment she imagined that she would be locked in, that Rufus and Martha had sealed her inside this huge mausoleum of a house. But the French doors opened easily, and she stepped out onto the terrace beyond, sucking in a breath of morning air. Helen looked up at the many windows of the west wing, wondering if she'd see a small face peering back, a little hand waving hello. But the curtains – all of them – were drawn. She looked to her left, to the mirror wing, but realized immediately that her assumption had been wrong. This wasn't another wing of the house – it had no windows, only narrow slits in the old stone. Could this be the peel tower? It was surely too big – the same size as the west wing, definitely not small and easily defendable. It looked more like an old barn.

Helen headed for the archway. Beyond was another garden, this one far more riotous than the immaculate lawn behind her. Here was the foliage she'd brushed through in the dark the night before, a jungle that Helen, who was entirely plant-illiterate, couldn't hope to identify beyond the obvious rose bushes, which she could only name because they were covered in flowers. They had been badly battered by the storm, their heads bowed by the rain still caught beneath their petals, others strewn like confetti along the winding pebble paths, their scent lifting headily on the morning air. It was easy to see how beautiful this spot must be at its prime.

'Ah ha,' said a voice behind her, 'survived the night, I see. How are you this morning?'

Helen turned to see Rufus behind her, pushing the wheelbarrow again. It was full of debris left by the storm – broken foliage and crushed blooms. She was somewhat taken aback to see that he was smiling, the frown of the day before replaced by a wide grin beneath sparkling blue eyes.

'Morning,' she said. 'I . . . I'm fine, thanks.'

'Look,' he said, setting the barrow down and brushing his hands off as he came closer. 'I need to apologize for my manner yesterday. I know I weren't very welcoming. Martha gave me an earful for being a grumpy old sod, she did.'

'Oh,' said Helen, who couldn't remember Martha being particularly friendly, either. 'Well, I—'

'It's only that Mr Gissing's passing has been such a shock, and then with the storm coming in – we knew it was going to be a bad one – to get the news that someone was coming to deal with the house . . . well.' He paused for breath. 'I let all that get the better of me and suppose I had my hackles up. But there's no excuse for rudeness, and you're only here doing your job, same as the rest of us. Shall we start again?'

He held out a hand for her to shake with a renewed and surprisingly disarming grin, and Helen felt her face softening into an answering smile. She took his warm, gnarled hand and they shook, his grip firm around hers.

'Okay,' Helen said. 'Yes, please. I'd like that.' In the moment she forgot her resolve of the night before to leave as soon as she could. She was intrigued by the garden, and turned towards it. 'This is so beautiful. I had no idea it was here.'

'The garden? Oh, aye,' Rufus said. 'Mr Gissing's pride and joy, this was. Well, one of them. It's no wonder he barely left the island, is it?'

Helen detected a strong note of pride in the old man's voice, too. She glanced at the wheelbarrow again, at his sturdy overalls and boots. 'Is this *your* garden, Rufus?'

He laughed, a booming guffaw that made her smile again. 'Mine, lassie? No, of course not. This place was all Mr Gissing's.'

'But I meant – you're the gardener, aren't you?'

'Oh, aye. Well, that was what I was supposed to be. That was why I came to Rathbrooke in the first place, too many years ago to count now, to be the undergardener to old Jack Burnaby. But then one thing led to another and now . . . now you could say I'm general help with a strong leaning towards groundskeeping.'

Helen frowned. 'You can't do it all yourself, though. Surely that's far too much for one person?'

'Well, there's Martha to deal with the house and the kitchen garden,' he pointed out. 'And there's Cora.'

'Cora?'

At that moment a figure appeared from the rose garden, a sullen-faced girl, possibly pre-teen but of otherwise indeterminate age, dressed in a pair of mud-spattered jeans and an old black sweatshirt that seemed far too big for her. She had both arms wrapped around a bundle of garden waste.

'This is Cora,' Rufus said, his cheer apparently unaffected by the unfriendly look on the girl's face. 'Cora, come and say hello to Helen. She's the visitor your mam and I were telling you about.'

Cora came closer, but only so she could drop her armload of foliage into the gardener's wheelbarrow. Helen saw that the sweatshirt was a Led Zeppelin tour sweater, the logo fading with age. There were bits of twig stuck to it.

'Hi, Cora. Nice to meet you.'

'Hey,' the girl muttered, then turned to Rufus. 'We should go and check on the puffins.'

'Aye, lass, in a minute. Let's get this lot in the incinerator first. And your mam will be wanting you to have a bite of breakfast soon too, I should think.'

'Puffins?' Helen asked. The pair looked at her. Were they grandfather and granddaughter? 'There are puffins on the island? I've never seen a puffin.'

Cora smirked. 'They're all over the Farnes. It's why I'm not allowed a cat. Cy wouldn't let me.'

'Cy?'

'Mr Gissing,' Rufus filled in. 'He and Cora got on all right, didn't you, lass?'

Cora shrugged one shoulder. ''Cept for the stupid "no cat" rule,' she said. 'We could have kept one in the house. It couldn't have got to the puffins then, could it?'

'That would have been cruel though, wouldn't it?' Rufus pointed out, gently. 'To shut an animal in like that.'

'Not for a stray it wouldn't be,' Cora pointed out, hotly and, Helen thought, probably not for the first or even the fifth time. 'And anyway, the house is so big it might as well be outside. And a cat would deal with the mice.'

'You know what Mr Gissing's thought about that was, though, don't you, lass?' Rufus said. 'It might only take it getting out once. And the puffins need all the help they can get.'

Cora shrugged, biting her lip as if she wanted to retort, but in the end said nothing.

'Ah, so you two live in the west wing of the Hall?' Helen asked, somewhat relieved to have solved the mystery of the noises behind the locked door. 'That must be pretty amazing, Cora, to live in such an historic house?'

Cora stared at her, perplexed, and then looked at Rufus and back again. 'What? I don't live in the big house. I live with Mum, in the cottage.'

'And I live in the lighthouse, lass.' Rufus peered at her. 'Cora is Martha's daughter.'

'The lighthouse?' Helen repeated. 'I didn't know there even was one on the island.'

The gardener turned and pointed back through the gardens in the vague direction of the harbour. 'It's built into the island wall at the south reach,' he said. 'The light hasn't been used for decades now.'

'Oh,' Helen said. 'Then . . . who lives in the west wing?'

The old groundsman shook his head. 'No one. That's been shut up for years. The place was already too much for one person and Mr Gissing decided to close it up. No one's even been in there for . . . oh, must be going on a decade now. Most of the rest of the house is shut up too. He only really lived in a few rooms, right at the end.'

'But, I've heard people in there,' Helen protested. 'Children, running around. Playing.'

'Ah, there aren't any kiddies on the island,' Rufus said, and then added with a laugh, 'not since Cora here decided she was all grown up, like.'

Cora rolled her eyes. 'Like you said, it's an old house,' she told Helen. 'It's always making weird noises. I was sure I'd heard someone shouting my name once and it turned out it was some random ancient cuckoo clock in one of the rooms that Cy didn't even know he had. You'll have heard something like that. Or it was the storm.'

There came the sound of a handbell ringing, floating to them through the morning air. Rufus leaned over and nudged Cora.

'There y'go,' he said. 'Breakfast time. Best get over there while it's still hot. Then we'll see about the puffins.' He looked up at Helen. 'We'll have ours in the cottage kitchen, but Martha will have put yours in the dining room. You show her, Cora.'

Cora reluctantly led Helen back into the Hall to the 'dining room' – a long, high-ceilinged cavern on the ground floor. It was lined with carved dark wood panels and down the middle of the room ran an immense wooden table. When Helen counted how many chairs were arranged around it, the answer was twenty-six. A single place was set at the very end, and a plate had been covered with a gleaming silver cloche, beside which stood matching cutlery and a silver coffee pot with a delicate cup and saucer.

'There you go,' Cora announced. 'Mum'll come and get the dirty stuff later.' There was a sullen pause. 'Or she'll force me to do it.'

'Wait,' Helen said, as she turned to leave. 'I wasn't expecting your mum to make my meals. I can cook for myself, if someone will show me where the kitchen is.'

Cora snorted. 'Rather you than me,' she said. 'Unless you don't mind living on toast. I've got to go.'

She went, leaving Helen standing, alone, in the doorway of a room bigger than most restaurants she'd eaten in. It even had an actual chandelier. Two of them, in fact. After a moment Helen went to the table and lifted the cloche, the smell of freshly cooked food making her stomach rumble. The plate was piled with a cheese omelette speckled with fresh herbs, accompanied by perfectly crisp sautéed potatoes, plump sausages and streaky bacon. Helen felt her appetite return with a vengeance. She sat down, poured herself a coffee and started to eat.

*

Cyril, my friend,

Well, here she is, as I promised – an excellent first-edition copy of Mary Shelley's Frankenstein. *I know this isn't quite what you were hoping for from my visit to Geneva, but the* Idyllia *that was once here is long lost. The library that housed it looks like a carcass picked clean, and I am glad you are not the one to have seen it. This Shelley had somehow been forgotten. I love how the private binding – contemporary, I think? – has been designed to fit the book, instead of the library. I am sure the original owner would be glad to know that it will be going to someone who will appreciate it. There is a little light foxing, but as you can see, the binding is sound. It is not quite the incunabula you were hoping for, but still, had Mary stayed where she was, I believe the worm would have found her monster, and I know that you would not abide that end for any book.*

As to the other matter – I agree, the lines you sent do sound authentic, though you know as well as anyone that I am not an expert. And in isolation it is surely very hard to tell. What you say about the handwriting and its position on the manuscript is fascinating, for sure. Como bien dices, un punto para la columna 'colaboración'. *Perhaps it is time for Folger. I know you have enquired before, but if you at least sent photographs, I think you'd receive a better reaction. You can use natural light and no flash – there would be no damage, I promise you. Do you have a camera? Perhaps not. I can send you one. Digital, no film. But then you would also need a computer, or at least a mobile phone . . . ah, Cyril, my friend. I forget how far you are from joining us in the 21st century!*

Tomorrow I set sail for Porto Seguro, to visit the church of São Francisco. No, I will not tell you why! At least, not yet. Let that be a surprise if my own investigations turn out to be right – and who knows, maybe a slight salve for the loss of Theocritus. I do not want to send you further disappointment should this little side-quest be a bust. I will write when I reach Brazil – wish me luck on the Bay of Biscay. It is for sure the wrong time of year to cross, but dear Alejandra is, as ever, determined.

Yours ever faithfully, your friend,

Thiago Montera

Chapter Six

By the time she'd finished her breakfast, Helen had decided to stay after all. It was partly Martha's delicious food – she never really bothered cooking properly for herself at home; it was always too much effort for just one person – and partly her rediscovery of her phone. Helen had actually forgotten about it until she sat down and felt the bulk of it in her jeans pocket. She pulled it out and looked at it. It had no signal, but the feeling of doom that instantly swooped into her stomach as she thumbed on the screen was enough to remind her of the terrible dread that had lurked at her shoulder right up until she'd arrived on the island. Yet Helen had been so preoccupied that until then she hadn't thought of the mess her life had become once since she'd got here. If Rathbrooke Hall could carry on being such a distraction, then so be it. She had a job to do that would keep her away from everything on the mainland, so she should just get on with it.

Then there was Martha herself. Helen was finishing her

coffee when the housekeeper appeared in the dining room, offering a soft knock at the great wooden door before pushing it open.

'Morning,' Martha said, with a genuinely friendly smile, though Helen saw that she was tired. There were dark shadows beneath her eyes. 'Cora said she'd helped you find your breakfast. Sorry I wasn't here myself, but I'd left the oven on.'

'Hi!' Helen shuffled her chair out from beneath the table. 'I was just going to gather these dishes up and come to find you. Thank you so much, that was amazing. The best thing I've eaten for ages.'

'I'm lucky you're so easily pleased,' Martha laughed. She was carrying an empty tray. She was far younger than Helen had realized – probably Helen's own age, mid-thirties, in fact. 'There's no need for you to worry about the plates – that's my job.'

Helen stood and held her hand out for the tray, which Martha reluctantly handed over. 'It might have been your job to look after Mr Gissing, but I'm not your responsibility. There's no call for you to wait on me. You must have more than enough to do.'

In the end they cleared the dishes together, stacking them neatly on the tray beneath the cloche.

'I'm sorry I didn't chat much last night,' Martha said. 'I realized afterwards that we really didn't give you a good welcome. Rufus can be such an old grump, but he's lovely really. It was just that the storm was so much worse than we were expecting. We were both worried and he was back far later than I'd thought he would be.'

Helen waved this apology away, although she appreciated it. 'It was bad timing on my part to arrive when I did. I hadn't even thought to look at the forecast. Thank you for making sure I had somewhere to sleep and something delicious to eat when you had so many other worries.'

'Did you sleep well? I've always thought those old four-posters look like you could curl up like a cat in them – so comfy.'

Helen grimaced, a little embarrassed. 'Actually, I slept on the sofa. I was a bit creeped out by the house. I kept hearing weird noises. I wanted to stay by the fire.'

'Ah,' Martha nodded, sympathetically. 'I remember what it was like the first few times I came in here. And with the power cut and the storm it would have been a hundred times worse. Sorry, I didn't think. I'm so used to the place now.'

'Really, it's fine,' Helen told her, picking up the empty coffee pot. 'I'll take this for you. Until your daughter told me, I thought you lived in the house.'

'Oh, we're not far away,' Martha said. 'We're in the garden cottage. It's this way. Cora and I usually go in and out via the old kitchen – it's quicker than coming right around the front of the house.'

She led Helen out of the room through a narrow door in the corner of the room that, when closed, disappeared into the wall – clearly meant for servants' use only. They traversed a short, dark corridor into a much larger room that Helen could see had once been a kitchen, but that was now mostly disused, although there was a newish-looking microwave and toaster on one counter that also housed short stacks of clean crockery, a canister of knives and forks, a kettle and an old wooden bread bin.

'Mr Gissing liked to be able to make himself a snack if he wanted one,' Martha explained. 'He had a tendency to keep odd hours, especially if he was reading, which was most of the time when he was well enough. Feel free to do the same – there's tea, coffee and canned soup in the cupboard, bread in the bread bin. The fridge will always be stocked with milk, butter and cheese and the water is fine from the tap. But I'm very happy to cook your meals for you while you're here, same as I always do for Rufus and my Cora.'

'That's very kind of you,' Helen told her, as they passed through the kitchen. 'How long have you lived here?'

'Me? Oh, it's going on six years now,' Martha said, reaching the far wall and opening another door that led out into the bright, storm-washed sunshine outside. 'Cora had just turned seven – so yeah, it must be six years. Rufus has been here man and boy, but I came to replace Mrs Burnaby, who passed away not long after her husband. Mr Gissing needed someone to live here permanently and I . . . well, I needed somewhere safe for me and Cora. He had trouble finding anyone willing to live out here. I said we'd give it six months to see if I could cope with life on the island, and we're still here.'

Helen smiled, wondering about the 'safe' comment. Perhaps she wasn't the only one who had used Rathbrooke to get away from a bad situation. 'It must suit you, then.'

'It does,' Martha agreed. 'I know a lot of people would find it difficult, but actually I love it. Cora does too. Or, at least, she used to.' She frowned. 'I think the teenage years are beginning to hit. She's been so difficult these past few weeks. I know she's still grieving, of course – she and Mr Gissing were thick as thieves. And I suppose I should be prepared for it to get worse before it gets better. Goodness knows I'm having enough sleepless nights about what's going to happen to us from here. The solicitors told Rufus and me that we should stay while they work out what to do with the estate, as it needs so much day-to-day maintenance. But after that, if you can't find the will . . .' She trailed off, a troubled expression passing across her face. 'Even if you do find it, who knows what it will say? He always said he'd look after us – Cora and me and of course Rufus, too. But I never thought to ask what that would look like. Maybe he didn't even mean it.'

'I'm sorry,' said Helen. 'It must be awful to be so uncertain about what the future holds.'

Martha managed a smile, but it was a small one. 'Ah, well. That's life, isn't it? Cora and I, we're survivors. We'll be alright, somehow. It's Rufus I really worry for, to be honest. Rathbrooke Island is all he's ever known, really.'

They left the house behind and Martha led Helen along a path that wound through a small coppice of trees. It took

Helen a few moments to notice that they were all laden with apples.

'Wait,' she said, stopping to look around. She could see the island wall through the leaves, standing to the north. 'Is this an orchard?'

Martha turned back. 'Oh, yes. Mr Gissing was so proud of it. We've got a lot of very old apple varieties here. There's the mulberries, too. They were his real passion.'

'I wouldn't have thought that anything would grow well here,' Helen said, with surprise. 'What with the North Sea weather.'

'Ah, well, that's what the island wall is all about,' Martha indicated the rise of stone just visible through the verdant canopies of the fruit trees. 'For shelter. I know it probably didn't seem it, what with you getting battered so badly by the storm on your way over, but that's what I meant about it being such a bad one.'

'Does the wall go right the way around the island?'

'Yes,' Martha turned again to point back towards the house. 'Except where the north wall of the Hall faces the sea. The island wall starts at the west corner of the house, there,' she pointed to the wall in which the door they had just left stood, 'and it runs all the way around the circumference of the island, finishing at the east corner of the old peel tower wall, which is at the opposite end of the house to where we are now. Maintaining it is a devil of a job. That and the gardens takes up most of Rufus's time.'

'I can believe that,' Helen murmured, trying to fathom

how difficult that task must be, let alone how long it must have taken to build in the first place. The workers must have brought tonnes of quarried stone by boat from the mainland. 'Is it worth it? Does it work?'

'Why don't you come and look at the kitchen garden, and you can tell me.'

Martha set off again, turning down a path that led beneath some particularly gnarled trees that made Helen think, obscurely, of Rathbrooke Hall's warped windowpanes. They had the same age-wrought quality of strangely attractive disfigurement to them. Looking closer, Helen wondered if these were the mulberries, but saw small apples beginning to bow the branches as they grew.

'I'm not sure I've ever actually eaten mulberries,' Helen said. 'You never see them in the shops, or at least you don't in London supermarkets.'

'You had some last night, in the cake I left you,' Martha said. 'Although they were from last season, out of the freezer. There are actually more mulberry trees in London than anywhere else in the UK, but they don't keep once they've been picked, that's why you don't see them for sale in shops very often. You've got to eat them fresh – straight off the tree, if you can. Otherwise they need to be frozen or made into some sort of conserve. Mulberry jam is the best – we've still got a store of that from last year, too. There's some in the cupboard in the Hall's kitchen. It's delicious. Mr Gissing adored it. Although I think that was also partly because of all the history.'

'The history?'

Martha flashed Helen a smile. 'Ask Rufus – he'll tell you about it better than I could. It's Rufus who looks after the trees. Every couple of years we sell saplings that he takes from cuttings here to a garden centre on the mainland – it's one of the island's regular income streams. Well,' she added, 'that and meat and wool from the sheep. Here we are.'

They had reached another wall, similar to the one that enclosed the lawn rather than the island itself. Built into it was an archway leading into another sheltered section of the garden.

'Wow,' Helen said. 'I see what you mean.'

Inside the wall, which intersected with a huge orangery that was built against the disused west wing of Rathbrooke Hall to their left, were dozens of raised vegetable beds. They were all full of verdant plants, rain from the previous night dissipating from their leaves in the morning sun. Some were netted, and Martha led Helen between them, pointing out varieties of potatoes, cabbages, cauliflowers and carrots, all of which seemed to Helen to be, to coin an Austenian phrase, exemplary vegetables.

'There are no rabbits on the island, which is a bonus, but we do still have to do battle with flying pests, as well as slugs and snails,' Martha said. 'Hence the nets and copper rings. Mr Gissing and Rufus were both very keen not to use pesticides. We have some very old beehives in the orchard, too – we don't want to interfere with our pollinators.'

'That greenhouse is beautiful,' Helen said, staring up at it. Inside she could see vines pressing against the windows.

'It's very old, though not as old as the house,' Martha smiled, with a touch of pride. 'Mr Gissing thought it had probably been added in the Victorian period. I'd show you inside, but that's Cora's province. She's been looking after it all herself for the past couple of years, and so I leave her to it. It's good for her to have something that's entirely her responsibility and she's really poured her all into it. It's got a little woodstove in it, so we have salad and cucumbers all year. Our strawberry season is far longer than you'd expect, too. Tomatoes not so much – there's rarely sun for long enough this far north, really. She's grown some fantastic squashes, though. We're still eating last year's now, they've kept so well.'

Helen smiled. 'It sounds as if your daughter has very green fingers.'

'She does,' Martha agreed. 'Rufus is a good teacher. I can see her ending up at agricultural college when the time comes.'

'Does she go to the school on the mainland?'

'She will when the summer is over. She's been home-schooled since we've been here, but she'll be starting her GCSEs in September. We decided together that it would be best for her to join a mainstream school for that. It's all the way down in Alnwick, which would be a long trip there and back every day, so we're looking at her staying with my sister and niece in Alnmouth during the week. I think that's probably playing on her mind too – it'll be a big change for both of us. But I want to make sure she has the best chance at whatever she decides she wants to do. Still, what with that, Mr Gissing's death and the uncertainty over where we'll be calling home . . . it's a lot for her to cope with. But she's a good kid, really.'

Helen smiled. 'I'm sure she is.'

The Darlings' cottage was a tiny stone-built square house that looked as if it belonged in a watercolour painting, built into the island wall with windows looking out towards the mainland. Martha took Helen into the kitchen, a small, cosy affair that instantly made her feel more at home than any room she'd so far seen in the huge and sprawling Rathbrooke Hall. There were photographs pinned to the fridge with magnets, a pile of paperback books on the small circular dining table. The curtains had a modern, colourful print and the air was scented by the vase of sweet peas standing on the windowsill above the sink.

'Ah, bless them, they've done the washing up,' Martha noted as she put down the tray of dishes beside the full draining board, and turned to take the coffee pot from Helen's hands. 'I expect they've gone off to check on the puffins after the storm. Cora was worrying about them this morning. She's in touch with the RSPB – she sends them reports throughout nesting season.'

'She mentioned the puffins when I met her earlier,' Helen said. 'I've never seen a puffin.'

'Next time you can go too,' the housekeeper told her. 'You'll probably be here a few days at least, won't you?'

Helen drew in a breath. She'd barely seen a third of

Rathbrooke Hall yet, but already the idea of cataloguing it was overwhelming in the extreme. And what was she to do about the gardens? About Martha and Cora's house – and Rufus's home, the lighthouse?

'I guess so,' she said. 'And I'd better get started, hadn't I?'

Chapter Seven

Helen decided that a sensible way to begin would be with a complete walk-through of the entire main house, and retrieved her iPad from her bag so that she could take notes. She started in the little parlour with the French doors and methodically walked through each room and hallway on the ground floor, pushing back curtains as she went, letting the morning light flood into spaces that had obviously been disused for a long time. She found herself traversing abandoned rooms big enough that her footsteps echoed. They were all full of dust sheets spread to hang like ghostly figures over furniture that had likely stood in the same place for centuries.

She made page headings for each room, including the dining room in which she had eaten breakfast and the ballroom that connected to it, which was of matching size with more windows facing out over the North Sea. There was also a huge foyer with a massive studded wooden door. It was locked, but when opened it would lead out onto the terrace and lawn Helen had crossed earlier – clearly it had once been the main entrance, but was now rarely, if ever, used. The foyer's staircase was even grander than the one she'd already climbed more than once. It swept up to a balcony on the first floor, which she decided to leave for later, determined to complete her search of downstairs first.

It was clear that Mr Gissing had, at least during the later stages of his life, primarily used a small suite of rooms on the ground floor to the east of the foyer, a warren of smaller parlours and reception rooms branching from the main entrance hall. Along a corridor here, Helen discovered a comfortable sitting room a little like the one she had slept in upstairs the night before, although this felt far more lived in. Besides a hearth, a sofa and an armchair, there were desks and tables overflowing with papers and books. In the adjoining room she found a bed, much more modern than the four-poster upstairs (and, she surmised, far easier to get in and out of for a man of advancing years), and a wardrobe of clothes, along with plenty of other personal effects that belonged to this century rather than previous ones. Further down the corridor, there was a small bathroom that, although spotlessly clean, had obviously been in recent use.

At the end of the corridor were a pair of wooden double doors which seemed of a similar age to Rathbrooke Hall's main entrance. Helen tried to turn their wrought-iron handles, but they were locked. She carried on back to the foyer and up to the second floor, where more sitting rooms, bedrooms and bathrooms revealed themselves, all unused aside from the one that had been given to her – all full of items that would need to be catalogued. She tried the doors to the second floor of the west wing again, but these were also still locked. Helen leaned one ear against the old wood for a moment, straining to hear anything from the other side, but all was silence. The storm had passed and, with it, it seemed, those strange noises.

At the other end of the house she found a corridor that matched the one below, but instead of another set of double doors at the end, there was a blank wall. Helen looked at the sketched layout she'd made of the building and saw that beyond these doors there must be an entire area – the corner that would join the main house to the barn that formed the east 'wing' – which she couldn't access. From what Martha had told her, this was the peel tower, the oldest part of Rathbrooke Hall. She left it for the time being and continued with her walk-through by making her way up the flight of stairs that led to the third floor.

This storey had no balcony overlooking the entrance hall and housed further bedrooms and bathrooms, as well as what had once obviously been a nursery. All these were large and, aside from the nursery, stuffed with art and more dust-sheeted furniture. Helen wondered when, if ever, all of these rooms had been used. She couldn't imagine Rathbrooke Hall as a thriving family home, but she supposed that at some time a long, long time ago, it must have been.

It took Helen a while to find the narrow servants' stairway leading up to the attic level, and when she did the door at the top was also locked. She made a note to investigate further, and went down to find Martha again.

'I don't have keys for the west wing,' the housekeeper told her, when Helen explained her need to get through the Hall's locked doors. 'That's never been open in all the years I've been here. I wouldn't be surprised if it's lost. But I've got the rest of the keys to the main house, including the library.'

'The library?' Helen repeated. 'I didn't know there was one. I was just told that Mr Gissing was a collector of antiques, and that included some books.'

Martha laughed. 'Well, I guess that's one way of putting it,' she said, going to a box on the wall and taking down a large, ornate black key from one of the hooks inside. 'Come on, I'll show you. It's where Mr Gissing spent most of his time even before his health grew worse. It was his favourite part of the house by far. I'll take you in there now.'

The library was beyond the locked double doors at the end of the corridor where Mr Gissing had slept. Helen followed Martha inside through a wall of red stone five feet thick, and then stopped. She couldn't move. For a book lover, this wasn't just a library. It was Aladdin's cave.

'This is the old peel tower,' Martha told her, as Helen looked around, trying to take in what she was seeing. 'I think it's probably been the heart of the house ever since Mr Gissing took it over from his uncle, back in the 1950s. There was already a very old library here then, and Mr Gissing was a collector himself, so he just . . . kept adding to it, I suppose.'

Helen hadn't seen so many books in one place since

she'd finished her Master's. She was completely surrounded. Countless volumes lined the walls in shelving that reached from the floor to the low ceiling, and there were more free-standing bookcases wherever Helen looked. The only place that wasn't crammed with books was the huge stone hearth, probably original, and its more recent wood burner. There were even discreet piles of books on the floor, having never quite found their place. Paperbacks, hardbacks, leather- and cloth-bound, there were books as far as her eye could see, many of them clearly the sort of antiquarian volumes she'd so loved to pore over at Edinburgh University.

'There are two more floors,' Martha told her, indicating a staircase tucked into the corner of the room. 'I'll take you up.'

Helen followed Martha up the stairs and at the top was surprised by the sight of a mezzanine above her – she could see a balconied level reaching up into the tower over their heads. She guessed that, at some point, one of the floors that would once have existed when this was a place of refuge had been taken out and replaced with this alternative.

'There's no way he'd get away with it now, not with this being a listed building,' Martha said, as if reading Helen's mind as she stood at the top of the stairs, contemplating the space above them. 'But one of the first things Mr Gissing did when he inherited Rathbrooke was to renovate the peel into what you see now. He put in electricity and took out the middle floor – or rather, he just didn't replace it. He told me once it had been in danger of rotting through, so he turned it into a balcony instead. He said he sometimes regretted that, because it meant less room for books. They were his ultimate passion. He spent most of his time here, and he told me that this place was the only achievement in his life that meant anything to him. I'm not really sure what he meant by that, to be honest. I do know there are a lot of very old and valuable volumes and manuscripts here. Every few years he'd send one to a specialist auction house on the mainland – Bonham's or Sotheby's, somewhere like that – and whatever he sent would always cause a stir, even though he kept his identity a secret. To be honest, I think that's what kept the coffers full and kept his living here on Rathbrooke the way he did viable. That's why, out of all the parts of the Hall that are still in use, he always kept the library locked, and he had the single key – he only gave it to me right at the end, when he got too sick to come in here. He told me it wasn't because he didn't trust me, but because it was his responsibility and no one else's. Although,' Martha added, 'this bit isn't the best of it, in my opinion. We need to go up one more flight for that.'

The housekeeper led Helen up another narrow flight of wooden stairs that curved beneath the first balcony. The peel did not feel cold, despite the cavern above them and how thick its stone walls were. Indeed, it felt impervious to any sort of attack, to any encroachment from outside, whether that be the elements or human warfare. The sound of their footsteps on the stairs did not echo, either, as she'd expected given the open space, the noise deadened by thousands – tens of thousands – of books, which also lined the walls beside the staircase. Helen peered at these as she passed, but didn't recognize any of the titles she saw embossed into leather and cloth. Some of them seemed to be in Spanish, French and German as well as English. Once they reached the top of the steps, Martha crossed two sides of the balcony, leading Helen towards a pair of very heavy curtains.

'Here we are,' Martha said, stopping in front of the drapes. 'Mr Gissing enjoyed sitting in front of the fire on the ground floor or at his desk down there, but if this place was mine, *this* is where I'd spend all my time.'

With a flourish, she drew back the heavy velvet to reveal a large alcove in the wall that faced east. It was about six feet wide, hewn out of the immensely thick wall of the peel tower and fitted with a huge, arched window. Though not the same age as those in the rest of Rathbrooke Hall, the designer had made the glass to match, so that it comprised small, diamond-shaped panes, but these had not warped in the same way as their ancient counterparts. The arch looked out over the North Sea – in fact, from this aspect, all the person standing in the alcove could see was the turbulent, grey water and matching sky, stretching on into the blurred horizon. The alcove had been fitted with wooden panelling and a comfortably wide bench seat that had been positioned right beneath the window. The bench was cushioned, and so was part of the wall either side of the window. Anyone sitting on the bench would have their back to the view, but Helen immediately understood that it had been positioned this way so that whomever was using it could sit sideways to the glass, with their back against the cushioned wall and their legs stretched along the cushions beneath the window.

'It's a reading nook,' Helen said. 'Isn't it?'

Martha smiled. 'I think so. I don't think he ever really used it, though. Isn't that strange? After he went to such lengths to create it. He kept the curtains drawn across it most of the time. He said he was worried about the light fading the spines of the books. But then why did he have it put in in the first place? It must have cost a fortune, even back then.'

*

3 Sunnyside Road
Seahouses
Northumberland

You know that rule I told you about where only people we really know are allowed to come to the island? Well, I guess Cy dying means that doesn't apply any more, because Mum and Rufus brought over some woman I've never heard of. She's here now. She's actually staying in the house, as if she owns it! Mum says she's from Cy's solicitor because they're trying to find his will, which sounds like rubbish to me. They're just looking for the most valuable stuff, probably so they can sell it, just like you warned me. She's trying to stick her nose into everything. Cy would be so mad if he knew.

Anyway, if that rule doesn't apply any more, you can come and visit too, can't you? You won't even have to wait until I go to school.

Chapter Eight

For the next week, Helen spent most of her time in the library. At first it was because that's where she saw most of Cyril Gissing's papers – piles of them on the small table beside the old sofa that stood in front of the wood burner, on the desk and in other places dotted around the room. But more and more it was because that's where she felt most at home in Rathbrooke Hall. It was comfortable, full of books and, perhaps more significantly, there she did not hear the kind of noises that were still plaguing her in other parts of the building, especially when she was in 'her' room.

Helen had become more and more attuned to the sounds emanating from Rathbrooke's shadowy corners, and increasingly suspicious as to their nature. They mostly came at night, often when she was on the verge of fitful sleep. She had finally decamped from the sofa to the four-poster bed in her suite. Martha was right; it was comfortable – a nest of soft mattresses and pillows in which to cocoon herself. But they did not cushion her from the thought that she was not alone in the house: that somewhere else in these rooms, something was moving. The noises frequently took the form of what she thought of as footsteps, although when she tried to describe them to Rufus or Martha, she always realized they sounded too quick for that, and too truncated in their movement. There was always a skitter followed by silence.

And so her sleep continued to be unsettled, both by these noises and by the haunting anxiety of what she had left behind on the mainland. In the library, though, she felt at peace, absorbed by her immense task. It was dark on the ground floor with so few windows, it was true, but the peel tower walls were so thick that it was oftentimes blessedly silent. When she needed natural light, she went up to the reading nook, spreading papers on the floor of the alcove and sitting cross-legged on the rug to examine them.

She'd tried asking the others about the strange noises, but they had looked at her doubtfully.

'Maybe we've got squirrels,' Rufus suggested.

'There aren't any creatures like that on the island, you know that as well as I do,' Martha pointed out. 'There aren't any rats, either.'

'There are mice, though,' Cora pointed out. 'Maybe they've got into the attic.'

'It's not coming from above, and it can't be mice,' Helen countered. 'Not unless they're gargantuan. They make too much noise for that.'

'Some of them have grown to a fair size,' Cora said, conversationally, seeming not in the slightest worried by Helen's descriptions. 'It's the island effect. I've been reading about it. Mammals grow to fit their surroundings, just like fish in a pond.'

Helen, who was not traditionally nervous of vermin, shuddered at the idea of being shut in an ancient house with giant mice. 'I really, really don't think it's mice.'

Martha patted her arm. 'I think it's far more likely it's just the house,' she said. 'I told you: it does make some strange noises. I won't lie – I don't think I'd want to live in it full-time. During the day it's fine, but the few times I stayed overnight to watch Mr Gissing when he was poorly were enough to convince me of that.'

'Ach, don't be spooking the poor woman,' Rufus said. 'You'll be telling her it's haunted next, when it is no such thing. There's nowt in there but you and memories, lass,' he told Helen. 'And the wind down the chimneys and the creaks in the stone. You've nothing to worry about. Although I'm with Martha – I wouldn't stay there myself. Unless it was in the peel. There's nothing untoward coming to get anyone in that place.'

It was all the excuse Helen needed to spend as much time there as possible. She thought anyone would find it fascinating, but as a book lover it was all-consuming. She excused this by telling herself that this was what her mother's firm had wanted her to do, wasn't it? To inventory the house. She was just starting with the books, that was all. *All* of the books – and what books they were.

Helen found first-edition volumes of Keats and

Wordsworth, of Coleridge and Browning, of Byron and Shelley. There were illuminated manuscripts, their colours so bright they took her breath away; huge leather-bound tomes illustrated by Gustave Doré; small, pocket-sized bindings of Austen and all the Brontës, even Branwell. Helen thought she had found a fortune within the first morning of her quest, although of course she couldn't use the internet to look anything up or ask for another opinion. Every volume she picked up seemed a rarity, and she had yet to really venture onto either of the mezzanine levels. Her old tutors in Edinburgh would be beside themselves.

Inside the peel, time passed with little note. Martha or Cora would appear with meals because she left it so rarely and although the housekeeper didn't seem to mind her sitting in the library to eat, it was clear that Cora didn't want her in there at all.

'No one ever ate in here but Mr Gissing,' Cora complained, the first time she brought Helen a plate of sandwiches at lunchtime. 'You shouldn't either. You shouldn't even be in here in the first place!'

Helen had looked up from the indicia page of a collection of *Household Words*. It was the third she had picked up, from a bookcase that held nothing but. It seemed to her that Rathbrooke Hall might be home to a complete set of every tale Dickens wrote and first published in that magazine, from *The Pickwick Papers* on.

'No one but Mr Gissing ever ate *anywhere* in the Hall,' she pointed out.

'Yes, they did,' Cora said, her face as sullen as her voice. 'Sometimes he'd invite us all over for dinner, and we'd all eat in the dining room.'

'Really?' Helen remembered what Rufus had said, the first day that she'd met Cora, after the storm. 'You and he got on well, didn't you?'

Cora was busy tidying something on one of the tables. 'Yeah. He didn't treat me like an idiot or a problem, the way everyone else does,' she muttered. 'He wasn't like Mum, who doesn't like me going over to the mainland on my own and won't even let me have a phone so I can get online like a normal person. But Cyril knew I could look after myself. He trusted me. Especially in here. He wouldn't have trusted someone he didn't know. Like *you*,' she added, in case Helen had missed her point.

'I'm trying to be helpful, Cora, that's all,' Helen said.

The girl let out an angry breath. 'You're just ticking up how much money this place is worth. That's all anyone cares about, isn't it? Not what's in the books, just what they're worth as objects.' She stalked off in a huff, and probably would have slammed the library doors shut behind her if they hadn't been quite so heavy.

Helen continued working as she considered Cora's words. Having spent more time in the library and seen what it housed for herself, Helen understood Cyril Gissing's meticulous care over it, but she was surprised that Cora seemed to care quite so much herself. Still, it seemed that Mr Gissing had somehow managed to instil an appreciation for the words in these dusty books in a girl apparently otherwise entirely unimpressed by the adults around her. Cora probably knew more about the library than anyone else except its owner. When she realized this, Helen searched Cora out to ask if she would help Helen, but the girl flat-out refused.

'I'm not helping you one bit,' the teen said, her jaw set in resolute disgust. 'Cyril would hate you being in there even more than I do.'

'Then he should have made sure his will was easy to find,' Helen pointed out. 'But because he didn't, this has to be done. It's either me or someone else, Cora, so why not help me? You can keep an eye on what I'm doing that way, can't you?'

All she got was a roll of the eyes and the sight of the teenager's back as she stalked away.

That was the day that Helen had found Cyril Gissing's diary. At first, she had no idea that's what the small notebook was – it wasn't a neat and tidy account of his days, but rather a receptacle of scrawled thoughts, at least at the beginning. She hadn't yet found the will or any sign of the owner of Rathbrooke Island's personal feelings about anything, so Helen found herself drawn to it. After all, she was staying in his house and spending her days in his favourite place – she felt oddly close to him in some ways, and yet she'd never be able to meet him. She hadn't even seen a photograph of the man – for all the trinkets dotted around Rathbrooke Hall, there were few photographs, and none that were taken in the last decade. Leafing through words he had written was the closest she'd ever get to conversing with the man himself. She set it aside and returned to it that evening, but soon realized there was plenty in it that she didn't understand, and not only because much of what Gissing had written had been put down in a rushed, florid hand.

'I feel like some of it's in code, or something,' she said to Martha, as the housekeeper delivered Helen's breakfast the morning after she'd first delved into the notebook. 'There are words I swear aren't really words. Acronyms, too. That sort of thing. Did you ever know him to use ciphers?'

Martha shook her head with a frown. 'Never. Although I'm probably not the person you should ask. Cora might know, though. Do you think there might be something in those notebooks about what he wanted to do with the island?'

'I don't think so, really,' Helen admitted. 'It mostly seems to be about the books he was reading – or at least, the books he was collecting. He bought a lot, didn't he? I've found references to auction houses in just about every part of the world.'

The other woman smiled sadly. 'Oh yes. In the last years, he never left the island unless it was to collect a book he'd bought that had arrived at the post office in Seahouses, or, as was more likely, by courier. The post office in Seahouses keeps anything for us until it can be collected. Mr Gissing was always so anxious that whatever he'd bought be brought to the island as safely as possible, and that seemed to mean him collecting it from the mainland himself. Part of the ritual, I suppose.'

Helen frowned. 'The ritual?'

Martha shrugged. 'That's just what I thought of it as. He had a very specific series of things he would do whenever a new book arrived at the library. I think that, in the end, when his health was really beginning to fail, it was the only thing he could control. It brought him comfort, I suppose. Perhaps the notebook you've found was part of that – he always really studied whatever it was he'd bought. Over the years he'd probably developed some sort of shorthand of his own to make notes about each volume. He probably never intended them to mean anything to anyone else.'

Helen nodded. 'That makes sense.'

Later, as Helen was heading back through the house towards the library, a movement out of the window caught her eye. She could see Rufus battling an ancient petrol-driven lawnmower, methodically trimming the grass of the great lawn into neat stripes. The sweat she could see on the old man's brow, even at this distance, gave her pause. She went out through the double doors of the east parlour and the warmth of the day enveloped her, a reminder of just how cool the inside of Rathbrooke Hall always remained. When she stepped out of its shadow, she realized that the late July day was already truly hot.

'Rufus,' she called, but he didn't hear her over the noise of the mower. He only killed the engine once he spotted her standing on the gravel path a few feet in front of him.

'Morning, lassie,' he said, cheerfully enough. 'How are you getting on? Cora tells me you've shown yourself to be a bit of a bookworm.'

'Rufus, don't you have anyone to help you with the garden?' she asked. 'It must be too much for you on your own, surely, especially in high summer.'

'He's got me,' said a young voice from behind them, and there was Cora approaching, with a large Thermos and two glasses. 'Mum's sent lemonade,' she said, as she deposited these on the path. 'Said we'll need it today.'

Rufus wiped a hand over his brow. 'Aye, that we will.'

'It still seems too much, even for two people,' Helen pointed out.

'Well, we get day help in from the mainland when we really need it,' Rufus said, as Cora poured two glasses that clinked with ice as it tumbled from the flask's chilled interior. 'Next week, for example, we've got a couple of lads coming out to shear the sheep. That's too much for me these days.'

'I keep telling him to let me do the mowing,' Cora added. 'He won't, though.'

'Not with this old beast, lassie,' Rufus said, patting the handle of the ancient machine on which he was leaning. 'Don't want you doing yourself an injury. Who am I going to get to run errands for me if you chop off a foot?'

Cora rolled her eyes, the very image of teenage disgruntlement.

'Listen,' Helen said to them both. 'Cora, you told me that you used to come and have dinner with Mr Gissing in the big house sometimes. Maybe we could do that again? I feel really odd eating in that massive dining room all alone.'

Cora wrinkled her nose in a frown. 'Maybe . . .'

'Your mum, too, obviously,' Helen added, and then realized something. 'And I'd do the cooking. I wouldn't want her to do it. She can have a night off.'

'Aye, well, she deserves that,' Rufus observed.

'Yeah,' Cora agreed. 'She'd like that.'

'Well, then, that's agreed,' said Helen, feeling cheerful about her plan for a moment before realizing something else. 'Oh.'

'What?' Cora asked.

Helen frowned. 'Well, I hadn't thought about groceries.'

'Martha will let you pick any veg you want to use out of the kitchen garden,' Rufus said. 'And there's the freezer.'

At this, Cora groaned.

'What's the matter?' Helen asked.

'Do we have to have lamb *again*?' the teenager grumbled. 'You know that's all the freezer's full of.'

'Never turn down free food, lassie,' Rufus said, his stalwart voice booming across the lawn. 'There's a life lesson for ye. Wait until you're fending for yourself and you'll thank me for it.'

Cora huffed. 'I'm not being ungrateful,' she said, in a tone that suggested this might be a track she was used to defending herself on. 'But—'

'I make a mean pizza,' Helen said, interrupting before the girl answered Rufus with a tirade of her own. 'I make my own dough and everything. How about that?'

Cora brightened. 'Mum never makes pizza.'

'There we go then,' Helen said, pleased that she'd found a way to connect with the moody teenager at last. 'Pizza it is.'

'Fair enough,' Rufus said, comfortably. 'I would imagine Martha's got everything you need in the stores.'

Helen wasn't sure about this. 'I think if I'm cooking for everyone, I should be doing it out of my own pocket, not the estate's.'

Rufus smiled a little at that. 'Well, I'm taking a run to Seahouses tomorrow. You can come with me and shop there, if you like.'

'That would be great,' Helen said. 'I'll charge my phone overnight – that way I can give the solicitor an update while we're in signal, too.'

She headed back to the Hall with a spring in her step, though by the time she reached the door, this had subsided. For a week now she had been inside the bubble of Rathbrooke Island, out of contact and, more importantly, far away from the mess that her life had become. She had been so absorbed by Cyril Gissing's vast collection of books that she had almost forgotten what was lurking for her back in the real world. The thought of it all made her not want to return at all. When she got back to the library, she stood on the threshold for a moment, breathing in the scent of old pages. It would be so easy to get lost here, she realized. In some ways, she already had. Helen knew she'd been neglecting her job regarding the rest of the house in favour of spending all her time in the library. But that couldn't last for ever, could it?

Besides, it had been more than a week since she'd hit the headlines. A week was a very long time in showbusiness, not to mention the tabloid news cycle. Perhaps the storm of her downfall had already rolled on to engulf a different shore.

Helen tried to get back to the job of cataloguing, but her mind wouldn't settle. Intrusive thoughts dominated her mind instead – frustrating, given how calming she had previously found the library to be. Even after half an hour she had failed to get through the shelf she'd been intending to finish. Then she pulled something unexpected from between the next books – not a volume, but a thin folder. For a moment she wondered if she'd finally found Cyril Gissing's last will and testament. When she opened the folder, however, she saw that it held not legal papers, but a sheaf of neat, handwritten letters.

Curious, Helen took the folder back to Gissing's desk. It didn't take her long to see that they went back years, and while they had been sent from all over the world, they were all written by the same correspondent.

His name was Thiago Montera.

Chapter Nine

In the morning, Helen found Rufus and Cora in the orchard. They were boxing a series of small saplings into a wooden crate, terracotta-coloured pots full of fronds of wispy trees staked with bamboo canes, their new leaves still furled into themselves.

'This is why I'm going over,' Rufus explained, as Cora closed the crate and nailed down the wooden lid with determined gusto. 'I've been promising these to the garden centre for a while. They've got folk who've been on the waiting list for them. They're big enough now. They'll not be planted for a few weeks, until autumn – but they can go to their new homes, climatize a bit in their pots.'

'Are they apple trees?' Helen asked.

'No, these are the mulberries,' Cora said. 'They're saplings from cuttings that we took two years ago. They're big enough to move now.'

'Mulberries,' Helen repeated, remembering what Martha had said that first morning she'd spent on the island. 'Martha told me to ask you about the one in the orchard, Rufus, but I forgot. It sounded as if there was a story behind it?'

'Oh, well,' Rufus said. 'Have you met the old dame yet?'

'The tree? No, I don't think so.'

'You'd remember it if you had,' he said. 'Come on, I'll show you.'

Rufus guided her to the centre of the orchard, where a great tree, verdant with leaves, spread out in an immense tangle. It bore branches that were so heavy they dipped towards the ground before reaching skyward in a huge sprawl. Rufus led the way, pushing between leaves and under the canopy. Helen followed, finding herself enveloped by the mulberry, its leaves closing behind the three of them – for Cora had followed, too – like a curtain. It reminded Helen of hideouts in forests when she was a child, little natural shelters hidden away from the grown-ups, except this one was adult sized. Above their heads she could see clusters of fruit, like large blackberries, not yet ripe.

Beneath the mulberry, the outside world was a myth held at bay. It was the library all over again, but here the shelves were branches. There was something intensely humbling about it. Helen reached out a hand, laid it against the dark, gnarled bark.

'Impressive, isn't she?' Rufus smiled. His voice fell against the wall of leaves as if against snow, silenced and contained. 'Do you know why we've got black mulberries in Britain? They're not a native fruit, you know.'

Helen shook her head. She didn't know, at all, but could

tell she was in the presence of great age – she could feel it through her fingers.

'See, the thing is,' Rufus began, 'mulberries are what silk worms live on. Silk worms and mulberries, that's what made that great industry. The story goes that there was a Chinese princess back in ancient times who observed caterpillars on the mulberry trees in her orchards, weaving their cocoons with the finest thread she'd ever seen. She was the one that first stole that thread so her weavers could make silk, and they were the folk who realized how important the mulberry was to the silk caterpillars.'

'The Silk Road,' Cora added. 'That wouldn't have existed without the mulberry.'

The gardener pointed at her. 'Exactly right. Well, time rolls on and we get to King James I. He liked the hunting of witches and had a terror of Catholics. He also had a taste for fancy clothes. And he decided that England should be able to produce its own silk to make them. He didn't want to have to import the cloth for his fine wardrobe any more. He wanted it to be produced here. And to be fair to him, he did do a tad of research on the subject. He was a bit of a scholar, that Jimmy the King. He learned a bit, and between 1607 and 1608, he brought many thousands of mulberry trees to England. He urged all the nobles of the land to plant mulberries on their estates and in their gardens. For a sliver of time there, mulberry trees became a symbol of wealth and aristocracy and owning one was a signal to the King himself that you were his loyal servant. Plenty of aspiring folk planted mulberries in their gardens. Thousands of saplings there were, and black mulberries, you know, they live a long time once they're established. Most were planted in London, and many are still there today: great, shambling, bushy trees, four hundred years old, reminders of great grounds that were once the gardens of great homes. The buildings are usually long gone, their grounds built on and concreted over so that only the mulberries are left behind in a little lonely square of dirt. They're still standing, still producing fruit, though few can remember what they are or why they were planted in the first place.'

'But,' Cora interjected, 'way back when, King Jim had made a big mistake. Huge.'

'He had,' Rufus said. 'Come on, we'd best get going. I'll tell you the rest as we get on.'

Helen let her hand slip from the bark of the Rathbrooke mulberry and followed Rufus and Cora out from beneath her boughs. She helped him and Cora load the saplings and then they began to head down the path towards the harbour, Cora and Helen stopping the pots from toppling while Rufus pushed the barrow.

'The mistake that King James had made,' the gardener said, picking up his tale again as they walked, 'was that his mulberry saplings were black mulberry, not white mulberry. Now, silk worms like any type of mulberry, but here's the thing. White mulberry grows much more quickly than the black mulberry. When your silk caterpillars hatch, they will munch away at the leaves around them. They eat a lot and they eat fast. On a white mulberry, that's fine, because the tree will keep producing leaves as quickly as the critters can eat 'em. But a black mulberry, not so much. It takes the black mulberry tree much longer to grow more leaves. If you raise your silk worms on a black mulberry, they'll strip its leaves and starve before the tree has a chance to produce more. It doesn't do the tree much good, either, losing all of its leaves so quickly in growing season. That's the main reason why Jimmy's great plan to launch an English silk industry was a miserable failure. But it did mean that there were now a great number of mulberry trees in England, in the gardens of notable folks.'

'Including William Shakespeare,' Cora added.

'Aye,' Rufus nodded. 'Aye.'

'Really?' Helen asked. 'Shakespeare had one of King James's mulberry trees?'

'Oh my God!' Cora crowed. 'This next bit is going to blow your *mind*!'

'What will?' Helen asked, as Rufus laughed.

'Wait a bit while we get underway,' he said. They had reached Rathbrooke's tiny harbour. 'I can't spend all day standing about telling stories!'

They loaded the boat and set off for Seahouses. The day was another sunny one, the light dancing on the North Sea as if to play on its soft waves. The summer sun illuminated the Northumberland coast in a haze of golden light, tumbling the dunes with shadows. In one direction curved Beadnell beach, long and yellow with its short but treacherous belts of rocks. In the other, Bamburgh Castle stood immense and impervious over the bay, big enough to house a city within its walls. Lindisfarne was hazy beyond and out in the sea in the middle distance, while the rest of the Farnes were strung like black bunting on the tide, their craggy black rocks and flat treeless tops transformed into glinting pennants, presided over by the two lighthouses. Everywhere overhead the seabirds wailed and dipped, hunting in the tide. Helen looked back towards Rathbrooke, her black cliffs looming over them as they departed her shadow, topped with that huge feat of the island wall. Even this was less forbidding in the summer sun. As they passed into open water, she saw the mass of little puffins around the promontory beyond the wall to the island's far south, throwing up plumes of water as they plunged into the water over and over, catching fish.

'Come on, then,' she shouted, once they were clear of the harbour channel. 'One of you tell me the story.'

Rufus looked at Cora. 'Do you want to?'

The teenager shook her head. 'You do it.'

'All right, then. Here we go. Well, old Bill Shakespeare, come this time, wasn't a mere glover's boy any more – he was a gent, and a famous and rich one at that. He planted a mulberry right there in the garden of New Place, his house in Stratford. He was proud of it and would show it off to visitors, which makes the people who consider such things think he probably did literally plant it himself, instead of getting a gardener to do it. Anyway, after he died, that tree – tall now, and strong, not even a quarter of its way into life – became a kind of pilgrimage for people who wanted to pay their respects to the great departed bard.'

'We're not just talking directly after he died, neither,' Cora shouted, over the engine. 'This went on for years, didn't it, Rufus?'

'It did,' Rufus agreed. 'It was there for at least 150 years and it would still be there now, alive and well, except that in 1756, the vicar who lived in New Place at that time – the man's name was Francis, by all accounts, unhappy man was he – got so tired of strangers knocking on his door asking to get into his garden to see Shakespeare's mulberry that he cut it down.'

'He didn't!' Helen said, shocked.

'He did!' Rufus laughed, with a shake of his head. 'He paid for it though – the story goes that he was so vilified for slaying Shakespeare's tree that he ended up having to sell the house and pack off out of Stratford for good.'

'I'm not surprised,' Helen said, indignant on behalf of this long-gone tree. 'What a terrible end for that part of Shakespeare's legacy.'

'Ah ha!' said Rufus. 'You can be forgiven for thinking that would be the end, for sure, what with it being hacked into a stump and all, but—'

'It wasn't!' Cora joined in, cheeks rosy from the wind. 'It wasn't the end. It was just the beginning.'

Rufus slowed to observe the speed restrictions in place in the harbour channel. The Seahouses they sailed towards was a world away from the one Helen had first encountered.

There were already tours leaving the harbour, the indistinct boom of the tour guides' voices carrying across the water. The fishing boats that had been out overnight were back, a colourful riot of red and blue lined up against the gleaming concrete. The sun was so bright that Helen wished she'd brought her sunglasses – spending most of her time inside the gloomy confines of Rathbrooke Hall meant she had forgotten that everywhere else, summer was in full swing.

'Cora's right,' Rufus continued. 'What happened was, the trunk and branches and what-not of that good tree became a kind of relic. Actually, it became many hundreds of relics – thousands, probably, like the body of a saint that turns out to have more fingers and toes than us regular folk. A timber merchant bought the felled wood and he turned it into all manner of goods. Trinket boxes, carved mementos, you name it, people wanted them. They wanted cuttings, too, which were saved after the tree was felled. And so Shakespeare's mulberry tree survived, in a way.'

'That's amazing,' Helen said. 'I can't believe I've never heard of this before. And if there were cuttings, does that mean that there are more of these trees still surviving today? Ones that came from Shakespeare's original mulberry?'

'Oh yes,' Rufus said, glancing at Cora with a broad smile.

'You're sitting next to some of them right now,' the girl said, patting her hand on top of the crate of saplings. 'Well – I guess these are third generation, because they're saplings of a sapling. But still. That's pretty close, right?'

Helen realized what this meant. 'Wait – so that mulberry

you just showed me, in Rathbrooke's orchard – that was once a sapling taken directly from Shakespeare's own felled tree?'

'Aye, that's right,' Rufus said. 'Don't ask me who planted it, because Mr Gissing never knew for sure. It was here when he inherited, though I don't think he knew about it until much later. He told me – when he told me the story that I've just told you, which became one of his favourites – that he'd found a very old bill of sale from when Abington Park was sold in 1841. That was a big manor house and grounds down in Northampton. All of its contents were auctioned off, and the then-owner of Rathbrooke bought a load of stuff for the Hall at that time. There it was, on the list of goods, an entry that said: "One strong tree of Shakespeare's mulberry, grown of a sapling taken from New Place".'

'And he thought it really was one of Shakespeare's mulberry trees?' Helen asked, trying to work out the timeline. 'That had been brought all the way here from Northampton, almost two hundred years ago?'

Rufus nodded. 'He always could spin a story, could Mr Gissing – maybe because he spent so much of his time reading them. Knowing him, he'd done a bit of research into it all to work it all out. Anyway, he started getting me to propagate saplings ourselves. Now we sell a few through the garden centre at Seahouses,' Rufus said, as he docked the boat at the harbour wall. 'He wanted to make sure that Shakespeare's trees took root up here in the north, and so here we are,' he leaned over and patted the crate of tiny trees, 'doing just that.'

Helen contemplated the box of saplings at her feet. It was a nice story, although she wasn't sure she could believe it was true, or how anyone would ever prove it either way.

Cora leapt out of the boat and tied her off as Rufus killed the engine. Helen helped them get the crate up onto the harbour arm.

'I'm going to go off on my own for a bit, all right?' Cora said.

'Eh?' Rufus looked perplexed. 'Why would you do that?'

The girl rolled her eyes. 'Because I've got my own life?'

'Oi, less of the cheek,' the gardener scolded, gently. 'Aren't you going to help me load the saplings into the van?' He indicated a black transit that had parked up on the harbour, the logo of a garden centre picked out in elegant script on the side.

'I need to post something. And I'm going to meet up with my cousin,' Cora said, as she looked towards the van, where a driver was just climbing out of the front. 'Graham's there, look – he'll help.' She was already walking away.

'Cora!'

'I'll be back here soon as,' she shouted back, still moving. 'Promise!'

Rufus gave a gusty sigh. 'Fine. Make sure it's not longer than two hours or we'll leave without you! I've got plenty to be getting on with back home! Cora! I mean it!' he called after her. 'You be back here in two hours!'

Cora threw up a hand but didn't turn, shifting into a run that took her up the curving slope that led past the booking huts of the boat trip companies and away out of sight.

'Should we go after her?'

Rufus shook his head. 'She probably could do with a bit of freedom, truth be told.' He glanced at Helen with a smile. 'Might burn off some of that mardy attitude. Right, I'd best get on. Meet you back here?'

Helen agreed and they went their separate ways. She went to check on Melanie's car, which seemed to still be safe where she had parked it on the Sunday she had arrived, although she moved it to a different spot, worried about causing annoyance to the locals. Then she sat in the driver's seat, gathering her courage before turning on her phone. She ignored the furious beeping as messages poured in demanding her attention and called her mother instead, giving her a brief update and describing the situation she had found on the island. Irene didn't seem phased by the months that Helen estimated it was going to take to catalogue the contents.

'Well, stick at it as long as you're able,' her mother said. 'We'll work something out if you run out of steam.' There was a pause. 'How are you doing . . . about the other thing?'

Helen didn't need to ask what. She shifted in her seat, leaning on the steering wheel and watching the crowds board another catamaran to take the Farne Islands cruise. 'I'm trying not to think about it,' she said, truthfully. 'Being on the island is helping . . . it's like being on another planet.'

'Good,' said her mother. 'Long may it last. Although . . .'

'What?' Helen prompted, her stomach dipping.

'Melanie called me,' Irene said. 'She just wanted to know

how you're doing. I said I hadn't heard from you either, but that I was sure you were fine.'

Helen rubbed a hand across her face. 'I've no idea when she'll get her car back. I should have come by public transport; I'm not even going to use it while I'm here.'

'I can call her for you, if you like,' her mother said. 'Let her know how you're getting on.'

'Yeah, if you could,' Helen said, passing the buck with guilty relief. 'I don't think I can face talking to her – it's not that I blame her; I just don't want to think about it. Tell her the car's fine, would you? And tell her I will be in touch . . . some time.'

After they said goodbye, Helen turned off her phone again, another wave of relief washing over her as she slid it away out of sight. This was the longest in years that she hadn't been anchored to contact every moment of the day. There was something liberating in it, something deeply refreshing. It wasn't just that it meant she didn't have to confront whatever muck was floating around in her orbit. Her mind was clearer. She hadn't doomscrolled in over a week. Helen felt more centred, more focused, than she had for months, years. *Long may it last*, she thought, and wondered if she could stay on Rathbrooke for good. It would, after all, be the perfect place for a writer. Not that she had much hope of ever publishing anything else again. Even under a pseudonym, her past would find her. Damn Brett Pottinger. If only she hadn't caught his eye, all those years ago. If only she hadn't been so naive and easy to manipulate. If only she'd been stronger, smarter.

She got out of the car and locked these thoughts in it behind her before they could become even more maudlin. Helen paused for a moment, looking out over the harbour, with the island she had left not long ago in the middle distance between her and the others on the horizon. From here, it and the other Farne Islands looked like a series of flat stones, as if someone had stood on the shore and tried to skim them across the North Sea. From this angle and in this light, Rathbrooke looked as featureless as all of them, the only building visible the slight turret of the lighthouse. This was Rufus's domain. It stood at the opposite end of the island to the house, and was built into the island wall, which from this distance simply looked like more of the impervious cliff face. It was the same with the other Farnes – the only distinguishing features that Helen could make out were the raised points of the two distant lighthouses, one at each end of the small archipelago, there to ward boats away from a watery wrecking on the islands. She could see small boats between the harbour and the islands, a series of pleasure crafts taking visitors on and off the nature reserves to see the sea birds, primarily the puffins. But none were anywhere near Rathbrooke Island. Helen wondered what stories the locals told about the place and its inhabitants.

She went to find the ingredients she needed for dinner. Seahouses had one street of shops, mainly given over to eateries and gifts themed for the seabirds and seals that made the islands off the coast their home for part of the year. It also had a large Co-op, a grocer's shop and a store specializing in

Northumbrian produce. Helen spent a long time choosing delicious charcuterie, olives and cheeses, as well as unbleached bread flour milled from Northumbrian wheat. It seemed ridiculous to buy vegetables when the garden on Rathbrooke was so verdant, but she bought chocolate, cream and condensed milk for an ice cream dessert. The condensed milk and cream she had to go into the supermarket to find, and this was when her downfall came. Waiting at the checkout, she glanced at a rack of magazines to see a photograph of herself, inset against a snatched image of a pale, exhausted Alice Marsh. WHERE IS SHE? The headline demanded. HOMEWRECKER GOES AWOL LEAVING ACTRESS DEVASTATED

Helen froze, staring at her own picture, unable to move. It had been taken at Daunt Books, at the party her publisher had thrown for the publication of *All of the Above*. Helen had had her hair done for the occasion and had bought a new dress. She looked happy and polished, a massive contrast to the pap shot of the actress, who had probably been snapped as she popped to the local shop for a pint of milk one Sunday morning. The contrast – Helen smiling, smug even, and Alice, pale and makeup-free – was striking. It was manipulated, an illusion, of course it was, but still Helen's gut clenched.

She stood there so long that the person behind her nudged her forward. Helen flinched and apologized and tried to keep her head down, which meant she did not see Cora in the queue behind her.

*

3 Sunnyside Road
Seahouses
Northumberland

Maybe you're right. Maybe it would be better for the two of you to talk about this face-to-face. But you know how paranoid Mum is. If she knew I was writing to you she'd go ballistic. And you wouldn't be able to get to the island without one of us bringing you over anyway. All of the boat owners know Rufus and they wouldn't come into harbour without telling him they were on their way and why. And I don't think he'd let them bring you, because I think Mum's told him a load of lies about you. He's always squirrelly when I bring you up, like he'd rather I didn't know about you at all.

Chapter Ten

Helen half expected for her and Rufus to end up waiting for Cora, but she needn't have worried. She and Rufus were loading her shopping onto the deck when the girl appeared, her earlier sunny disposition replaced once more by a sullen scowl, which she directed at Helen before turning to Rufus.

'Told you I'd be back,' she said.

'Aye, you did,' Rufus said, and it was then that Helen saw how much he loved the girl, like a granddaughter, for sure. 'A good thing too.'

'Did you have a good visit with your cousin?' Helen asked, but Cora ignored her, covering her rudeness by climbing aboard the *Lady Jane*.

'Come on, you wee scoundrel scrap,' Rufus said to Cora, oblivious. 'You can pilot us back.'

'Really?' Cora's eyes widened – her face, a second ago aged with cynicism, now youthful again with excitement. 'All the way to the island?'

'Aye, why not?' Rufus said. 'You've been practising,

haven't you? Just take it easy out of the harbour. Watch for traffic; there's a lot about today. And no speeding; we don't need to make an enemy of the harbour master.'

Cora took the wheel and Rufus moved out of her way. He glanced at Helen with a smile as Cora took them out of Seahouses. Helen turned back as they left the dock, watching the village glow in the sun, the banality of a working harbour turned glorious by the simple benevolence of warmth and light.

'What did you do before you came here?' asked Cora, as they all sat around the great dining table later that evening. The room had echoed with their laughter – well, the adults had laughed, anyway. Cora's mood had turned churlish and stubbornly silent again. Still, amid the chatter it was possible to imagine other such gatherings throughout the ages, the warm and convivial breaking of bread stretching back centuries. With other people in it, Rathbrooke Hall seemed less imperious, less a wreck of itself, as if in feeling joy the house had reflected back not just what had been generated this evening, but what it remembered of all those bygone decades. 'Did you always do this? Go to sort out people's houses after they died?'

'Oh – no,' Helen said, the laugh she had ended her last sentence on dying a little, fading away. 'No. Actually, this is the first time I've ever done something like this.'

Cora stuffed her mouth with more ice cream. The food, at least, had seemed up to her standards. 'What did you do before that, then?'

Helen tried to think about her past in a way that was explainable, though she'd rather not talk about it at all. 'I wrote a book.'

'Just one?' Cora asked, shovelling a mound of chocolate ice cream into her mouth.

'Cora!' her mother said. 'Writing one book is a big thing!'

Cora shrugged. 'You must have done something else, though. I mean, you're here because you're doing a job, so you must need to earn a living. You're not rich, is what I mean, so you can't have spent your whole life until now writing just *one* book.'

'Depends when she wrote the book,' Rufus pointed out. 'What's it called, lass? Would we have heard of it?'

Helen suddenly wished she had used a different name than her own when she had come here. Was she destined always to make the same mistakes? 'Helen Thorne' was easily remembered, even if only from glancing at one of the posters that had been everywhere when *All of the Above* first came out, and never mind the magnitude of discussion generated over it since, particularly recently.

'You're right, Cora,' she said, dodging the question, burying the lede. 'I started off as an actress. Or at least, I tried to. I didn't get very far.' Helen looked down at her own bowl of ice cream, which was beginning to melt into a puddle.

'Well,' Cora said, 'I suppose it's not easy getting parts with a broken nose like yours. They want pretty faces, don't they, on screen. Mostly, anyway.'

'Cora!' Martha said, and this time her tone was outraged,

mortified. 'What's got into you? Why are you being so rude? Apologize, right now. And after Helen put all this effort into making you this lovely dinner.'

Cora shrugged, her concentration all for her bowl of dessert. Helen watched the girl's bowed head and wondered if this was deliberate animosity or only the vagaries of teenage contrariness rearing its head. The apology came, but belatedly enough for the delay to be pointed. 'Sorry.'

'You might be right,' Helen said. 'But my nose wasn't broken when I started acting. Actually, when it happened it pretty much ended my career.'

Cora looked up. Helen could see the girl wanted to ask the obvious question: *How did it happen?* But she couldn't bring herself to reveal her interest. She wanted to project indifference, so that Helen would understand that nothing about her mattered. Yes, this was definite animosity, of the sort that hadn't been there yesterday, or even this morning, before their trip to the mainland. Helen's heart sank, remembering that screaming headline in the supermarket, that photograph of her at her happiest, as if that's how she always was. Had Cora seen it? Very possibly, and the picture was recognizably Helen. That would account for this renewed hostility.

The conversation had dipped in the wake of Cora's rudeness and Helen was suddenly too mired in her own worries to be a good host and pick it up. Rufus stepped into the breach instead, trying to jolly them back on course.

'How's it going in the library, then, Helen?' he asked. 'I

wondered why you were spending so much time in there. Makes sense if you're a writer.'

'Slowly,' Helen admitted. 'It's all too much for one person. Especially as I've been trying to decipher Mr Gissing's diary, too.'

Cora stared at Helen with full outrage. 'You're reading his *diary*? You can't do that! It's private! That's . . . you're not allowed!'

'Cora!' her mother said, yet again, but this time the girl would not be dissuaded.

'No! It's not right!'

'I'm trying to find Mr Gissing's will, Cora, that's why I'm going through his papers,' she said, keeping her voice as even as possible. 'There must be one somewhere. And if there isn't, there could be something in the diary. If he wrote down what he wanted to happen with the island, it would help. That's why I'm here – to *help*.'

'You shouldn't even be in the library,' Cora carried on, dismissing Helen's words as if she hadn't spoken. 'He'd hate that. I know he would. I've *told* you that. He wanted it kept safe. He wouldn't want some stranger poking around in it.'

'I want to keep it safe too, Cora,' Helen tried. 'It's a very special place.'

'You don't know a thing about it!' Cora shouted. 'And you never will!'

With that, she got up and stormed off, out through the kitchen. Martha called after her, but the only response was the bang of the door as she went out into the orchard and away.

'I'm so sorry,' Martha said. 'I don't know what's got into her. Rufus, did something happen when you went to Seahouses?'

Rufus shook his head. 'Not that I know of, lass. She's just uppity, that's all. She's had a lot to deal with of late, eh? She's a good girl; she probably already feels bad about all that malarkey, Helen. She'll come back to apologize, you'll see.'

But Helen was sure that Cora wouldn't and she was equally sure she knew why. The evening was over. Together they cleared the plates, but Helen wouldn't let Martha or Rufus help her wash them. She did that herself after they'd left, finding herself with tears on her cheeks as she did, and then told herself to stop being so self-pitying.

It was another two days before she saw Cora again. The girl appeared without fanfare, carrying Helen's breakfast like a peace offering, although she did not look especially contrite.

'Mum says I should take you to see the puffins,' she said. 'We can go once you've had your breakfast.'

Helen studied the girl's face, which was a studious blank. 'You don't have to do that.'

'I do,' she said. 'It's to apologize for the other night.' she paused. 'And to say thank you for the dinner. Both, I guess. If I don't take you, I'll be in trouble. I don't want to be in trouble, so if you don't come and that happens, I'd have to tell her why I was pissed off with you in the first place and I don't think you'd want me to do that. Because the thing is that my mum *really* hates cheats. My dad cheated on her and that's why we're here.' The girl shrugged. 'And I can see how matey the two of you are getting, so you probably don't want her to hear that you've ended up here for being on the other side of the same thing, do you?'

Helen wondered whether to address what had caused this hostility. Perhaps Cora, as young as she was, might understand. But she decided almost immediately that no, it wouldn't help. Cora wasn't really angry at Helen. She was angry at everything else going on in her life and Helen was a convenient outlet.

'Fine,' she said. 'I'll come.'

Cora nodded and stalked to the concealed door, throwing her parting line over her shoulder. 'Wait for me outside the greenhouse when you're ready to go.'

Helen ate her breakfast quickly, washed the plates in the kitchen and stacked them on the rack to dry before going upstairs to use the bathroom. As she came back down past the doors to the west wing, she heard a thump, followed by the echo of something rolling, then another thump, then another, then the patter-and-silence of the swift footsteps she had heard so often. The strange sounds from behind the closed doors had faded into the background of her sojourn at the Hall in the past few days, perhaps because she was spending so much time at the other end of the house. She listened for another minute, but a silence descended that seemed stiller than it should be, as always happened when her attention was focused on trying to decipher something that may not even have been there in the first place.

Helen went back downstairs, pulled on her walking boots, and went out of the kitchen door into the morning light. She stood for a moment amid the light breeze and brightness of the day, listening to the rustle in the orchard leaves. For days now she had barely been outside, the now fateful-seeming trip to Seahouses notwithstanding. Instead, all her daily energies had been focused on the library, on Cyril Gissing's diary and the letters she had found in his desk. Something told her she'd discovered something significant, if only she could decipher the hidden meaning within. She felt a little like a detective, piecing together fragments of information into something more or less whole, although what picture that whole would form when she did, she had no idea.

Helen went through the orchard arch and passed into the kitchen garden. Since her last visit, a stitch of carrots had been lifted, the neat bare line of earth left behind, dark and drying in the warm sun. She went to the door of the greenhouse and peered inside, the plants within so verdant it was difficult to see between them. She realized, though, that there were windows in the wall against which it stood – windows that must look out of, or, more importantly, *into* the lower floor of the empty west wing. This seemed odd to her – were greenhouses usually built like this? But of course Rathbrooke Hall was a mishmash of historical eras and building styles, added to over the centuries. Presumably the greenhouse had been built where it would best serve its purpose and over existing features of the house.

There was no sign of movement beyond the glass, no

visible indication that Cora was inside. Helen went to turn the round wooden handle, to push the door open and call a greeting, but before she could the girl appeared inside and turned a key in the handle on the other side of the door – clearly it had been locked. She opened the door and stepped quickly outside, so that Helen had to step out of the way, back along the path. Cora pulled the door shut and turned the key again – Helen saw over Cora's shoulder that she had a keychain heavy with several keys in her hand. The girl stuffed the whole lot back in her pocket.

'Come on, then,' Cora said, briskly, turning and leading Helen away down the path.

To Helen's surprise, they did not cut through the rose garden and along to the harbour gate as she had expected. Instead, the girl led her into the sheep pastures that she hadn't yet visited. The sheep were small – short-legged creatures with small tips of horns above friendly little black faces. Their fleeces were wiry and thick, a colour mottled between chocolate brown and cream. They were surprisingly pretty, not something Helen had ever considered sheep to be before, and so small that she wondered whether they were all lambs, but that seemed unlikely.

'What cute sheep,' she said, to Cora, who strode along just ahead of her. 'I've never seen this breed before.'

The girl cast a glance towards the flock, who as one had lifted their woolly heads to chart their progress. 'No, you wouldn't have,' she said, nonchalantly. 'They're Rathbrooke Cheviots. There are only two flocks of them, this one and one over at a rare breed farm on the mainland. And that one's only there so we can swap rams to limit inbreeding.'

'Really?' Helen looked over at the flock again. 'The island has its own breed of sheep? How is that even possible? Where did they come from?'

'They're descended from the mainland Cheviots,' Cora said. 'That's about all I know. It was another thing that Cy was really proud of.'

Helen looked again at the sheep's distinctive fleeces and thought about Rufus's many layers of knitted jumpers. 'The fleece – does it get turned into yarn?'

'Yup,' said Cora, still striding on at a fair pace, so that Helen had to hurry to catch up. 'My mum spins it. She learned how to do it when we got here because it's what the old lady used to do who had the job before her. People buy it for tons of money because the flock's so small that there's not that much of it and only Mum spins it. It's really good and super warm.'

They had reached a door in the island wall, the thick greying wood flaking gently with age. Helen watched as Cora pulled out her bunch of keys again, selected a large one that looked a similar age to the door itself, and fitted it to the lock.

'Cora,' Helen said, as something occurred to her. 'Have you got a lot of keys to Rathbrooke Hall?'

'Nope,' the girl said, even as the huge bunch of keys jangled in her hand. 'These are Mum's. I just borrow them when I need them.'

Cora stepped through into the wind that cut beyond the

wall. Helen followed as the girl waited for her, and then pulled the door shut behind them. The keys vanished once again into her voluminous pockets.

'We have to keep all the wall gates shut, always,' Cora shouted, over the combined sound of the waves on the rocks below them, the wind and the screaming seabirds. 'If the sheep got out here it would be a nightmare to round them up.'

She led the way along a path that ran close to the island wall, but still not far enough from the cliff edge for Helen's liking. She'd never been particularly scared of heights, but a person was so vulnerable out here – one slip could take you tumbling over the edge, crashing down the pinnacles of black rock into the roiling water below. Cora forged on ahead, unconcerned and without pause, until the wall curved in a tighter turn than the island's edge. The path still kept close to the stacked stone, but here a narrow promontory spat itself out into the ocean waters.

'We don't go any closer than this,' Cora shouted, fighting with the sound of water crashing beneath their feet. 'We don't want to disturb them.'

The promontory was crowded with little sea birds. There were puffins as far as the eye could see, the colourful bursts of their red and yellow beaks adding a carnival air to the day. There were some peeking out of burrows and some in flight, some roosting and dozing, some stuffing down silver fish that seemed far too big for their tiny shapes.

Helen laughed, delighted by the sheer aliveness of the

birdy chaos in front of her. Cora cracked a smile despite herself.

'They're gorgeous!'

'Yeah,' agreed Cora. 'They are. The numbers are good this year, too. There were a lot of pufflings. They're all about fledged now. They'll be starting to think about going back north in the next few weeks. They'll all be gone by the end of August.'

She had pulled out a notebook and pencil and was jotting something down, raising the pencil to count off numbers.

'Thank you,' Helen said. 'Thank you for bringing me, Cora. I know you didn't really want to.'

The girl shrugged and went on counting, and didn't answer.

'Cora,' Helen said, trying again. 'Maybe you can help me with what I've got to do. I know you don't like me reading Mr Gissing's diary, and I understand why. But maybe if you help me, I won't need to carry on.'

The girl looked at her suspiciously. 'What sort of help?'

Helen looked out at the water, at the wheeling seabirds, feeding their young. 'Well, like I said, what I'm really trying to do is find Mr Gissing's will. Have you got any idea where he might have put it? Even if he hadn't actually got around to making the new one he was planning yet, did he tell you what he wanted to do with Rathbrooke – or even the library? He must have had a plan.'

Cora shook her head.

'Really? Only I thought that maybe he might have

talked to you about it? It sounds as if you two were great friends.'

Cora stared out to sea. 'He said he'd make sure that we were all looked after, that's all. That nothing would have to change if we didn't want it to.'

'Really?' Helen said. 'He said that – that nothing would change?'

The girl glanced at her. 'It wasn't true, though, was it? Because he died and you're here instead, poking around where you shouldn't be.'

'But I'm only here because Mr Gissing didn't send his will back to the solicitor,' Helen pointed out. 'If we could find it—'

'I don't know where it is,' Cora said, staunchly. 'So you might as well stop asking.'

'All right,' Helen conceded. 'In that case, what *did* you two talk about?'

The girl chewed her lip and went back to making her notes. 'Books. We talked about books a lot. He'd been teaching me Shakespeare so that I'd have a jump on what we'd be studying next year when I go to school in Alnwick. And we were reading *Don Quixote*.'

'Really?' This was a surprising choice. Helen couldn't imagine that the Spanish classic was on the school curriculum.

'Yeah.' Cora looked up at her with a frown. 'Do you know it?'

'Only vaguely,' Helen admitted. 'I've never actually read it.'

'I like it,' the girl said. 'I like the way it's about a man who so desperately wants to live inside the stories he reads that he ends up seeing them everywhere. He makes his own story and lives inside it. But there's all this other stuff that goes with it. It's a parody and even if it's got a load of in-jokes that would have made more sense at the time, it makes me laugh. Although the women in it are rubbish.'

Helen allowed herself a little smile at that. Then something else occurred to her. 'Cora – did you ever hear Mr Gissing talk about someone called Thiago Montera?'

Cora froze, just for a second, just long enough for Helen to see that the name meant something to her. 'Yes,' she said, though in a way that suggested she would rather not say anything at all. 'Thiago Montera is a librarian. In Spain. Cy used to write to him all the time and he wrote back.'

'He wrote to a librarian in Spain?'

'Yup.'

'What about? Was it about *Don Quixote*?'

Cora sighed with great gravity, as if she were being asked to hold up the world. 'They talked about all sorts of books. He was just a friend of Cy's. They'd been writing to each other for, like, *ever*, okay?'

'Like a pen pal.'

'Yeah, whatever,' Cora said, bored of this now. 'Come on. Let's go back. I can't leave you out here, I have to lock the gate again.'

The conversation with Cora, although short, gave Helen an idea. Back in the library she pulled out Cyril Gissing's diary again, taking it from the nook in the desk in which she had found it and opening it on the tabletop beneath the small lamp. She saw now that the odd words that she had thought were in some sort of code were actually written in a different language. Could it really be that simple? Could Cyril Gissing's fascination with a classic Spanish novel and the fact that he had a Spanish friend with whom he apparently regularly corresponded be the answer? She searched the shelves until she found a Spanish–English dictionary bound in red leather, with a spine weathered enough to suggest constant use. She opened it and a handwritten letter fell to the floor at her feet – another that matched the ones she'd already found. She picked it up and saw neat lines of slanted handwriting, which appeared to be mostly in English, aside from a few lines. *Cyril, my dear friend* was the salutation, and the writer signed off his name with a flourish: *Until next month – Thiago Montera.*

Helen took both the book and the letter back to the desk and looked up a random word from the diary that she had not been able to decipher. Sure enough, that was the key. It wasn't a code at all. It was only that his diaries were interlaced with Spanish. Why? Why not write the whole thing in Spanish, if he'd been worried about someone on Rathbrooke reading them? But the door to the library was always locked, wasn't it? And even if it hadn't been, to Helen it seemed that the residents of the island were all loyal enough to their employer not to breach his trust in any way. Cora's outrage that his privacy was being violated even after death was enough for her to see that. Why, then?

Helen supposed the answer probably lay in the words she now had the chance to decipher. She took the diary, a notepad and the dictionary, and painstakingly translated each mystery line: one hesitant, probably-not-quite-accurate word at a time.

*

Cyril, my friend,

I am writing quickly, sending you this before Alejandra and I embark from Cairo en route to Heraklion. This is something a little different for you, which I came across completely by surprise in the house of a former aide to a British diplomat in Egypt. A different beast to what I usually send you, and not what you will have been expecting to hear news of from this trip.

You may have opened the parcel already, and perhaps even have it in your hands as you read this. Isn't it a crisp copy? In perfect mint condition, I would say. I'm not even sure the spine has ever been cracked – we may be, you and I, the first people to flick through its pages since it came off the press. Perhaps it was sent to a service colleague of Fleming's, who took one look at it and lost it amid his shelves out of disinterest or envy. Yes, it is a pristine first edition of Casino Royale*, complete with a dust jacket that could have been folded around it by the fingers of the gentlest angel. I have never seen corners so sharp on a book that has been out in the world since 1953. And the colours are so bright! Not a hint of foxing or fading. Anyway, it belongs with you. It will be the perfect find for someone.*

And now for the sea, the sun above it, and a welcome breeze.

As ever, your friend,

Thiago Montera

Chapter Eleven

Helen had brought back wine from the mainland when she'd shopped for the four of them, and since there was a bottle remaining, a few days later she invited Martha over for a glass and a chat. She missed her girlfriends back home – especially Melanie, whom she saw most of all of them. Besides, she couldn't work all the time, and anyway, she wanted to talk to the housekeeper about some of the things she had found in the diary. There was guilt there, too. *Mum really hates cheats.* Helen wanted to prove that she wasn't one of those women, while knowing that she couldn't, because it was too late – she already was. It was a barrier she'd carried with her for years, that feeling that she was other than the women around her, that she had separated herself from them in an invisible yet fundamental way and, moreover, had only herself to blame for it.

They took the wine and the olives and other nibbles that Helen had left over from that night into the library. It felt odd to Helen, that here she was, entertaining as if

Martha were the guest, when really it was the other way around.

'I've only ever been in here for short bursts,' Martha admitted, as they settled themselves by the wood burner. Helen was getting proficient at lighting it – she'd done it so often that now she only needed to use a couple of bits of kindling to get it roaring. 'Just to collect plates or bring tea, and even then, only sometimes. It was Cora who came in here mostly. It's quite a place, isn't it? How are you getting on with the cataloguing?'

'I've got through most of that bookcase over there,' Helen said, indicating the far wall. 'There must already be three hundred books on the list and that's, what, not even a tenth of what's here? I've still got so far to go.' She poured a glass of wine and handed it to her new friend.

Martha looked over at the desk, where Helen had spread the old man's diary, its pages opened like a pinned butterfly. 'How are you getting on with Mr Gissing's diary? Has it been any help?'

Helen took a mouthful of wine. 'Not really. At first, I thought it might tell me where he'd put it, although now I'm not so sure. The more I read of it, the more I think he was researching something he had here, something that he was completely consumed by but wanted to keep secret. I've found letters from scholars all over the world, people he'd written to asking questions.'

'Questions?' Martha said. 'What kind of questions?'

'That's the thing,' Helen said. 'He seems to be talking

about a manuscript, but he's obviously very cagey about talking openly about it. There's only one person who seems to really know what he's talking about – a librarian in Spain called Thiago Montera. There are a lot of letters from him. Some had been collected together but others are tucked into volumes all over the place. They all seem to be about collecting books, some of which Montera was clearly doing for Mr Gissing. Did you ever hear Cyril mention him?'

'A librarian in Spain?' Martha frowned, thinking. 'No, not directly. But he did write a lot of letters, to places all over the world. Half of his day seemed to be spent doing just that. I thought it was because he was buying books from all over the place, though. I didn't know he was writing to the same people over and over, or that they wrote back except to send the books he bought. That's what Cora told me he was doing.'

'Cora?'

Martha nodded, sipping wine. 'He could still read, but he suffered from such terrible arthritis. It had become much worse in the last few years. He found it difficult to write, so she became . . . well, his secretary, kind of, I suppose. He used to pay her to take down dictation for him in the evenings. Maybe you should ask her about it.'

Helen thought about this – thought about Cora's pause when she'd asked her whether the name Thiago Montera had meant anything to her. She hadn't wanted to say anything, which suggested she knew more than she'd let on. Perhaps out of the same loyalty that had made her so angry at Helen for spending time alone in the library.

'I don't think she'd tell me,' Helen admitted. 'She obviously doesn't like me going through Mr Gissing's things.'

Martha sighed. 'I'm sorry about how rude she was the other night.'

'It's not your fault. And I get it, I really do.' She wasn't about to explain the depth of her understanding, or where it came from. She liked Martha and hated the idea that the woman would look at her with disgust if her transgressions with Brett came to light. Perhaps it was inevitable that it would come out eventually, but Helen wanted to maintain the bubble for as long as she could. 'I just wish I could convince her that I'm not the enemy. I'd love to find a will that makes it clear that he wanted you all to stay here, on the island. From everything I've learned about him from the three of you and from his diary, I can't believe he didn't want that to happen. And Cora told me that he'd said he'd make sure nothing had to change after he was gone.'

Martha sighed. 'He did always say we'd be looked after,' she said. 'But that could have meant anything, couldn't it? A few thousand as a goodbye, maybe. We don't have any claim over this place, and I wouldn't expect to have one. I always assumed that we'd eventually move on, Cora and me. But I can't believe he didn't leave a will here somewhere, or at least some indication of what he wanted to happen to all his precious books, if nothing else. It doesn't make sense that he didn't.'

'You don't have any idea why he'd decided to update it?' Helen asked.

Martha shook her head. 'Not that I can think of. Nothing much has changed in all the years I've been here, to tell you the truth.'

They were both quiet for a while, watching the crackling fire.

'I'm glad he had you,' Helen said, eventually. 'You, and Cora and Rufus. This Thiago person, too. They seemed pretty close friends. He never came to visit? Thiago, I mean.'

'Not since I've lived on Rathbrooke. I never knew him to have any visitors. Rufus has never mentioned any, either. I always thought of him as such a lonely man, although he never seemed sad, particularly. He was so very engrossed in his books. They say that, don't they? That you can never be lonely if you've got a book. I suppose he proved that right.'

Helen wasn't sure that was quite the saying. She would have substituted 'lonely' for 'bored'. Certainly there were entries in the diaries that made her think the old man was very lonely indeed.

'Although,' Martha added, 'if he did have a friend in this Thiago, I'm glad to know it. You think they had been writing for a long time?'

'Cora said so,' Helen nodded. 'They certainly talk to each other like very old friends.'

'What do they talk about?'

'Old books, mostly. What new acquisitions they've bought, what they've been reading. It sounds as if this

Montera character used to go on "quests" to find books that Cyril couldn't chase after himself. There are questions from Thiago about whatever it is Mr Gissing was researching too, but he talks as if it's an old conversation that's been going on for just as long as they've known each other. It's as if I've come in in the middle and I missed what it was they were talking about, and they never actually say what it is again, so I've got no idea. There are loads of references in Spanish, for some reason, so I have to translate it – or try to as closely as possible, anyway. I'm trying to go back to the beginning, trying to sift through Thiago's letters to find a reference to what exactly they're discussing, but it's like searching for a single sentence midway through the middle of a book. I don't know what I'm looking for, or even if it's there at all. Or if it is there, what shape it will take. A title? The name of an author? And it's made more difficult by the fact that I've only got one side of the conversation. I can't know what was in the letters that Cyril wrote to Thiago; I've only got the ones Thiago wrote back.'

'Sounds complicated.'

Helen laughed. 'It is. But it's kind of compelling, too. I like their relationship. Cyril loved Thiago, I think. And Thiago definitely loved Cyril.'

'Really?' Martha looked a little shocked at this. 'Romantically, you mean?'

'I'm not so sure about that,' Helen said, drinking more wine. 'But there's a definite affection there when Cyril writes about him in his diary, and plenty of trust. They were true friends, I suppose. They seem so sympatico in their interests. They'd obviously had a lot to say to each other over the span of years.'

'I wonder how they met?' Martha wondered. 'Mr Gissing never talked much about his past, but it's not as if he was always here, living on the island. When he was younger, he travelled quite a bit, according to Rufus. He'd go off searching the world for books in person in the way he later did from this armchair.' She patted the leather reverentially.

'That's definitely what Montera seems to be doing for him in most of the letters,' Helen said. 'Maybe that's the answer. Perhaps they met decades ago in Spain, on one of those trips.'

'In a bookshop,' Martha said, with a smile. 'Over a copy of . . . I don't know, what would it be?'

'*Don Quixote*, probably,' Helen said, joining in with this fictional meet-cute between two old book lovers. 'A book about reading books leading the reader into a never-ending quest, bringing together two readers each on their own quests – how about that?'

Martha watched the fire, smiling. 'I like that. That two people can find each other, however unlikely it may seem that they'll ever meet at all.' She frowned. 'We should write to him, shouldn't we? He might not even know about Cyril's death – in fact, he probably doesn't. Who else would have told him? I'll ask Cora tomorrow. We'll let the poor man know. She must know his address.'

The conversation moved on then. Helen steered the talk away from her own past and towards Martha's, and if the housekeeper noticed, she didn't mention it. Martha had been born in Northumberland, not far from the coast.

'Way back in the chain, we're actually the Darlings of Grace Darling fame,' she said. 'She was a distant cousin ten times removed or some such nonsense connection like that. Rufus likes to joke that it was written in the stars that I'd end up here – we're destined to live surrounded by sea.'

Helen had seen the bright glare of Longstone Lighthouse, warding the shipping of the North Sea away from the archipelago of dark rocks. It was solar-powered and automated now, but for more than a hundred years it had been staffed, and it was from Longstone that the daring young figure of Grace Darling had famously helped her father rescue a group of sailors wrecked and stranded, rowing the little wooden boat herself against the rage of a hellish storm. It was difficult for Helen to imagine what daily life had been out there in the days when the only transport to take a person to and fro across that stretch of water was oar and sail.

'This coast is truly your home, then,' Helen observed.

'Maybe,' Martha said, with a sardonic laugh. 'I think I can accept that now that I'm older. When I was younger, though, I just wanted to get away. Bright lights, big city, that's what I wanted. I got as far as Edinburgh, as a student. I liked it there, too.'

'You were at Edinburgh University?' Helen said, surprised. 'That's where I did my postgrad. What did you do there?'

'I did a Fine Art degree,' Martha said. 'Most of one, anyway. I loved it. And then I messed it up by marrying an arsehole. He wasn't an arsehole at the time, of course. That's what caught me out.' She sighed, sipped more wine. 'Ach, I'll not moan tonight. Suffice it to say, I'm glad I had Cora, but if I could have had one without the other, it would have been far better.'

'Sorry,' Helen said. 'I sympathize.'

'What about you?' Martha asked. 'Have you had to leave anyone behind to do this job?'

Helen's heart gave a slight jiggle in her chest. For a moment she considered coming clean. But, 'No,' is what she said in the moment. 'I've not had the best luck in meeting good men, to be honest.' Unconsciously, she brushed her fingers across the crooked bridge of her broken nose.

'Ah, pet,' Martha said, reaching out to pat her knee. 'I think we might both have had a similar experience. There are good ones out there, I promise.'

'For you too, if you want it again,' Helen said.

'Maybe, aye,' Martha agreed. 'Not fussed for now, to be honest. Too keen on making sure Cora's sorted out. She can be a handful, as you've seen. And in between – well, this is a perfect place for painting. Mr Gissing was always so kind about it. Called me Rathbrooke's Artist in Residence. He liked my seascapes.'

'Wait,' Helen said, pausing with her glass halfway to her lips. 'Are there paintings of yours hanging around Rathbrooke Hall?'

Martha nodded. 'There are quite a few. He kept telling me to take out the old ones and use the frames – it was embarrassing! I made sure to store all the ones I took out properly. They're in the attic – I should show you, actually, you'll need to catalogue those, too.'

Helen stood up. 'I need to see your paintings!' she exclaimed. 'Where are they? Take me now!'

And so Martha took her on an entirely new tour of Rathbrooke Hall, this time to specifically look at the art on the walls. Martha's paintings were impressive – large canvasses in oils, clearly depicting the land and seascapes around them.

'These are beautiful, Martha,' Helen said, as they contemplated a crashing ocean scene, a storm that was so vivid it was almost possible to feel the spray crashing against the crags of black rock standing out amid the deft strokes of paint. 'Do you sell them?'

'No,' Martha admitted. 'It's not as if I even finished at art school. I'm just an amateur, really.'

Helen regarded her new friend. 'That's ridiculous. These are truly amazing. Look at where we're standing,' she indicated the grandeur of the great house around them – faded, yes, but still extraordinary. 'Your work fits in here perfectly. It should be in galleries all over the world.'

The housekeeper gave a lopsided smile. 'That's what Mr Gissing always used to say,' she said. 'He was always so kind.'

'He was right,' Helen insisted. 'Martha, this is what you should be doing. Not cooking breakfast, lunch and dinner for chancers like me.'

'I can only paint here because Mr Gissing gave me the

room and the job gave me the time, not to mention free accommodation, so I had the money for materials. Anywhere else . . .' she shook her head. 'Anyway, they're not that good. You're just being kind, like he was.'

Helen thought about this for a while, until Martha turned to look at her. The two women looked at each other and Helen gave a small smile. 'Just thinking about how often talented women don't have the confidence that men with half their abilities do,' she said. 'Why is that?'

Martha lifted one shoulder in a half-shrug. 'Experience,' she suggested. 'Anyway, I'm happy as I am. I wouldn't want to be famous, not even a little. It's never seemed like a good thing to be to me.'

Helen nodded. 'No,' she said. 'It isn't.' Martha gave her a questioning look, but before she could ask what was in her mind, Helen pointed at the wall on which the seascape hung. 'I've been meaning to ask about the wallpaper,' she said. 'I've never seen anything like it. All these tiny gold triangles behind the painted birds. They've each got little embossed ridges in them. It must have all been done by hand – I can't imagine how long it took and how much it cost.'

'Ahh,' Martha said. 'Yes, it's extraordinary, isn't it? Mr Gissing told me about it when I first arrived. It's really rare, actually – for a start, it's not paper, it's actually tooled leather.'

'Really?' Helen looked more closely at the background between the painted exotic birds. She reached out a hand to touch the wall, gently feeling the ridges with her fingertips. 'I've never heard of anything like that before.'

'The panels would have been imported from Italy in the 1600s. There aren't many houses that had a wall covering like this in the first place, and even fewer where it's survived. Levens Hall in Cumbria is the only other place Mr Gissing knew about. The idea of all the gold and the ridges is that it would catch and amplify candlelight. You've seen for yourself how dark these hallways are when the electrics are out. Imagine living here when all you had was candlelight once the sun had set.'

Helen glanced around the rest of the hallway and had to suppress a sudden shudder. She could imagine it very well. She stepped back from the wall.

'This house is full of so many wonders,' she said. 'I can't help feeling that it's a museum in its own right. I wonder why Mr Gissing never thought about approaching the National Trust to take it on, like the other Farnes?'

'It's a good question,' Martha agreed, a troubled frown passing across her face. 'Maybe that's what will happen anyway. Or maybe even what he intended all along. There are worse things that could happen to this place, I suppose.'

'Sorry,' Helen said. 'But I was just thinking that would mean you could all stay here then, too. You, Cora and Rufus. They'd need caretakers for it, wouldn't they, and they'd never find better ones than you three.'

Martha gave a thin, worried smile, and Helen regretted making her think of trouble that she had perhaps managed to forget for a while. 'We can but dream, eh?'

*

3 Sunnyside Road
Seahouses
Northumberland

Yes, I have got my own boat, but I'm not supposed to take it out alone. Maybe it'd be best to wait until I'm staying on the mainland after all.

Chapter Twelve

'*Another* storm?' Helen asked, when Rufus came to tell her of the forecast for the coming days. 'Are you sure this is summer, Rufus?'

The gardener laughed. 'Aye, well, we're heading for the end of the hot weather,' he said. 'They get worse as we roll towards autumn.'

'Is there anything I can do to help?'

'You could help us close up all the shutters on the Hall,' Rufus said. Then he brightened, a mischievous look in his eye. 'Cora told me you'd been showing an interest in the sheep – fancy helping us get them in, too?'

'Absolutely,' Helen said.

'Oh, Rufus,' Martha laughed when she arrived and heard about this plan. 'You can't make the poor woman lurch about in the pasture muck – she's only got one suitcase of clothes with her!'

'There's nowt to worry about there,' Rufus said, stoutly. 'I can lend her some overalls. Some wellies, too. Come on, lassie, come back to the lighthouse and we'll get you sorted out.'

This is how Helen ended up seeing the inside of Rufus's diminutive home for the first time. She'd seen the lighthouse from the water: the small, square tower built into the southern reach of the island wall, but she'd never yet had a reason to visit. The overalls he'd promised her were kept in a small shed beside the tower, but still the gardener took her inside his home. He mumbled some apology for the 'clutter', but as soon as Helen had stepped over the threshold, she found herself enveloped in a cosiness that she experienced with an intense kind of envy. Rufus's home was almost the exact opposite of Rathbrooke Hall. It was three storeys, but each of these was tiny – one room with a little kitchenette and a bathroom downstairs, a small bedroom upstairs and then, right at the top, the lighthouse apparatus. Rufus evidently sensed her curiosity, because he offered her a tour without Helen having to ask – which she never would have, because as desperate to explore the tiny building as she was, Helen was loathe to invade his personal space. Yet Rufus showed her round cheerfully, bidding her to dip her head to avoid bashing it against the low lintels as they went up the tiny staircase to the second floor. His bed was neatly made, topped with the thickest duvet Helen had ever seen, covered by a quilted throw that seemed as old as the building itself. There was just room for a single chair and one small wardrobe, squashed in beneath the second set of stairs – though these were even more basic than the one they had climbed into his bedroom, barely more than a wooden ladder leading up through a trapdoor in the ceiling.

At the very top of the tower, which was only just higher than the island wall, was the light that had once been lit every night, but now wasn't used at all.

'When this was first built, there wouldn't have been all this technical gubbins here,' Rufus said, as they squeezed into the tiny space together. He pointed towards the Farnes. 'Like Prior Castell's tower on Inner Farne, way back when Rathbrooke Hall was first built, they would have gathered a pile of whatever dry wood they could find, put it on the roof – that's what we're standing on now – and set fire to it to warn the passing ships they were near land. Later, when electricity came, they enclosed this room and added the big light that's still here.'

They were standing in a room – to Helen it felt like a cabin on a ship – that was largely glass, though the framing and the roof was of sturdy oak. The light was large and Helen could see eight huge bulbs, their strong, coiled filaments intact inside their thick glass. They were stacked together within another external glass tube, which was strengthened still further by a cage, one side of which was a sheet of tooled metal.

'The cage would rotate when the light was on,' Rufus explained. 'It was on a timer, set to flash out a warning or, in times of emergency, it could send an entire message for the mainland to see. There are records of wrecks striking the island's promontories, so they took it seriously.' He gestured to the switchboard beside them. 'All controlled from here.'

Helen looked at the plethora of knobs and dials beneath Rufus's hand. 'It's not used at all now?'

Rufus shook his head. 'Oh no. There's no need for it any more. I test the old girl every now and then, because I want to know if she's still hanging in there and that her generator is still working, but I do that during the day so as not to cause any consternation in Seahouses. The people would get a right shock if she started up without warning!'

Helen ran her fingers lightly over the bank of switches, a little sad that this fascinating place had slipped into obsolescence. Rathbrooke held so many secrets she'd never even imagined, and she hated the thought of them fading. More and more, she realized she didn't want anything here to change, not even slightly. There must be a will, somewhere, mustn't there? Who would own such a wonderful place and not make sure its future was certain when they weren't around to look after it themselves? Or had Cyril Gissing been so taken up with his obsession – whatever it was – that he'd genuinely neglected to update it as he'd intended? And what had made him decide he needed to update it anyway?

The rain began in earnest then, hammering against the glass all around them as the storm made landfall over the island.

Outside, Rufus dug out a set of khaki overalls and picked up a pair of almost-clean wellies from the shed. 'There you are,' he said, thrusting both at Helen as they sheltered from the rain. 'Those should sort you out. Best get on with it – I've got a feeling this is going to be a bad one.'

He was right. By the time they'd got the sheep into the barn, Helen was soaked through and the wind was howling over Rathbrooke's roof. She found it spooky, how calm the atmosphere on the ground was by comparison. If not for the rain, which fell on them despite the island wall, she would feel as if the whole place were beneath a huge umbrella, or inside a jar, isolated from the vagaries of the outside world.

As the hours went by, however, the storm grew in intensity. The generator was prepped and ready to go, but Helen had made sure she had the storm lamps charged and candles at hand too, just in case. They all ate dinner together, but by nine o'clock had retired to their respective homes. Helen felt another stab of envy, thinking of Rufus tucked away in the sturdy little tower she'd seen earlier. The memory of it seemed so much more welcoming than the great, empty expanse of Rathbrooke Hall. She decided to spend the night in the library. It was the place she always felt safest, insulated from everything that went on outside its thick stone walls. She would make herself a flask of tea, she decided, just in case the power went out, because Martha had already warned Helen that if they did lose electricity, she wouldn't bother to set the generator going overnight, but would wait until the morning. A flask of tea, a packet of biscuits, and that would be enough for Helen until the sun came up or the storm blew itself out – whichever came first.

As Helen headed from the kitchen towards the library with her supplies, however, there came a thunderous, echoing bang, followed by another, and then another. For a confused second, she mistook it for lightning striking the roof – thinking that one of the chimneys had been struck and was falling, despite the sudden silence beneath the whistling of the wind outside. But then the cacophony came again, three times in quick succession – *BANG! BANG! BANG!* – and she realized it was coming from the main door. Someone was clanging the great iron knocker that hung in the centre of the ancient wood of Rathbrooke Hall's huge, disused front entrance. She froze, staring at it. It settled for a second and then shook as the knocking was repeated, swifter this time, perhaps more desperate: *BANG-BANG-BANG-BANG!* Was it the ghosts of the west wing, making themselves known at last? As soon as this thought occurred to her, Helen cursed herself for it. Of course it wasn't – there was some poor soul outside, in this hellish rain. She had no key for the main door and shouting through it was pointless – it was too thick, and the growing maelstrom outside too loud, for whomever it was to hear her. She ran instead to the French doors of the little parlour and unlocked them, holding out the lamp as the rain turned towards her, lashing her with its cold anger. She could see nothing beyond the small halo it cast out into the endless darkness, a pale circle of uncertain light on the slick stone slabs of the terrace. She leaned out of the door with the light and shouted.

'Hello?'

She could barely see a foot in front of her – all was darkness and the wind was so strong and the rain so potent she could not look directly into the storm. Then, suddenly, there was a figure before her, standing right inside her circle of light. Helen yelped in shock and backed up, whereupon the shadow followed, until they both stumbled over the threshold and into the shelter of the room. The figure was large and shrouded in a leather jacket that had been hoiked up over his head: but now this was dropped to reveal a man, soaked to the skin, with dark hair slicked against his face by the rain. In each of his ears glinted a gold ring, and as he lifted his hands to push his sodden hair back, Helen saw there were rings on his fingers too. He was gasping, catching his breath from the onslaught of the storm, wiping rain from his cheeks and dark eyes.

'Thank you,' he said, the word muffled as his hands passed over his face again, his voice outlined not only with relief but also by an accent she couldn't immediately place. 'Thank you, thank you.'

'Who are you? What are you doing here?' Helen asked, as his rasping breath settled, and it was then that she remembered the men who had been booked to come and shear the sheep. This had to be one of them, surely, looking for Rufus – he must have got turned around finding his way on the island in the storm. 'Rufus will be back at the lighthouse.'

A frown rippled across the stranger's face. 'Rufus?'

'He's the groundskeeper. He looks after the sheep.'

The very wet man was looking more perplexed by the second. 'The sheep? I am not here for any sheep.' His jaw was square enough to set a right angle by it, and now that he had squeezed some of the rain from his hair, the ends were curling a little. With his dark eyes and hair, the gold rings in his ears and on his fingers and his battered jacket that looked as if it had weathered a hundred battles of indeterminate sort, he looked like a pirate. Helen took a step back, glanced at the poker that stood beside the unlit hearth of the parlour.

'Then who *are* you? What are you *doing* here?' Surely he wasn't a pap? Not in this weather? But who else would come here unannounced? She lunged for the poker, brandished it as she would a sword.

'Whoa, whoa!' The stranger held up both hands, took a step back of his own. 'I am here to see Cyril. My name is Thiago. I am his friend. Is he here?'

Helen almost dropped the poker. 'You're . . . *what?*'

He was still holding up both hands. More droplets of rain had slid down his face, but he didn't move to wipe them away. He spoke slowly, as if to a frightened horse. 'My name is Thiago Montera. I am a friend of Cyril Gissing. This is his house, yes? I have that right? Or . . . or have I come to the wrong island? I thought this was Rathbrooke, my chart said that this was Rathbrooke? But perhaps, in the storm . . . I have been mistaken?'

She stared at him, mouth open. *This* was Thiago Montera? This was the man whose letters she'd been reading? 'I . . . it is. This is Rathbrooke Island. What do you mean, your chart?'

Now he did swipe a hand across his wet face again. He really was soaked through. 'My sailing chart.'

'You sailed here?' Was this man a complete idiot? 'What

possessed you to leave in this?' Helen waved a hand at the weather outside, the rain still battering against the French doors.

'It wasn't like this when I left,' he said. 'I thought I had time to get here ahead of the storm.'

'From Seahouses?' she asked, mystified.

'No, of course not,' he said, beginning to shiver, a violent tremble that she heard in his voice. 'From Bilbao.'

'You sailed here from *Bilbao*?'

He looked at her, jaw clenched tight against the chatter, eyes narrowed, as if his patience might finally be wearing thin. 'Where is Cyril?' he asked. 'He is why I came. To see him.'

Helen blinked, trying to get her brain to shake itself back into gear. For days now she'd been reading about Thiago Montera from his own hand. In her mind, he was as old and fusty as this ancient house. She couldn't equate the man before her with the image in her head, or with the Thiago who exchanged wordy, longhand letters about antiquarian texts with a man who must have been old enough to be his – what? Grandfather?

'He's . . . ' she began and then stopped, suddenly at a loss. She hadn't expected to be breaking this kind of news today, or in these circumstances. 'I'm afraid Mr Gissing passed away some weeks ago. His funeral was a month ago. I'm sorry.'

Thiago's shoulders slumped and he let out a breath, accompanied by a word that might have been a soft curse in Spanish. 'I was worried that something might have happened when I did not hear from him. That's why I came. Ah, Cyril, my friend. I should have come sooner, but I kept hoping to get his letter. I had written last – it was his turn.'

Something about all this still didn't sit right with Helen. 'You came all this way – unannounced –' *and uninvited*, she thought but did not say, too British to say something so blunt, even to this utter stranger, 'because you didn't get an answer to a letter?'

He watched her steadily for a moment, as if trying to work out if she were accusing him of something. She wasn't, but only because she wasn't sure what he could be guilty of aside from arriving like the pirate he most definitely resembled. She'd have to be careful, Helen thought, or she'd end up calling him that outright. *Pirate.* He'd certainly sailed here like one.

'Cyril and I only ever communicated by written letter,' he said, then. 'Twenty years, or more, he had never missed returning mine, even though I was often late with my correspondence to him. Besides, there are no phones here, are there? How else would I have found out without coming here myself?'

'There's a phone in the housekeeper's cottage,' Helen pointed out. 'The only reason there isn't one in the Hall is that Mr Gissing didn't want one.'

Thiago stared at her, his teeth chattering now. 'I did not know that. Cyril never said. I just assumed there was no way to have one on the island. And you – who are you?' he asked. 'Could you be . . . Martha?'

'What? No. My name is Helen. Helen Thorne.'

His dark eyebrows rose. 'Helen?' And then he repeated it, but as a statement. 'Helen. Whoever you are, I have something to beg of you.'

She was still wary, still clutching the poker. 'What?'

He raised his hands again, just a little, a kind of shrug. 'I am . . . very cold.'

Of course he was. He'd just sailed here through a storm. It had soaked him so thoroughly that he was dripping the part of it that he had carried inside with him into a damp circle on the ancient wooden floor. Helen did not lower the poker.

'I don't know who you are,' she said. 'You've just turned up in the middle of the night with no warning.'

'I am sorry,' he said. 'There is a barn, yes? I will stay there.' As if in answer, the wind blasted harder against the doors behind them. The rain seemed to hammer with renewed rage.

He was still dripping. Helen saw him shiver again, and knew it wasn't an act. She couldn't send him back out there, not on a night like this. And she knew he was telling the truth, didn't she, about him being a friend of Cyril's? Just because this man was so utterly unlike the one she had constructed in her head out of the letters she had read did not mean it wasn't him. And being that man, Cyril Gissing would want him looked after. Just because he looked like a pirate didn't mean he was going to act like one. Not that she was going to just believe him wholescale on the strength of this conversation. Could it really be true that he hadn't known his friend of twenty years was dead? If he was playing a part and he *had* known, then the only reason Thiago Montera could possibly be here was the library and its wealth of valuable books. Helen had been planning to spend the night on the sofa inside it – she would have barely heard the raging storm within the peel walls – but now she changed her mind.

'No,' she said. 'Come on. You need to get dry.'

She led him upstairs to the living quarters that had been hers since she'd arrived on Rathbrooke.

'I'll get the fire going,' she said, turning to the bulk of him, standing silent at her shoulder once she'd pushed open the door onto her 'living room'. 'Then I'll go and make some hot coffee. The power will probably go out at some point, but there's a gas burner in the kitchen.'

Thiago stopped her with a light hand rested on her arm, strong fingers cold on her bicep, even through the layers of her clothing. 'I can light the fire,' he said, his jaw still clenched against the cold. 'Coffee – *Sí. Please.*'

She left him there, for a brief moment pondering the idea of turning the key in the lock as she went so that he could not wander about the house. But as she glanced back from the door he was already attending to the fire. And anyway, what did she imagine he was going to do? Shove a painting under his drenched coat and rush out into the storm with it? Even if he did, he couldn't get off the island, not in this storm. It was a miracle he had made it here in one piece in the first place.

Helen made coffee as quickly as she could, loading a tray with the full percolator, mugs and a jug of milk, and then carried it back upstairs. She was halfway up, passing the ancient window with its myriad unsettled diamond panes, when the power cut out. She stopped for a moment, blinking in the darkness, cursing herself for not remembering to take the storm lamp with her, and then felt her way up the final short flight of steps to her floor. The storm raged outside, but Helen thought she could feel something inside it, too, something other than her and her strange Spanish visitor: an ephemeral presence, sketched by uncertain movement, as always beyond the locked doors of the west wing. There came a sound to her left: the patter of feet running towards her, amplified in the darkness. She fled in the opposite direction, through the short stretch of cavernous pitch black, put her back to the door of her rooms and backed through it, her heart a base drum in her chest.

She turned to find the fire now roaring and Thiago Montera standing in front of it, stripped to the waist. He had spread his drenched sweater and the layers he'd been wearing beneath it over the backs of chairs to dry, but he was holding his jacket in both hands, standing on the flags of the stone hearth so that it and he were uplit by the orange glow of flames as the coat dripped onto the flags at his feet.

'I should not trust this,' he said to her, not looking up, his attention all on the old coat. 'It is worse than useless. The seams – all weak and no longer waterproof, they let everything through them. Still, it was my grandfather's, and I am a sentimental fool.'

She could find nothing to say, and he looked around at her silence, arms dropping a little so that the firelight cast the contours of his torso and shoulders in deep relief. With his hair now drying in the heat from the flames, the curls were more pronounced, drifting across his brow in a tousled, careless mess. He seemed suddenly aware of his state of undress and apologized, dropping the coat so that it formed a shapeless heap on the hearth and moving quickly to the sofa, taking a blanket that was folded there and wrapping it around his shoulders.

'My dry clothes are all on the boat,' he said, by way of explanation, as Helen put the coffee tray down on the table.

'I'm sorry, I don't have anything I can lend you instead.' If he tried to fit into one of her T-shirts, he'd split it at the seams.

He gave a crooked smile. 'The fire will dry mine quickly.'

She nodded and he went back to the hearth, rearranging the coat and crouching on his haunches beside it. To dry his trousers, she supposed, which Helen was relieved he had kept on. They looked like some kind of sturdy work kit, presumably made for sailors, quick-drying to withstand the conditions of life at sea. *Pirate*. Her heart had not quite calmed from her sudden terror on the darkened stairs. She found herself tracing the defined muscles of his lower back, visible every time the blanket shifted.

Helen sat on the sofa and poured them both coffee, trying

to work him out. 'You're a lot younger than I thought you'd be,' she said.

He looked over at her with surprise, dark eyebrows shooting up towards his curls. 'Than you *thought* I would be? What do you mean? Who are you, Helen Thorne? Cyril never mentioned you in any of his letters. He talked about Rufus and Martha and little Cora, described them, even. But not you. Even though you seem familiar, I do not think it is from his letters. I think I would have remembered that.'

'I'm no one,' Helen said. 'I didn't know Mr Gissing at all, more's the pity. I was sent here by Mr Gissing's solicitor, that's all. At the time of his passing they didn't have his will on file, so I'm trying to find it. Part of that has been going through his papers and I found some of your letters. That's how I . . .' – she nearly said *know you*, but of course she didn't know him, not at all, not *this* him, which she was having a very hard time aligning with the Thiago whose words she had read, ' . . . heard about you.' She didn't mention the diaries, or why she'd already felt an odd affection towards someone she'd never met and thought was an old man.

If her visitor found it strange that she had read his private letters, he didn't say so, just nodded silently as she passed him his coffee. Thiago held the mug in both hands, dwarfing it.

'He did not leave a will?' Thiago asked. 'That cannot be right. Cyril . . . he was fastidious about such things.'

'It seems strange to me, too,' Helen agreed. 'Not that I knew him, but having learned even the smallest things about him that I have since I've been here, I can't understand why he wouldn't have made one. According to the solicitor he'd wanted to change it, but they don't know why he hadn't done that yet. I'm hoping he'd at least written his own version of it and I just haven't found it yet. Although why he wouldn't send a copy back to his solicitor is anyone's guess.'

She felt Thiago's eyes on her as she spoke. He was studying her, as Helen herself had studied Martha's paintings.

'This is what you do?' he asked. 'If you don't mind me saying so, you don't seem to me much like a lawyer.'

That stung a little, for some reason too obscure for Helen to understand at that moment. Why *shouldn't* she be a lawyer? She looked more like a lawyer than he did a member of his profession. 'Yes, well, Mr Montera, *you* don't seem much like a librarian.'

He grinned at her – rakish, bold and brilliant. 'No? Then how do I seem?'

'Like a pirate,' she said, undoing all her intentions not to say it aloud. 'You seem exactly like a *pirate*.'

'Pfft,' he said, his eyes laughing at her. 'Racial profiling! You say this because I am Spanish and have gold rings in my ears.'

'I say this,' she countered, 'because you turned up on an island, uninvited, on a boat in a storm in the middle of the night. And,' she admitted, 'because you have rings in your ears and hair that looks like it was drawn by a Disney cartoonist. If you had a beard I would have locked you out in the wind and the rain to fend for yourself. Better that than share a house with Blackbeard himself.'

He threw his head back and laughed aloud. Helen found herself smiling as she swallowed more of her coffee. Here she was with a strange man in this strange house, stranded and alone with him, smiling. She tamped down on her reaction. He was too easy on the eye, too smooth. She'd been burned by that before, she reminded herself. Never again.

His laughter died down, though his smile remained. 'I have been called worse,' he said. 'But I am not a pirate. In truth I am . . . the opposite.'

'And what is the opposite of a pirate?'

He considered this as he poured them both the last of the coffee. Behind him, the fire was roaring in the grate, warm and welcoming. 'I am a collector of books that would otherwise vanish. But not for myself. For libraries and museums. It means I travel a lot to find them, often to very distant and out-of-the-way places, so . . .' he shrugged, 'perhaps this is why I look like a pirate.'

Helen frowned, alarm bells ringing. 'Is that why you're here?'

He looked up at her, one hand still holding closed the blanket, clenching it over his heart. 'Is what why I'm here?'

Helen put down her mug, leaning back. 'The library.'

Something flickered across his face, gone too quickly for Helen to identify it. 'The library of Rathbrooke,' he said, letting go of a breath, 'is a place I have heard tell of since I was eighteen years old. But I have never seen it. I always wanted to come here, to meet Cyril in person, but I never did. I was too afraid to be honest with him, even though he was my friend. Besides, there were always other places to go. Always other places that Cyril would send me.'

'Places Cyril would *send* you?' Helen asked. She already knew from his letters that Montera had often gone on 'quests' to find books as a result of Cyril Gissing's research. But this made it sound as if Thiago Montera was following his instructions, like an employee. And what did he mean, he was too afraid to be honest? About what?

'*Sí*,' Montera said. 'I learned almost everything I know about old books from Cyril Gissing. He had . . . a talent for finding them, tracing them. He had whole histories of their journeys, through years, through countries, from one shelf to another, from one family to another, one collector to another. He wanted to save them. Not just the stories, but the books themselves. When he knew there was a chance that they might vanish, in one way or another, he would go to rescue them. If he could not get there himself . . . then I would go.'

'Then the books *are* why you're here.'

'No,' Thiago said. 'I told you: I came because I had not heard from Cyril. I was worried for my friend, and I thought it was time I revealed that I was not quite what he thought I was. Although now I *am* worried about his books. You must know he had collected many, many valuable volumes over his life. What will you do with them?'

'That's not up to me,' Helen told him. 'It's not my decision. My job is just to catalogue them. If I don't find a will with clear instructions, that'll be up to the solicitors, since there is no family.'

Thiago lapsed into silence again, apparently troubled. He got up to check on how his clothes were drying. Helen wondered why he hadn't asked to see the library, if it was such a fabled place to him. As she studied him, he shrugged her blanket from his shoulders and pulled his T-shirt back on over his head. Then he returned to drop down beside her on the sofa, a pensive look on his face.

'None of this makes sense,' she said. 'You say you've known about the library here since you were eighteen and that everything you know about books you learned from Cyril Gissing. But how, if you never came here, and he never met you in Spain? You can't have been a librarian when you were *eighteen*. And what do you mean when you say you weren't honest with your friend?'

Thiago stared into the fire, his brow furrowed. Helen wondered if he was trying to evade her question, or whether he was thinking of how to frame his answer. He rubbed a hand across his face.

'It is a long story,' he said, eventually.

Outside, the rain lashed at the windows. From somewhere there came the sound of a loud crash, of something falling, being knocked over. The noise sounded closer than the muted noise of the storm outside – as if it had come from inside Rathbrooke Hall, perhaps even just outside the door of Helen's room. Thiago froze, startled, staring at the door.

'What was that?'

Helen tried to shake off the chill skitter of fear that traced across her shoulders. 'I don't know. I hear strange noises all the time. I'm really beginning to think this place might be haunted.'

She expected Thiago to dismiss this as easily as Rufus, Martha and Cora had, but instead he looked at her uneasily.

'Ghosts?'

Helen shrugged, trying to laugh it off. She was glad she was not alone – glad for him, glad to have another human here with her in this strange, lonely house crouching beneath the weight of the summer storm, pirate or not. It was ridiculous. She should be afraid of him, or at least not at all ready to trust him. And yet, despite herself, despite all that was sensible and all that history had taught her, she found herself doing just that. She was Don Quixote, wasn't she? Wanting to believe that the stories she had read were real, were the whole truth.

'Maybe. I haven't seen anything like that. Mostly I hear them. Noises like that one we just heard. Footsteps, sometimes. Laughter, too, or at least that's what it sounds like to me. I can't be sure; it echoes so much.'

He crossed himself, a gesture that surprised her. A religious man, then. 'I have seen ghosts,' he said. 'These old houses, they hold such histories.'

'I never hear them in the library,' she said. 'It is always peaceful there.'

He smiled, a little sadly. 'Cyril thought so, too. He loved it so, his library.'

'We aren't going anywhere, are we?' Helen pointed out

then. 'I won't sleep, and I don't think you will, either. Tell me the story, even if it's a long one.'

Thiago stared into the fire again, as if contemplating. Then he looked at her.

'Do you have anything to eat?' he asked.

Chapter Thirteen

They hurried down the stairs through the dark, huddled together inside the puddle of light cast by the lamp like friends united against the world instead of new acquaintances. They heard no more noises aside from those of the storm, muffled and distant outside the strange bubble of Rathbrooke. They went back upstairs armed with provisions and toasted thick slices of bread stuck on the end of Helen's poker, holding them over the flames before spreading them with butter and jam as if they were characters in a children's story from the 1930s. Helen curled on the sofa, her head on the cushioned arm. Thiago remained on the floor, closer to the fire, and when he began his story, he sounded more like the voice she knew from his letters.

'I was not a good student,' he said. 'No one thought I had prospects, least of all me. I was . . . difficult. I hated authority. Hated school, hated rules. Never listened to anyone. Never studied. I was just counting down the days until I could get out of lessons for good. But there was one teacher, just one, who would not write me off. She saw something in me no one else did, though I don't know how, or why. She kept giving me books to read – I read them in secret, because my friends would have laughed at me otherwise. I loved all of them, even the ones that I didn't like: the adventure, the way a book can take you to another world, let you become another person, make you walk in another person's shoes. We would talk about them and every time we did, she would end by telling me I must go to college. In the end I told her that boys like me did not go to college, that reading stories was all very well, but it was not a job, and I needed a job. Besides, I had proven that I could not study: *would not* study. It would be a waste of money I did not have. She told me she would get me a job, if I would at least think about it. I don't know why she had such faith in me, but I agreed. Either way, I knew she was good for the money, and all I had to do was tell her no at the end of it. I thought she'd get me to dig her garden or paint her walls. But no. She had a friend who turned out to be a professor of literature. He needed an assistant – someone to keep up with his mail, that kind of thing. He didn't trust me any more than I trusted him and I have no idea how she managed to talk him into giving me a chance. On my very first day he gave me a stack of letters and told me to write back to the sender in England. It had to be written, because the writer did not use email. I was to write that there should be no more letters sent to this address, because my professor would be retiring in a few months and moving away. They would no longer be read.'

'The letters . . . were from Cyril Gissing?' Helen guessed.

'They were. There were a lot of them. My professor told me I didn't need to read them, but I glanced through a couple and then I couldn't help myself – I read them all. And what I learned there turned me into a librarian.'

'How?' Helen wanted to know. It was easy to imagine Thiago Montera as a troubled teen. It wasn't as easy to see how the letters of a man who would have been aged even twenty years ago could have set such a boy on any new course in life, let alone one dedicated to the stewardship of books. 'What was in the letters?'

'Cyril was a collector, as you know,' Thiago said, tipping his head back against the sofa so that his curls brushed her ankles. 'But he didn't collect only to possess. He collected to *preserve*. He sought out books that were in danger of extinction. Not just famous books, but forgotten ones, too, or ones that had never been known in the first place. He was passionate about the words in those books, about why they had been written and what it meant that they survived even when no one remembered them. Often, if he thought the books he had rescued belonged somewhere in particular, he gave them away. That was why he had first contacted my professor. He had traced a first edition, first printing, signed copy of *Don Quixote* to an abandoned estate outside Buenos Aires. He had reason to believe, as a result of his research, that it had been gifted to the original owner by Cervantes himself, who had taken it with him across the globe. The inscription in the front when he finally held it in his hands proved this to be true, an intriguing aspect of history in itself given the colonial history of Argentina. It was in Spanish, of course, and for any collector of notable literature it would be a prize, even for one who did not speak the language fluently. Besides which, it could have fetched a fortune on the open market. But instead of selling it to the highest bidder, Cyril contacted the National Library of Spain, because he thought it should be returned to us. That was how he first came to contact my professor, who was at the time the director of the Rare Collection as well as lecturing at the university. He asked a fair price and said he wouldn't take it anywhere else. That if we wanted it, we could have it, and if not, he would keep it in his own collection. And not only that, but any time we changed our minds, it would be here for us.'

Helen frowned. 'But . . . your professor turned him down? And he couldn't even find the time to write back himself – he asked you to do it for him instead?'

'No, that particular contact had happened years before. That was the first time that Cyril had written to the professor. The Rare Collection took the book, of course. It is still on the shelves, even today. But after that, I think Cyril imagined he had found a like-minded man in the professor. And I think he was lonely, perhaps, in his quest. He wrote frequently, recounting his trips all over the world, searching for the books he had tracked down. This had gone on for years. I was riveted by his tales. It was like reading about the adventures of Indiana Jones, but instead of gold or statues, it was books he was seeking. All Cyril was interested in was preserving those volumes. He did not want them to end up in landfill, or to crumble like the Cervantes would have, had he not found it, or be torn apart for use as kindling or packing. He seemed to me, in those letters, like a . . . a sort of Robin Hood.' Thiago smiled wryly, perhaps at his own youthful idealism. 'Anyway. He could tell a story as well as any I had read in the books my teacher had inspired me with. He made his quests to find these books exciting. And he made me want to do the same.'

'You did write back to him, then,' Helen guessed.

'I did,' Thiago agreed. 'And I was a bold kid. I told him that although the professor was about to retire, I would be taking his place.' Thiago shrugged. 'An outright lie, but I could write well enough to disguise my youth. That was where my correspondence – and friendship – with Cyril Gissing began. And eventually, it became the truth, or something like it, even though he never learned my real age and lack of experience. I avoided meeting him in person, at first because it would reveal my subterfuge, and then because I was so often travelling. I became the one who went out and found the volumes he tracked down. I still am.'

Helen tried to work this out. 'Then . . . were you employed by Mr Gissing?'

She watched as Thiago thought about this for a moment.

'He paid me sometimes, but no, I wouldn't say I was employed by him.'

'Then – how do you live?' Helen asked. 'When I asked Cora about you, she said you were a librarian in Spain.'

Thiago turned to look at her, a question in his eyes. 'You asked Cora about me?'

Helen felt her cheeks growing warm. 'When I found the letters you'd sent. I wanted to know if she recognized the name.'

He nodded, as if this seemed to make sense to him. 'Little Cora. I look forward to meeting her. Cyril thought of her as the granddaughter he did not have, I think. She's half right – I work for the National Library of Spain. For some of the time, anyway.'

'The same one your professor worked for back in the day?'

'The very same.'

'But only some of the time?'

He looked back at the fire, a dark shadow passing through his eyes. Then it was gone, and he smiled. 'There are too many books out there in the world to find,' he said. 'And besides, once I found Alejandra, I never wanted to be anywhere but out on the high seas, with her.'

Helen braced herself, then wondered why she needed to. It wasn't the first time she'd heard the name, after all. Thiago wrote about her all the time in his letters. 'Alejandra?'

Thiago flicked his gaze back to hers. 'My boat.'

'Oh!' Helen said. 'Your *boat*.'

'You'll have to meet her,' he went on. 'I think you two would get on. And there, now you know my whole tale.'

'I doubt that.'

'Everything that matters,' he conceded.

She wasn't sure about that, either, but the cadence of his

voice had been as soothing as reading his letters, and the fire was warm, and it was late. The storm outside seemed very far away. She could feel herself drowsing, drifting on a tide of sleep.

'And now it is your turn,' he said. 'What brought you here, Helen Thorne? Way back when, what turned your tide to bring you to this shore?'

She was already half asleep.

'When I was very young, I made a mistake,' she said, sleepily. 'A terrible one. I trusted the wrong person. And it ruined my life.'

'That,' Thiago said, though his voice was fading from her, as if she were falling away from him as she slid into slumber, '*that* I can understand.'

Chapter Fourteen

Helen woke the next morning with her head still on the sofa cushion. For a second after she opened her eyes, she did not remember the night before. Then it all came to her in a rush. She sat up, pushing back the blanket that had somehow found its way over her in the night. The fire had died down but the room was still warm. There was daylight pushing its way in around the edges of the heavy curtains, and it was quiet: she could hear no noise from outside, no storm still lashing against the ancient windows. There was also no sign of Thiago, either. His clothes had gone, as had the tray of plates and mugs she'd brought up, as if he'd been no more than a figment of her imagination.

She was suddenly filled with horror, her heart thumping. He'd gone in the night, hadn't he? What had he taken with him? What had he pilfered while she slept? She checked for the library key, stomach turning with sick anxiety until she found it in the pocket of the jeans she still wore. At least he hadn't got into the peel, but how on earth had she allowed herself to be taken in by a total stranger in a house that was not hers? Helen scrambled up from the sofa and went to the window, dragging back the curtain to look out on a calm day, the sky grey-washed but dry overhead.

Below was a scene of carnage, far worse than that left by the last storm Helen had seen hit Rathbrooke. The lawn was strewn with torn leaves, which had also gathered in the bowl of the dolphin fountain. Through the arch beyond she could see that the rose trellis on the outside of the wall had collapsed, taking with it the climbing roses that Rufus had so lovingly trained against it. She saw movement, and there was the old man himself, struggling to haul a large section of the splintered framework into his arms. Another movement, and Helen could see that there was someone there with him, bearing the greater weight as between them they tried to lift it.

Thiago.

Helen pulled on her coat and went out. The morning was blustery, wind picking at her unbrushed hair, but the air held none of the fury of the night before.

'Good morning,' Thiago called when he spotted her.

'Hi,' she said, her feet crunching on the gravel path as she neared. The trellis had snapped in multiple places. Surely there was no saving it. Perhaps the rose could be pruned and coaxed to climb against a new one. 'I thought you'd gone.'

He looked surprised, his dark eyes darting to hers. 'I saw Rufus from the window. I thought I should help. Sorry.'

She shook her head. In her pocket, her fingers closed around the library key. 'I just—'

'I know,' he said, grinning. The wind played with his hair, throwing his curls about. 'Pirate, no?'

She smiled despite herself. 'Something like that.'

'Lad says he got here last night, in the middle of that maelstrom,' Rufus said, in a tone of blank amazement. 'Mad! I didn't know a thing about it; I was hunkered down with the shutters locked tight while that monster tore around out here. Thought I was going to get up this morning to see the roof had gone. Found this instead,' he said, hoisting the broken trellis in his arms.

'I'm sorry, Rufus. Will you be able to save the plant?'

'Oh aye, no doubt,' said the gardener. 'A year or two and she'll recover. The woodwork though, that's another story. This will all have to go into the incinerator.'

'Perhaps we can save some of it,' Thiago said, examining the framework in his hands. 'I will put anything that looks as if it might be rescued over there . . .' He walked a little way away to begin a pile of the broken trellis.

'Rufus,' Helen said quietly, while their new visitor was out of earshot. 'Had you heard of Thiago Montera before he turned up this morning?'

'A mention, here and there,' the gardener said.

'Really?'

'Oh yes. He was a friend of Mr Gissing's, by all accounts. They used to write back and forth all the time. Thiago was one of his sources for his library collecting, I think.'

'Yes,' Helen said, relieved. 'That's what he told me, too.'

'You should see Cora this morning,' Rufus said, with a

grin. 'She lost her head when she found out who he was. Knows all about him, she does. You'd think he was a rockstar come to visit.'

Helen smiled again. Of course, she wasn't the only person on Rathbrooke who knew Thiago Montera through his letters. And if anyone was a harsh judge of character, it was Cora Darling. Helen watched the Spaniard continue to stack the broken trellis. Then there came the now-familiar sound of a handbell ringing, calling them all to breakfast.

Any residual uncertainty as to whether the Thiago Montera that had presented himself during the storm was the same one whose letters she had read was dispelled once and for all when she finally took him into the library. This happened directly after breakfast, which the inhabitants of Rathbrooke ate together around the big house's dining-room table, and at which the librarian had made everyone – including Cora – alternately laugh and sit entranced by his tales of travel all over the world in pursuit of rare volumes. To Helen, even as she listened to him and laughed along at the tales of his exploits, it seemed a somewhat lonely life. Yes, he had a home in Madrid, a small apartment not far from the library, and by all accounts a loving if fragmented family spread out across the northern reaches of Spain. But the months that Thiago Montera was not researching lost texts seemed to be spent on the road, or more often the ocean, moving, always moving from one side of the globe to the other and back again. It made her wonder what he was running from.

They helped to clear the breakfast plates and told Rufus and Cora that they would join them later in the garden to help clear more debris. Then Helen led him through the quiet, dusty rooms of the great house towards the library that had played host to his written words for years, but never once to him in person.

Thiago followed at her shoulder, a broad presence, though quiet. She thought there were things she should ask him, that there were important matters to discuss, but she was also aware of a tension in him, an anticipation. It was all about the library, she realized, and did not want to spoil his first true experience of it with chatter. When they reached the peel doors, she pushed both open and went in, while Thiago stood on the threshold, in much the same state of wonder as Helen had found herself on her first visit.

'It's something, isn't it?' she said, turning back to him as he stood in the doorway.

He nodded, a look of wonder on his face. 'He told me, and I visualized it, of course. But this . . .' He raised a hand into the book-lined space, but said no more. Helen understood. She left him there at the door – he needed to come at this at his own pace. She wove around the bookcases and furniture to reach the great hearth, a path she had traversed so often in the weeks that she had been resident on the island that it had become as well known as her own flat in London. She knelt to sweep out the grate and re-lay the fire, and by the time she had it lit, Thiago was standing at one of the piles of books that had never found a shelf, holding an ancient leather-bound volume and turning its pages reverently, before carefully putting the book back on the pile and beginning to look around the rest of the library.

Helen gave him space, not wanting to intrude on what seemed to be an important private moment. She went to the desk and sought out Gissing's notebooks instead, looking for the entries that had caused her so much consternation. A few minutes later she saw Thiago making his way up to the mezzanine. A little after that she realized she could no longer hear his footsteps. She went up and found him standing in the reading nook, looking out over the North Sea. He glanced at her with a sad smile as she went to stand beside him.

'He made this for a lost love,' he said, quietly. 'Did you know that?'

'No, I didn't,' Helen admitted. 'But I wondered. Martha told me he never used it and kept the drapes drawn over it most of the time.'

Thiago nodded, reaching out one hand to trace his fingers across the old wood panelling on the nook's walls. 'Cyril was still a young man then. Her name was Eleanor. They met at a hotel in Switzerland, on the first trip he had taken to locate a book he had traced. She was the daughter of the hotelier. The old house it had been converted from had once had a grand library, and some of the books were still packed away in the attic. Eleanor was going to join Cyril here, on Rathbrooke. They were to be married, and he made this nook for her as a wedding present.'

'What happened?'

'She died,' Thiago said. 'She was in a car accident a few months before the wedding. It broke his heart so badly that it never healed. I think that's when he really threw himself into his quest. He couldn't save her; he'd never had a chance. He saved every book he could, instead. He wanted to make sure that all those stories had a better ending than theirs had. That became the focus of his life, instead of the future they would have had together.'

'What a tragedy.'

'Yes.' Thiago said nothing more, gazing out of the window, and Helen wondered whether he was mourning for the love his friend had lost so long ago, or for something in his own past. A moment later he glanced at her again and smiled, wider this time, as if making an effort to shake off the melancholy of the moment.

'There's something you want to ask me, isn't there?'

'About a million things, actually,' Helen admitted.

'But one more than any other, I think?'

She nodded, glancing past him at the grey waters beyond Rathbrooke's crumbling, ragged edge. 'Come downstairs. There's something I want you to see.'

They sat on the sofa, and she showed him the notes she had been taking from Cyril's notebooks, the cipher she had found that still made no sense even after her translations.

'Can you tell me what all of this means?' she asked. 'From your letters, I know the two of you discussed it – I've translated the sentences you put in Spanish, and you're obviously talking about a book. But I still can't work out what book, or why he was so careful when he wrote to you about it.'

Thiago pored over the pages. He seemed to be deep in thought again. 'This is not about a book,' he said, eventually. 'But we did discuss it a lot. It was probably Cyril's greatest obsession in his later years. He thought he had found a copy of *Cardenio*. He'd spent years trying to build a case that would authenticate it.'

'*Cardenio*?' Helen said, with a frown. 'You mean . . . the lost Shakespeare play?'

'You know of it?'

'A little,' she told him. She knew of it because it connected to her general areas of interest, but it hadn't been part of her postgrad studies in rare books, for one very good reason. 'No one's ever found a manuscript, have they?'

'No,' Thiago agreed. 'It has been lost for at least three hundred years. But Cyril was convinced that he had a copy – probably the only copy that exists – here, in Rathbrooke's library.'

Chapter Fifteen

'Are you serious?' Helen said, stunned by this idea. 'But . . . how would that even be possible?'

'Exactly,' said Thiago. 'We know it existed because there are documents from 1612 that record it being performed twice at court in that year. It was definitely a play that had Shakespeare's name on it. It might have been co-authored by another playwright called Fletcher, but even so, it was a Shakespeare play. To find it? And *here*, of all places? It seems very unlikely. If it *was* here . . .' He spread his hands and Helen understood. Any lost manuscript – even a partial one – with a connection to Shakespeare would be priceless, in both monetary and historical terms.

'Do we even know what the story of the play was?' Helen asked.

'We do,' Thiago said. 'The full title of the play was *The History of Cardenio*. Cardenio is a character in one of Don Quixote's adventures.'

'*Don Quixote*?' Helen said, surprised. 'Cora told me that

Cyril was reading that with her. It must have been a favourite of his?'

Thiago smiled. '*Sí*. We talked of it often. Cervantes' book had been published in 1611, and was popular all over Europe, especially in London. That is probably why Shakespeare and Fletcher decided to bring a version to the stage – perhaps even at the king's request. The book was too long for them to dramatize whole, so they chose a portion of it – one of Don Quixote's many separate adventures on his madcap quests – and what they chose was Cardenio.'

'I didn't know that,' Helen said, fascinated.

'Anyway,' Thiago went on, '*The History of Cardenio* was performed and then ... nothing. We don't know how it was received by the audience. Whatever scripts still existed at that point were lost. We assume, with our modern sensibilities, that Shakespeare must have kept a copy, at least for himself, yes? But perhaps he didn't. After all, he barely left any papers behind when he died. It seems inconceivable to us that the greatest playwright of all time did not have a library, papers, all the early notes about and drafts of his own work. And yet, nothing of that sort has ever been found. In his will, he famously makes mention of his 'second best bed', but there's nothing about a library, papers, or a body of work. Imagine that – how hugely Shakespeare has influenced the world around us, and yet we have almost none of his original writing.' Thiago shook his head, as if wondering at this conundrum. 'There aren't even many examples of his signature.'

Helen was quiet for a while. 'From what I've learned about Cyril Gissing, that's a mystery that would have been right up his street.'

Thiago laughed. 'Yes. And he's not the only one. A hundred years after Shakespeare died, another playwright called Lewis Theobald produced a play that he said was *Cardenio*, rediscovered. He called his play *Double Falsehood*, and there was some reason to believe that he really had used fragments of an actual Shakespeare script, or perhaps more than one, to build the play around.'

'Where would he have got those from, a century later?' Helen asked.

Thiago shrugged. 'He did not say. He was a scholar and a collector himself. Perhaps he had found versions that would have been used by the prompters at those court performances. But if Theobald did have such a thing, no one ever saw them and they have since been lost again. There have been other versions since then, trying to take the play back to what it might have been originally. Scholars have written fascinating works on the history and the politics of the time around when it would have been staged and so on. But an original script? No, there has never been one found.'

'It doesn't mean there isn't one out there, though. Or bits of one.'

'*Sí*. Indeed.'

Helen turned to look up at the vast library around them. 'And Cyril Gissing really believed he'd found one?'

'Yes. At least, that's what he told me.'

'You didn't believe him?'

'It was not that I didn't believe him,' Thiago said, carefully. 'I did believe him, of course I did, or at least I trusted that he had something of great age and literary interest. But such things are so complicated to authenticate. And finding a lost Shakespeare play? That would be . . . monumental in the literary world. *Me* believing him meant nothing. I am nobody. What I believe doesn't matter. But he refused to do the things that would mean it could be authenticated or discounted by the people who *do* matter. He would not allow experts to visit Rathbrooke to look at it. He would not photograph it. He could not scan it, because he didn't have the equipment – even if he did, it's unlikely he would have used the process. He refused to provide an account of how he came to have it. There was no provenance.' Thiago shrugged. 'He was known in our small, strange and spread-out community, but he was also elusive. Few had met him, and those who had were of a similar age to Cyril himself. They were retired, and in many cases his peers had begun to pass away. The younger generation did not know him.'

'I suppose he was easy to dismiss as a daft old man.'

'Perhaps not as disrespectful as that, at least not directly,' Thiago said. 'But what he was claiming to have, with nothing to verify it, was fantastical. Especially when you consider where we are. How would such a thing end up here, on an island so far from any of the places we know Shakespeare's life inhabited?' He spread his hands. 'Such is the way of things. And to be honest, while I trusted Cyril – his judgement *and* his knowledge . . . I did not take this claim too seriously either. I believed that *he* believed he had what he said he had, but . . . I thought it unlikely that whatever it was could actually be *Cardenio*.'

'Why?' Helen asked. 'He found a lot of other lost texts, didn't he? Why not this one?'

Thiago shrugged. 'He hadn't travelled himself for a long time. As I said, I became his legs in that respect, in the later years. It must be fifteen years since his last trip to locate a book personally. But he had only been talking about this manuscript for the past eight years, perhaps ten. Where would he have found it? How would he have acquired it?'

They lapsed into silence. There was something niggling at the back of Helen's mind. 'Do you know that he also believed that Rathbrooke has a Shakespeare mulberry tree? One of the original saplings?'

Thiago went very still. 'What?'

'It's in the orchard, along with others grown from cuttings taken from it. You know the story of Shakespeare's mulberry?'

'*Sí, sí*,' said Thiago. 'Cyril told me of it, in fact. But what made him think it was one of the mulberries taken from Shakespeare's own tree?'

Helen thought about the story that Rufus had told her. 'Rufus told me that Cyril had found a bill of sale from the 1841 auction of goods at Abington Park in Northampton. The tree was listed as a Shakespeare mulberry, although why there would have been a Shakespeare mulberry in the grounds, I don't know. That's a long way from Stratford-upon-Avon.'

'Abington Park.' A flash of excitement passed across his face. 'I have heard of this place before.'

'Oh?' Helen asked. 'In what context?'

Thiago got up and began to pace, as if he was too agitated to sit still. 'Cyril wrote to me of this. I did not understand the significance. Ah, Cyril, my friend,' he went on, as if addressing his friend's dear departed spirit, 'why must you always be so cryptic? He told me the story of Elizabeth Barnard. She was Shakespeare's last living relative – his granddaughter.' Thiago stopped and looked up at Helen, his dark eyes shining. 'She was lady of Abington Park. She had no children. She was the last of the Shakespeare line.'

Helen looked at him, her mind whirring. 'Wait,' she said, standing up too. 'Wait, wait. You're telling me that the last family connection to Shakespeare lived in the same place that a Shakespeare mulberry had been planted? But,' she shook her head, trying to follow the line, 'the auction was in 1841. She can't have still been alive then, surely?'

'No,' Thiago agreed. 'She died in 1670. The house was taken over by someone else after that. Shakespeare's mulberry had not even been felled by then. But still. It is a connection. Isn't it? It must mean something. When did Cyril find this bill of sale?'

Helen shook her head. 'I don't know. I'd have to ask Rufus. When he told me the story, I assumed it was a long time ago – but I don't know that for sure.'

Thiago looked around the library, as if that suddenly significant piece of ephemera might present itself for instant inspection. 'Have you found anything like that?'

'No. Although, I wasn't looking for it,' she admitted.

Thiago was quiet again. A subtle tension had entered his shoulders, as if an almost unbelievable possibility had occurred to him. 'What about the manuscript? The one he thought was *Cardenio*? You haven't found that, either?'

'No,' Helen said. 'But again, I wasn't looking for it. I'm not sure I would have known what I was looking at even if I had.' She waved at the stacks of paper on the desk. 'There is a lot to go through.'

Thiago stood, slowly, as if contemplating. 'This was without doubt the most precious thing he owned,' he said. 'And it would be fragile. A stack of paper, four hundred years old. If it were in a museum—'

'It would be in a climate-controlled room. It would be packed away in an archive box, in acid-free paper,' Helen said, standing too. 'There's nothing like that here.'

He turned to look at her. 'Really? Are you sure? There was a manuscript, I am sure of it. I never doubted that, even if I couldn't be as sure of its origin as Cyril. It is here somewhere. It must be. And if there is an actual link to the Shakespeare line – that's a provenance, Helen, or at least the beginnings of one.'

She thought. 'If propagating the trees is more recent than I assumed . . . if he only began to do that once he'd found the bill of sale . . . perhaps he found the manuscript at the same time. That would explain why he only began talking about it a few years ago. He didn't have to go looking for it. It was already here, at Rathbrooke. It came with the mulberry, from the sale at Abington.'

Thiago turned to look at her, and now there was a gleam in his eye. 'We have to find it.'

Chapter Sixteen

Helen took Thiago to see the mulberry before they went to find Rufus. The afternoon sun was warm, suspended high in an azure blue sky streaked with wisps of white cloud, as if there had never been a storm at all.

'Here,' she said, stepping off the orchard path and ducking beneath the boughs of the apple trees.

Thiago followed her through the small orchard. There were birds hopping about in the branches, and Helen wondered whether they nested on the island, or flew back to the mainland to roost. What was the range of an average sparrow? It seemed a long way to come for bugs, but she could imagine that Rathbrooke was a good place to raise your young if you were a bird. No cats, no cars, no predators, and crumbs from Martha's kitchen. Rufus left most of the orchard unmown. Now the long grass was scattered with the colourful splashes of daisy, harebell, cornflower and buttercup. The air was full of the lazy drone of bees, searching the wildflowers for pollen. Here, Helen thought, enclosed by the island wall, they were so far removed from modern life that it was easy to believe they had travelled back in time to Elizabethan England, so distant seemed the rest of the world. A secret garden: another fairy tale.

Thiago parted some of the mulberry's greenery, stepping in and leaning close to place a hand flat against it in the same way that Helen had. Thiago shut his eyes: a moment of communion, perhaps, a hope that this could connect him back to that time and place four hundred years ago. Around them the leaves susurrated in a light breeze. Above their heads the fruit hung heavier now, ripening quickly in the late summer heat.

'I've never heard of anything like that,' Rufus said, once they'd found him. He was with Martha and Cora, gathering the sheep ready for the shearers to arrive that afternoon. 'A secret room in Rathbrooke Hall? I suppose it's possible – you know what a warren the house is. But Cyril never told me about such a place.'

'Or me,' Martha said. 'And if Rufus doesn't know about it, then there's no reason Cora or I would.'

'Sounds made up to me,' Cora said, picking at her nails. 'Like something out of a kids' book – not real.'

'Do you remember any unusual renovations being done in the past few years?' Helen asked. 'Any of you?'

Martha gave a small, bemused laugh. 'Renovations? *Here?*'

Thiago turned to Rufus. 'Helen showed me the very old mulberry in the orchard.'

The old gardener smiled. 'Aye. It's taken from Shakespeare's one at New Place in Stratford, did she tell you that?'

'She did. Remarkable,' Thiago said. 'I'd love to hear the whole story. Do you know when Cyril realized what the tree was? Did he know even when you first came here?'

'Oh no,' Rufus said, with a quick shake of his head. 'It were only a few years back. He came out to find me here in the garden, all excited to tell me about it.'

'Can you remember exactly when that was?' Helen pressed. 'It could be important.'

Rufus rubbed his chin. 'Well, let's see now.' He looked at Martha, and then at Cora, who was standing, silent and sullen despite Thiago's presence. 'You girls hadn't got here yet, had you? That means it must be more than seven years ago. But Jack Burnaby had already passed away, which was ten years ago. I've a hunch it wasn't too long after, in fact, because Mrs Burnaby was struggling, bless her, with just us two old curmudgeons and her grief. It wasn't long after she decided to go and live with her sister in Bamburgh – so eight, nine years ago, I would say.'

Helen glanced at Thiago, who gave a subtle nod. Yes, that matched up.

'And you said he knew it was Shakespeare's tree because he had a bill of sale about the tree's original purchase?'

'Aye,' Rufus agreed, 'so he said.'

'You didn't see it for yourself?' Thiago asked. 'He didn't show it to you?'

'No – like I said, he came rushing out here into the

gardens to find me. He wouldn't have brought anything precious with him, he never did like his books and whatnot – ephemera – leaving the library.'

'Is there a blueprint of the house anywhere,' Helen asked, 'or a map to it of any kind?'

'I'm sorry lass, but no, there isn't,' Rufus said. He seemed a little perplexed by their fervour – not surprising given that neither Helen nor Thiago had explained exactly what they thought they were going to find inside this fabled hidden room.

'Any locked rooms?'

Martha snorted. 'Plenty. You came across them when you first arrived, remember? I gave you the keys I had.'

'Apart from the one for the west wing.'

'I've never had that,' Martha reiterated. 'Cyril didn't either. It's been shut up longer than Cora and I have been here.'

Helen's ears pricked up. 'But not for ever. Maybe only for the past ten years?'

'No,' Cora said. 'It's longer than that. Much longer. That's why there's no key. Cy told me. He and the previous housekeeper – Mrs Burnaby – decided it was too much to keep looking after it – cleaning it and all – when it wasn't being used. It was cleared out and locked up way back when.'

'How do you know it was cleared out?' Helen asked. 'Did Cyril tell you?'

'Yes,' the girl said. 'But you can see it is, too. There are windows looking into the ground floor from the greenhouse.

The rooms are completely bare. I can show you if you think I'm lying.'

'I don't think you're lying, Cora,' Helen said. 'Of course I don't. I'm just clutching at straws.' Helen turned to look up at the bulk of Cyril Gissing's home, looming behind them. 'Because if we can't narrow it down, we're just going to have to search the whole place, aren't we?'

'Well, I suppose you don't have to worry about the west wing,' Cora pointed out, helpfully. 'That's narrowed it down a bit, hasn't it?'

They started with the attic, which they weren't hopeful about given how many stairs it would have meant the octogenarian Cyril Gissing would have had to climb to get there. But since, even though it was locked, Martha had a key, they thought it the best place to try first. Helen knew as soon as they'd pushed open the door that they were already onto a losing streak. Here, too, the rooms that had once belonged to busy servants had been emptied of everything except the bedframes and the carefully stored paintings that the housekeeper had removed from their original frames. There were no cupboards to search. They knocked on the dividing walls and found them universally thin, just wattle and daub. There were no hidden passages or spaces beneath the floorboards, or at least nothing larger than a shoebox.

'This just doesn't feel right, does it?' Helen asked.

'No,' Thiago agreed. 'It's not up here.'

Helen went to the door of the last room and looked

back down the narrow passageway to the stairs. 'There are service passages between some of the rooms on the lower floors, aren't there? Like the one that connects the small kitchen to the dining room. He could have repurposed one of those.'

Thiago pointed at her, a gesture of agreement. 'Let's check them out.'

But none of these searches bore any fruit either.

'I told you,' Cora said, when she and Rufus finished in the garden and came to find them. 'You're wasting your time. There's no secret room at Rathbrooke Hall. I would have found it if there were. Cy would have told me about it. He told me everything.'

'Maybe you're right,' Helen admitted, defeated.

'I *am* right,' Cora said, definitively.

'I am not so sure,' Thiago said. 'That would mean that the manuscript didn't exist at all, and that for years Cyril was making up everything he said in his letters.'

'Not necessarily,' Helen said. 'Perhaps we're just wrong about the idea of it being in a specific hiding place.'

'But then you would have already found it,' Thiago said. 'This was his main obsession. He talked about it in every letter I received from him for almost the whole of the last decade. It would be on his desk or very close at hand somewhere else nearby. But you say you haven't seen it?'

'No. But look at the size of this place. That doesn't mean it isn't here.'

By this time it was after six. They had searched all day

through the great house's dusty rooms and found nothing. They went back to the library, defeated.

'I don't understand it,' Thiago said. 'He had that manuscript. It is a real thing, I am sure of it, as sure as I am that he must have left a will somewhere.'

'Could he have sold it?' Helen asked. 'Could he have become so frustrated at no one taking his claim seriously that he just . . . gave up and got rid of it? You said you weren't the only person he'd written to about it. What if one of those people did believe him, at least enough to think it was worth putting money into?'

'I can't believe he would have let it go,' Thiago said. 'Especially if someone else was convinced enough that it was real to offer to buy it. That would have fired him up more, I think. And anyway, he still had it in the last letter he wrote to me, just months before he died.'

Helen looked at the fire. 'Then perhaps he burned it,' she suggested. 'Perhaps he came to think it was worthless too, at the end?'

'Never,' Thiago said. 'Even if he'd decided at last that it was not *Cardenio*, it would have been valuable to him. All words were to Cyril, especially old ones – and it must have been old. Perhaps another Elizabethan play. Perhaps a forgery, even, but an old one, from antiquity. Even that would be of interest now.'

'Then perhaps the manuscript was why he wanted to change his will,' Helen suggested. 'The care of it would have been important to him. When he began to get ill he realized he needed to make sure it would be looked after beyond his death.'

Thiago's expression was downcast. 'But then why not actually do so?' He asked. 'Why delay? Why not trust one of us with it? He could have given it to anyone on the island to file properly. Or even me.'

Helen gave a small smile. 'Perhaps infirmity simply overtook him,' she suggested. 'I think we all probably always think we have more time.'

They fell into silence. Helen regarded Thiago, seated on the sofa in the great room full of books, and realized that it was only his second evening on the island, and yet he felt as if he belonged there. They hadn't discussed him staying a further night; it had simply seemed inevitable. Her initial discomfort at his method and time of arrival had soothed into ease in his presence, as if he was as much a resident of the island as Martha or Rufus or Cora. As if he had always been there.

It made her nervous, in an undefined way. She couldn't be this comfortable with him this quickly. She *shouldn't* be, should she? She knew nothing about him, not really. Trusting him would be a mistake.

'Where else can we look?' she asked, pushing away this nebulous anxiety. 'There are still other parts of the house we can go through. Perhaps tomorrow we'll strike lucky. In his last year or so Cyril had mainly been living in the rooms closest to the library, along the corridor just outside the peel entrance. Maybe there's something there.'

Thiago shook his head. 'My gut says that if it is not here, in the library, it is not anywhere.'

She smiled a little. 'You go by your gut a lot, don't you?'

He looked at her, face stern, though she could detect a twinkle deep in his dark eyes that belied the expression. 'You too, I think, yes? You must, as a writer yourself.'

Her heart gave a slight jump. 'What do you mean?'

He leaned towards her, clasping his hands together. 'There has been something familiar about you to me, ever since I first arrived. At first, I thought Cyril must have talked about you, but of course he hadn't. And yet – your face. Your name. These are not things easily forgotten. I realized it earlier today. You are an author. You wrote that book, *All of the Above*, didn't you?'

Helen's mouth was suddenly dry. She swallowed, feeling sick. Did this also mean he knew of her recent ignominy? Had he seen the papers, as she had – as *Cora* had?

Thiago frowned. 'I . . . am sorry. I did not realize this was a sore subject? But you are here incognito, doing a clerk's job. I should have realized. Unless,' he added, with a smile and that twinkle back again, trying to lighten the moment, 'this is some elaborate plot worthy of Cervantes or Shakespeare themselves and you are the other half of a twinned pair?'

Helen forced a smile. 'No, nothing like that. You just shocked me, that's all. I wouldn't have thought *All of the Above* was the sort of book you'd be interested in.'

Thiago tilted his head to one side, brushing his dark curls back with one hand as he regarded her. 'I love all books,' he said. ‘All books are equal, because every book tells a story about the world in which we live. Who am I to say whose stories are more important?’ He looked up, gestured to Cyril Gissing’s magnificent library. ‘I learned from Cyril, and his reason for living was to save stories from being lost. Any stories. All stories. Besides,’ he added, with another grin, ‘you were a bestseller in Spain, also. There was a very large poster of you and your book in the biggest bookshop in Madrid. I walked past it every day for weeks.’

Helen let out a slow breath. ‘Right.’ She wanted to ask him if he’d heard anything about her more recently, but she couldn’t bring herself to and he mentioned nothing further about it. If he didn’t know, she didn’t want to tell him. She didn’t want another relationship to turn sour because of her past, the way her interactions with Cora had. Pirate or not, she did not want to be despised by Thiago Montera.

Chapter Seventeen

'What *is* that?' Thiago asked, later that evening. They had retired to Helen's rooms on the second floor to eat the dinner that Martha had insisted on preparing for them both.

Mostly the ghosts were quiet, but they seemed agitated now. Perhaps it was Thiago's presence in the house. Perhaps another person, another life, and such a vivid one at that, had disturbed them. She wasn't sure when she'd begun to think of them as actual ghosts. They had become a fact of Rathbrooke, with the same level of reality as possessed by the staircases or the art on the walls or the crossed swords that seemed to be mounted over every fireplace in the building. In the background, a presence – or a lack thereof – that was an immutable fact of life on the island.

'They'll settle down,' she said.

He turned to look at her, amused. 'You are growing fond of them, these ghosts,' he said.

She shook her head. 'I'm just becoming used to them.

Whatever they are, they've never done me any harm. I've never seen anything, only heard them.'

Thiago seemed to ponder this, turning his wine glass around in his fingers so that the ruby liquid within shifted and glinted in the light from the candles they had lit on the table.

He sipped the wine, the same candlelight dancing through his hair. 'I've seen too much not to believe. But that's the point. I've *seen* things, Helen. Figures that look as real as you do to me now, sitting as close to me as you are now, but that could not possibly be there. Books moved on shelves by unseen hands. I have heard sounds, too, but never *only* sounds.'

'Until now,' Helen said. 'Rathbrooke is a unique place. Perhaps her ghosts are unique, too. I mean, look at the meal we just ate.' She indicated their empty plates, resting on the low table in front of the sofa. They had been sharing a bottle of wine over a dinner of lamb chops with summer salad and new potatoes. 'Everything was produced here on the island. Everything! Isn't that amazing for such a small place?'

'Apart from the wine,' he pointed out, with a gentle smile. 'Unless there is also some mythical vine I haven't been told of yet.'

'Apart from the wine,' she conceded, taking another sip. 'Although I wouldn't be surprised if Rufus had managed that too.'

Thiago smiled again. 'You are proud of this place.'

'I suppose I am,' she said, a little surprised at the

realization. It was a pride that was misplaced, of course. Whatever Rathbrooke was or had could be no achievement of hers. But still. She had, at some point over the month of her residence here, come to love it. Helen realized that it was going to be a wrench when she had to leave, and not only because it would mean a return to a world she knew would not welcome her.

Thiago said nothing more, instead reaching for his slice of the cake studded with mulberries from the orchard that Martha had given them for dessert. He contemplated this for a while. Helen was content to let the quiet between them expand – as she had predicted, the ghosts had once again subsided into silence, as they so often did – because quiet time spent with Thiago was not strained. She wondered if she could ask him to stay and help her catalogue the library properly. He was, after all, the perfect man for the job. Perhaps she could ask her mother to put Thiago on the payroll too. She should consult the island's inhabitants before she did that, although Helen thought she already knew what the reaction would be, certainly from Cora. Martha and Rufus both seemed to like Thiago too. He was a likeable guy.

'I keep coming back to the mulberry tree,' Thiago said, eventually. 'Why was Cyril so convinced it had been grown from a sapling from the tree at New Place?'

'Because of the bill of sale he'd found,' Helen reminded him. 'You heard what Rufus said.'

'Yes, but that came from Abington Park, not Stratford, and long after the Shakespeare line had ended. Besides, you have not found that, either, have you?' Thiago pointed out. 'And if it existed, it must be somewhere. He would not have misplaced that. The same with his will. He *must* have made a valid one. There's no way the Cyril that I knew would have left the fate of his books to chance. The library was his life's work. The whole point of him searching out those thousands of books was to make sure they would be preserved. Why, then, wouldn't he make sure that was going to happen after his death? It makes no sense that there was no will, it makes no sense that we cannot find that bill of sale, and it makes no sense that he spent years talking about a manuscript that does not exist. These things must be somewhere. There must be a place in the Hall that we haven't found yet.'

'Then it has to be in the west wing, doesn't it?' Helen said. 'It's the only place we haven't looked.'

Thiago frowned. 'It seems that way, and yet—' he stopped, shaking his head.

'And yet what?'

'Why would he keep it so far away from the library?' he asked. '*Cardenio* at least. And he spent all his time in the library. When he grew more frail, he moved his bedroom as close to the library as he could get. Why would he keep something he considered so precious at the other end of this huge old house, in an empty wing that he had to walk a long way to reach, that he had to unlock with a key that everyone who knew him best said he didn't have?'

'I don't know,' Helen said. 'You're right, when you put it

like that it doesn't seem to make sense. But I can't think of anywhere else to look.'

He nodded, his dark brow drawn together in a frown that formed his face into a glower as he stared into his wine glass.

'We'll open it up tomorrow,' Helen said. 'We'll have to do it carefully, so as not to cause damage, but there will be a way. For now, I don't know about you, but I'm ready for bed.'

Thiago looked up at her. For a brief, charged second, she wondered whether he had read more into her statement than she had intended. It was early, after all, by all usual metrics of an adult bed time. They had spent the day together, they were comfortable in each other's presence, they had shared a dinner by candlelight. Perhaps he had caught her staring at him, the way she kept catching herself, kicking herself. Helen could feel the blood rushing to her cheeks.

'If you'll be okay here on the sofa?' she added, in a voice she hoped had not been strangled by her sudden mortification. 'Tomorrow we should ask Martha if there's another room you can take for your own. If you want to stay longer, that is. Although I suppose that depends on what we find tomorrow, doesn't it?'

Stop gabbling, you idiot.

Thiago smiled. 'I will be fine on the sofa. No—' he said, catching her fingers briefly in his as she went to gather the plates to take them down to the kitchen, 'Please. Leave that to me.'

While he was out of the room she used the bathroom, fleeing into her bedroom before he could return. Nested in the deep mattresses of the huge four-poster, Helen lay back and stared at the canopy above her. There was something niggling at the back of her mind, a splinter of a thought embedded there, but she couldn't pull it out to see what it was. She found herself thinking of Thiago, instead, as she heard him return and move around next door.

She thought again about what he knew about her, what he did not know. She would forever be haunted by her past, by the narratives others had constructed for her and the ones she had failed to write for herself. Perhaps that's why she had turned to the keyboard in the end: a need to tell her own story, any story better than the one in which she had imprisoned herself. It was another version of Cyril Gissing's drive to preserve lost texts, of Don Quixote's absurd, mythic quests. She fell into a fitful sleep, her last conscious thoughts of Cyril Gissing and his haven of forgotten books.

In her dreams that night she chased a figure, indistinct and ephemeral, always just out of reach. It was trying to lead her somewhere, she thought, but would not wait for her to catch up. At some point Helen realized it was Thiago, and knew this despite not being able to see his face. He remained elusive: every time she tried to catch hold of him, he slipped through her fingers. They were in an endless hall of books that was the library of Rathbrooke, except it wasn't, because it was too vast for that – so many halls and galleries and stairways, unknowable, unmappable, always another corridor around another corner, all lined with book after book, too many to ever read, to ever know. The figure kept opening more doors, showing her more rooms full of books. Some were as huge as Rathbrooke's ballroom. Others were barely more than cupboards, secreted in corners any reasonable person would consider too small for anything useful, yet these were crammed with more books, though the apertures through which they could be reached were infuriatingly small. There was only one window, a huge eye that looked out into darkness, as if there were nothing in the world besides this one place, this library of lost corners, lost stories, lost books.

Helen woke with a start, tangled beneath her sheets, with just one thought in her head. She got up and dressed quickly, opening the door to her bedroom. Thiago was fast asleep, oblivious to her unsettled night, although he stirred when she came into the room, her feet stepping on a creaking floorboard.

'Helen?' he asked, sleepily.

'There's something—' she began, but then couldn't frame her thoughts. 'The library. I need to—' She couldn't explain. 'I need to go to the library, now.'

He scrambled to follow her, dragging on his jeans quickly, still yanking his sweater over his head even as she left the room.

Once back inside the peel, she climbed the stairs without pause. Thiago followed, silent, apparently content to let whatever was going on play out.

She led him to the reading nook and pushed back the curtains. Beyond them the first spears of dawn light were piercing the horizon. Through the arch of diamond panes, the North Sea stretched away from them, shadows on the water edged in morning light.

Helen looked around the little nook, at the wooden panels that lined it, at the bench that Cyril Gissing had shaped for the bride who was never to be. She turned in a circle in that small space, imagining the depth of vision it must have taken to hew this small haven out of the stone it had once been. With them both standing in the nook, there was barely enough room for her to move, and yet. It was space enough to read a book.

She looked at Thiago, who had followed her gaze around the nook as if he could divine from this her train of thought. His dark curls were as edged by morning light as the waves that surrounded this tiny fin of rock on which Rathbrooke stood, out of the oldest part of which its owner had reclaimed a small portion.

'What if there are other spaces like this?' Helen asked, eventually, into the silence. She raised a hand, gestured to the tiny room in which they stood. 'Here, in the library walls?'

Thiago went very still. Then he turned his head and looked at her. The morning light reached his eyes, and Helen knew he understood.

They found it that afternoon. Or, at least, they found what could only be a door to it, although it was so small as an entryway that anyone stepping in or out would have to bend almost double to duck beneath the lintel. It was little more than a wooden panel, ancient, hidden behind a bookcase on the mezzanine level that had been set on hinges so that it would pull away to reveal the wall behind it. The motion was smooth and silent – well-oiled, well-used.

There was a keyhole in the old wood, and they did not have the key.

'Probably means it isn't what you think it is, doesn't it?' Cora said, when she, Martha and Rufus were brought to take a look at this new discovery. 'It's just a forgotten cupboard, that's all.'

'I don't think so,' said Thiago. He pointed to three small holes that had been bored through the wood, roughly demarking a triangle. 'These are airholes, for ventilation.' He ran his index finger over the wood, where a handle would be had the door had one. 'This feels old, yes?' he said. 'Far older than the reading nook?'

'Yes,' Helen agreed. 'This door – it looks as old as Rathbrooke's main entrance, or the door to the west wing.'

Thiago nodded. 'And yet here, the wood has been worn smooth. By a hand pushing it open, pulling it closed, and not only in ancient times. More recently than that. I think this is exactly what we've been looking for. There must be a key.'

They searched again, all of them, but had no more success than in their first attempt.

'This is crazy,' Helen said, eventually, when they had spent so many hours riffling through the great house's corners that outside the sun was once again sinking towards the horizon. 'We're never going to find it. Look at the size of this place!

It could be anywhere. Even if we only looked inside every book in the library, it would take weeks.'

'And it probably doesn't exist in the first place,' Cora said, helpfully.

Thiago spread his hands. 'Then let me pick the lock.'

Helen gave him a sideways look. 'You can pick locks, too?'

He tilted his head to one side, gave a little grin. 'When the occasion calls for it.'

'Why am I not even slightly surprised?'

Thiago shrugged. 'It's a life skill.'

'Can you teach me?' Cora asked, eagerly.

'No, he cannot,' Martha said, firmly. 'And I'm not sure I like the idea of you doing it on that old door either, Thiago, truth be told. What if you were to damage it? Rufus, what do you think?'

'It's a fair point,' the gardener agreed. 'But I'm not sure what other choice we rightly have, Martha love. If Mr Gissing's will is nowhere else, then in a hidden locked cupboard none of us knew about is probably the likely spot, isn't it?'

They all turned to look at Helen, who seemed to have been tasked with making the decision. She didn't like the idea of causing damage either.

'You'll be careful with the lock?' she asked Thiago.

'I won't damage it,' he told her. 'I'll be careful, I promise. But I think Rufus is right. This has to be it, doesn't it? We've looked everywhere else.'

It took him what in retrospect could be considered

disturbingly little time to pop the old lock. The barrel turned with a faint click and then the door shifted on its hinges, quiet and smooth. All the inhabitants of Rathbrooke gathered closer to see what was beyond, and Thiago glanced back at them before pushing on the old wood. They all craned forward, ducking their heads to see. The door shifted open, silent, into darkness. Rufus fumbled in his jacket pocket and pulled out a little torch, flicking it on and directing the beam past Thiago's shoulder.

'Well, I'll be . . .' the old man muttered, quietly.

The beam illuminated a tiny room with a ceiling just high enough for a grown man to stand tall in. The floor, walls and roof were stone, hewn out of the peel's bulk like a purpose-built cell. It was smaller than the reading nook, with no windows or other inherent features besides a ledge along the wall opposite the door, which perhaps in desperation could serve an occupant as a place to sleep. On this had been placed a small wooden bookshelf, which housed a collection of boxes and archive folders beside a few lone books. Against the wall to their left was a small and roughly made wooden table and a chair. The cushions on the latter looked younger by several centuries than the seat they graced, and Helen recognized them as matching several others she'd seen in Cyril Gissing's rooms. On the table was another cushion, oblong and made of grey velvet with a dip in its centre. Helen had seen its kind before – the dip was shaped to hold a book, so that it could be opened gently, without damage to its cover. Beside this was a stack of thin white cotton gloves. Aside from these things, the table held a few other papers, weighted by what looked to Helen like a small figure carved out of dark wood. A netsuke, perhaps.

'It is a priest hole,' Helen said, quietly. 'It must be. A place made to hide Catholic recusants during the Reformation. That's why there are airholes in the door but no windows. This was built to stay secret.'

'Mr Gissing never mentioned it,' Rufus said. 'I had no idea, none.'

'Is that a key?' Martha asked.

Helen glanced over to see that she was pointing at the table on which was, sure enough, a very large and very old wrought-iron key, black with age. She picked it up, weighing it in her hand, and then pushed it into the lock that Thiago had just jimmied open. It fitted perfectly, turning with surprising smoothness to shoot out the bolt that would seal the door again once closed.

'Why would the key be *inside* the priest hole?' Rufus asked. 'That doesn't make sense, does it? It was locked, for sure.'

'There were probably two,' Thiago said. 'One would stay in here in case someone became trapped, or if the person who had locked the door from the outside . . . did not survive to reopen it.'

Helen shivered a little. She imagined being locked inside this dark, windowless room, terrified of being discovered and equally terrified of being forgotten. That had happened sometimes, she knew. Places like this were still being discovered in old houses just like Rathbrooke Hall, so hidden away that four centuries later they had not been found. Some of them held skeletons: unfortunate souls secreted in fear of their lives who had never again seen the light of day, because the person who had locked the door behind them – often the only person who knew where the hidden room was – had perished or been imprisoned, never to return. She took the key and kept it with her, putting it in her pocket for safe keeping.

'I wonder where the other one is?' she asked. 'Has anyone—'

'I've got to go and feed the chickens,' Cora cut Helen off to announce, apparently completely disinterested in what they had found.

'And I'd better get us all some supper on,' Martha said, turning away too. 'You'll not catch me setting foot in that hole, that's for sure.'

Helen understood the sentiment. Just looking through the tiny door was enough to make her feel as if the walls were closing in. But they'd found what they were looking for. Standing beside her in the narrow doorway, Thiago's gaze was fixed on the bookcase, though he had not moved. She could feel the tension radiating from his shoulders. He jumped a little when she touched his arm.

'Thiago?'

He shook his head once, then ducked to step into the room. He reached out for a pair of cotton gloves and put them on before carefully lifting a volume from the shelf. It was oversized, with a spine of red leather embossed with rich gilt. He held it gingerly, turning to show Helen what he held. When he opened the cover, she realized it was a box, within which was a book, bound in the same red leather with the same gilt decoration.

'I have seen one of these before,' Thiago said, quietly. 'Though we are not lucky enough to have one in our collection. There are 235 known to still survive, and I do not think this is one of that number.'

Thiago opened the book's cover to reveal the frontispiece. Helen recognized the famous portrait. She looked up at him. 'It's a First Folio,' she breathed.

The last time Helen had seen one of these was as a student in Edinburgh, and even then she hadn't touched it. The 'First Folio' was the first time Shakespeare's works had been collected. In some cases, it was the first time some of the plays had ever been printed, certainly officially. The book in front of them had been produced in 1623, but looked as if it had been printed yesterday. It was over four hundred years old, and utterly pristine.

Thiago closed the cover, closed the box, and turned back to the bookshelf to replace the folio where he had found it, picking up a much smaller book from beside it instead. It was bound in yellowing paper and it was clearly very fragile. When he saw the cover, Thiago drew in a sharp breath.

'What?' Helen asked. 'What is it?'

He looked back at the shelf, where the series of volumes exactly like the one he held had been lined up for who knew how long.

'It's a quarto of *Titus Andronicus*,' he said. 'This was printed in 1593.'

Helen moved until she was at his shoulder. Together they looked at the shelf. 'There are eighteen here,' she counted. 'I didn't even know it would be possible for these to survive so long unbound.'

Thiago muttered something in Spanish, replacing the slim volume with the utmost care. 'The people who first owned these would have seen the plays performed while Shakespeare himself stood backstage. How did Cyril manage to collect all of these? Why did he never tell me of them?'

Thiago replaced the slim volume as Helen picked up another small book from the collection. She murmured in shock as she realized what it was, looking up at Thiago as she held it up.

'Shakespeare's poetry,' she said. 'Also published during his lifetime. Actually, from what I remember, it was a more official publication than the quartos.'

Both lapsed into silence as they continued to examine the contents of the bookcase. It was clear to both of them that even without Cyril Gissing's fabled lost Shakespeare manuscript, they were standing inside a treasure trove of literary wonders.

The last item Thiago picked up was an unassuming modern archive box. The box, unlike everything else on the shelves, was not upright but lying down. Thiago picked it up, and it was clear to Helen that it was very light, possibly even empty. Yet when he opened it, the silent, wide-eyed glance that he gave her spoke volumes. Helen moved to look over his shoulder at the contents – sheaves of paper; not full sheets but oddments, different sizes, weights and thicknesses, though all obviously very old and all covered with handwriting, tight letters formed in sepia-tinted ink. They both looked down at this collection of fragile paper, and Helen was not sure that either of them were still breathing.

'This has to be it,' Helen whispered. 'Doesn't it?'

'I think it might be.' Thiago was equally hushed, equally in awe of what they might be looking at.

'Should we bring it out?' she asked eventually, her voice little more than a whisper. 'Or look at it in here?'

'I think,' Thiago said, 'we should look at it in exactly the way that Cyril himself did.'

*

3 Sunnyside Road
Seahouses
Northumberland

I do want you to come! Of course I do, Dad. I miss you, you know that. Tell me when you're going to be here and I'll be in Seahouses to meet you. Promise. Can't wait to see you. I love you.

Chapter Eighteen

Helen took another pair of thin gloves: soft cotton, white and clean. Thiago placed the box file carefully on the table and went out to find a second chair that would fit through the tiny door of the priest hole. Helen could not bear to remain inside alone, which gave her further cause to wonder as she stood outside waiting for him to return. Cyril had been willing to close himself inside that small stone box repeatedly, for hours, with no one knowing where he was. What if the door had refused to open once he was inside it and he'd become trapped? With the false bookcase automatically closing back into place, no one would have known where he was. If the key had failed to open the door from the inside, he would have been trapped. Would they have heard him eventually, shouting – and then screaming – for help? Or would they have dismissed the cries as nothing but the house, breathing, like the noises she – and Thiago too, now – had heard from the west wing?

What would compel him to take such a risk over and over, if not for total conviction?

Thiago returned with the smallest stool he could find, and still struggled to get it through the narrow door. They sat side by side at the table, which was hewn of ancient wooden planks so thick that Helen bashed her knees against it as they shuffled around for space.

The archive box was one with sides that could be folded flat. Neither Thiago nor Helen spoke as he undid the ties sealing it shut and they looked at what was inside. An untidy sheaf of yellowing paper, leaves curling at the edges, uneven sheets of different sizes. It was not bound in any way; there were no staples or fasteners, no ribbon holding the whole together. If not for its obvious age and the sepia tone of the ink forming the tight scrawl of handwritten words across each sheet's surface, it could have been a collection of random, unconnected pages of notes and letters.

'I am afraid to touch any of it,' Thiago said, after a few moments of silence. 'This is not right. Whatever this is – whether it is what Cyril thought it was or not – it should be studied in a museum, not here.'

Helen leaned forward, looking more closely at the yellowed page that had been placed on top of the uneven pile. The handwriting was so small, the words so closely packed in lines that straggled to the very edge of the page, that it was impossible for her to make out any meaning. To the left, though, the words were more spaced, and occurred every few lines, after which had been left a gap before the mass of words began again. Characters, followed by dialogue. A playscript, though not like any she had seen before.

'I'll be careful . . .' she said, 'but—'

Helen reached out, tentatively, to lift this first page out of the way enough to reveal the one below it. Thiago said nothing, and she had the sense that he was holding his breath as she moved the first fragile leaf. To her relief, nothing flaked from the ancient paper, no tears appeared, no marks were left by her gloved fingers. Though she thought that the scribe – whoever that was – had probably used both sides of the paper to write, she didn't risk turning it over, instead laying it face up on the open archive box so that it sat alongside the next page. This bore similarly tightly packed writing, the left-hand side of the page once again bearing single or in some cases a double name. Helen squinted at one of these for a moment.

'Look.' Still bent over the page, she pointed. Between the longer written lines were others – notes, perhaps – appended in what might have been different handwriting, even smaller. 'Revision notes?'

'Probably,' Thiago agreed. His voice was strained, thoughtful, his eyes fixed on the conundrum before them.

'This isn't a playscript though,' Helen pointed out. 'Or at least, it's not a complete one.'

'No,' Thiago said. 'I don't know what this is. I don't know—' he stopped, shook his head. 'I wish Cyril were here. I wish I could talk to him. He wrote so much about this, about his theories, in his letters. But now—' he stopped, shook his head. 'I am ashamed to say I do not remember it all. After a while . . . I stopped paying close attention. I was too convinced he was wrong, too busy with my own quests.'

Helen leaned back in her seat, thoughtfully. 'Did you keep them? His letters, I mean? He kept yours, after all.'

Thiago looked at her, a light sparking deep in his dark eyes. 'Yes,' he said. 'Yes, I have them.'

Helen spread her hands. 'Are they easy to find? Could you ask someone to send them to you?'

'They're not back in Madrid,' he said. 'They are on my boat.'

Helen stared at him in surprise. 'On your *boat*? You mean the one you came here on? The one moored in Rathbrooke harbour right now?'

He gave a lopsided shrug. 'I spend a lot of time on it.' He pushed back his chair. 'I'll go and get them.'

Helen looked down at the pile of ancient paper before them. 'Let's put these away,' she said. 'I want to come with you.'

Thiago smiled, quirked an eyebrow. 'You want to see my boat?'

'Do I want to see where a Spanish book-pirate makes his home?' she asked, gently sealing the fragile pages of manuscript back into the archive box and leaving it square on the small table before stripping off her gloves. 'Why yes. Yes, I most definitely do.'

After they had closed up the secret doorway behind them, Helen stopped for a moment, regarding it carefully, trying to fix its position in her mind.

'Worried you might not find it again?' Thiago asked her, amused.

She looked up at him. 'Worried that we'll come back and discover it never existed in the first place,' she said. 'I was just inside, and even now I'm not sure it was ever really there.'

He brushed his fingers against her arm: gloveless now, too. Thiago's touch lingered against her skin for a moment as he also studied the closed bookcase. The cell's entrance really was indistinguishable from the rest of the room, entirely hidden. He reached for a volume at the end of one of the shelves. He turned it around so that the pages were facing out, and then replaced it.

'There,' he said. 'A librarian's version of white pebbles in a forest,' and for a moment Helen did feel as if she were in a fairy tale, as if Rathbrooke itself had spun a yarn of story just for them.

Thiago's boat was sleek but tiny, modern beside the island's old runabout, the *Lady Jane*. The name *Alejandra* was emblazoned in an elegant curlicue of black lettering on the hull. Thiago climbed down the harbour wall and onto the gleaming white deck, digging a set of keys from his pocket to unlock and fold down the entrance to the space below before disappearing inside. A second later he returned to peer up at her, squinting a little in the sunlight.

'You can come aboard if you like,' he said.

Thiago vanished again as Helen followed. She paused once she'd got to the short set of steps that led down below decks. These living quarters didn't give much more space than in Cyril Gissing's secret cell. She stood there in the sunlight, taking in the diminutive space: the narrow banquette sofa on one side, the same on the other but with an added fold-back table. Thiago himself was riffling through the contents of a cupboard at the prow, beyond which she could see a narrow triangle of cushions arranged to form a mattress, on which was a scatter of untidy, pushed-back sheets. She could see how he could find the sofa in her borrowed Rathbrooke rooms so comfortable if this is where he usually slept.

When she looked back at him, Thiago had pulled out a series of boxes, all designed to be lashed securely into the cupboard. It made her think of the night he had arrived, which seemed an age ago now. How could a boat this small have weathered that storm? She could imagine him clinging on for dear life in the tiny cockpit, making his way towards the island's forbidding black cliffs. Cyril and Thiago: united in the humble tenacity of their determination.

He turned, holding up a handful of envelopes, some more dog-eared with age than others. 'Here they are,' he said. 'Or, at least, these are the ones from the last ten years.'

Chapter Nineteen

'You know, I think this has to do with the code I found in Cyril's diary,' Helen said, sometime later.

'Code?' Thiago asked, sleepily, from where he lay stretched out with his feet up on the sofa behind her.

It was late. They had taken the pile of letters back to the library, but not into the priest hole. Instead they had sat down in front of the great fireplace and opened them one by one. There were at least four for each year, sometimes more, and so they had cleared space on the floor and pieced them together in chronological order, until they had a grid of one-sided correspondence laid out in a sea of paper before them.

'I didn't know Cyril had kept a diary,' Thiago added. 'And he wrote it in code?'

'It's more of a notebook, really. A stream of consciousness. And "code" makes it sound far more linear than it actually is. Hang on—'

Helen got up and picked her way to the desk to retrieve the volume full of Cyril Gissing's notes.

'I found it the first week I was here, but couldn't decipher some of what he'd written. After a while I realized that certain repeated words or phrases had been written in Spanish – like in your letters to each other – but that still didn't help. Even when I translated them, they seemed meaningless, or at least not noting anything important. Then I . . . got distracted by other things, I suppose. At the time I had no idea about the *Cardenio*.'

Thiago swung his legs back to the floor as he sat up, rubbing a hand across his face. They'd been at this for hours. Thiago, far more experienced at reading his old friend's hand than Helen, was going through each letter and reading out every reference he could find as she typed it into a document that was slowly building into a map of Cyril Gissing's increasing preoccupation. The mentions were cryptic, though, even when he'd been talking to Thiago, whom he obviously trusted. Still Gissing referred to nothing implicitly, instead employing numbers and letters, apparently to refer to explicit documents, except even from the context of each letter it was impossible to infer what this was supposed to mean. Singly, dropped into conversation about his day-to-day life or added almost as an afterthought to a 'PS' after his signature, these references were seemingly throwaway, inconsequential.

After comparison, am further convinced it is also B in Sv, sheet 12. Clear when seen beside C in iv, following.

Or this, scrawled in a margin:

C is revision only! Probably 6B. See 13.

Helen returned to the sofa and sat beside Thiago, opening the diary on her lap. She found one of the instances of 'code' and pointed it out. Thiago's fingers brushed against hers as he took the book from her to hold it closer, reading out the scrawled note.

'*This is clearly* –' he glanced up at her, 'the next words are in Spanish, it says *segunda mano . . .* '

'I looked that up – it means "second hand", doesn't it?' Helen said. 'I thought it was probably talking about one of the books, or perhaps a bookshop?'

Thiago frowned, and read the line in English. '*This is clearly the second hand, refer to 17a.*'

Helen leaned closer. 'There's an article in there?'

'It's implied,' Thiago said. 'In this context. He's talking about a different person. As in – a person's handwriting. Or author. "The second hand". To differentiate, I suppose. So: *This is clearly the second author, refer to 17a.*'

'Well, that . . . ' Helen stopped, this sudden glimpse of clarity taking her by surprise. 'That seems a lot more useful. Doesn't it?'

Thiago let the diary rest against his thigh and stared into the middle distance for a moment. 'It does.' He closed the diary and set it between them on the sofa, nodding at the laptop she had beside her. 'Can I see the document you have compiled?'

She passed him the laptop and Thiago scrolled through for a moment before making a soft sound in his throat and shaking his head.

'What?' Helen asked. 'What are you thinking?'

He looked up at her. 'I know what this is,' he said. 'I know what Cyril was doing. He was compiling evidence. This is his version of breaking down Hand D.'

'Hand D – you mean, as with *Sir Thomas More*?'

'*Sí*. Exactly.'

Any antiquarian worth their salt knew the painstaking and protracted process that had equated what had become known in the rare book world as 'Hand D' with Shakespeare's own handwriting. It was one of four different examples of handwriting – the others known as Hands A, B and C respectively – that had been found across three pages of revisions to a manuscript of an Elizabethan play called *Sir Thomas More*. The play was known to have had several collaborators working on it, and in the 1920s a process of elimination and comparison with other examples of each of the individuals' handwriting had finally concluded that the fourth hand – 'Hand D' – was indeed that of William Shakespeare himself. Most contemporary scholars now agreed. Helen had studied the process that those scholars had followed as part of her Master's degree.

Thiago tapped the cover of Cyril's diary, then looked down at the expanse of letters at their feet. 'Cyril was doing something similar with what he kept upstairs in the priest hole. He was identifying the handwriting. That's what convinced him it was real, and that it was *Cardenio*, even if what he had wasn't a fair copy of the manuscript, or even, as far as I can see from what we have here, the foul papers of a final draft.'

Helen looked at her notes again. 'Foul papers' were what a manuscript was referred to in Shakespeare's time before it had been sent to a scribe to produce a 'fair', or final, copy. They often contained revisions, and in collaborative works could include pages written in different hands. There could be lines crossed out, whole pages added and removed, that kind of thing, but somewhere amid all the changes and corrections there would be a complete playscript that a scribe would then write out as a clean copy. Although Helen wasn't convinced that what they had found in Cyril's archive box was even that far along. It really was all over the place. Some of it seemed no more than notes.

Helen looked at the letters on the floor – the tightly packed writing of Cyril's own hand. 'But was Cyril a handwriting expert?' she asked. 'Could he do the kind of analysis that would need?'

'No,' Thiago said. 'Even if he were, he'd need other verification. Nowadays the pages would be scanned and computer techniques would be used, scientific methods – AI, even. All Cyril had was a hunch and what he could work out from that mass of papers. I told you – he wouldn't let anyone else see what he had. That was what made him so easy to dismiss.'

'What he had here convinced him, though, didn't it?' Helen pointed out. She indicated the letters in front of them.

'He spent years of his life on this, piecing it together. Almost a decade. And it doesn't look as if he wavered in his belief at all. In fact, looking at the notes we've put together, I'd say his conviction only got stronger. Do you think that was just hopeful delusion?'

'I can't believe it was, no. He never struck me as delusional, just passionate.' He looked so pained that Helen reached out to him, touching his hand with hers. He smiled sadly and turned his over, so that their fingers twined together against the old leather of the couch.

'Now that we know what all of Cyril's notes mean,' Helen said, 'perhaps we should look at the pages again. Match the notes he made in his diary to the actual pages he made them about. I mean,' she took a breath, 'if that really is a lost Shakespeare play up there we need to work out how to finish what Cyril started and who best to take it to.'

Thiago watched her quietly for a moment. Helen thought that she should probably withdraw her hand, but didn't. His fingers were warm between hers. She couldn't remember the last time she had felt connected to someone in this way, or at least someone that wasn't one of her friend group. He looked less of a pirate to her now, as if some of his rough edges had been smoothed away over the few days of their acquaintance. She'd come to the island running from a past that had taught her how very vicious some such connections could turn out to be, how damaging. But now here she was, wanting to believe that the future and the people she met in it could be different. Was that hope, she wondered, or stupidity? She pulled her hand from his, and Thiago let her go.

'Aren't you tired?' he asked. 'It's late.'

She shrugged a little. 'I am, but I don't think I'll sleep.'

He nodded. 'I'm the same.' He stood up. 'Alright, then. Let's do it.'

Together they squeezed back into the tiny space, although they left the door open, wedging it so that it could not shut behind them. As they settled at the bare table, in that almost-not-there room, Helen wondered whether anyone really had hidden in here in the past, afraid for their lives. That could surely be the only reason that anyone would subject themselves to the experience. Even with Thiago beside her, even though she knew they had the key and the door could not close on them, she felt hemmed in, trapped.

Perhaps this is the origin of Rathbrooke's ghosts, she thought, and then wished she hadn't. Now was not the time to get spooked. And anyway, Helen reminded herself, she had never heard hide nor hair of anything even slightly ghostly inside the library.

They both donned gloves again. Helen laid Cyril's diary out before them while Thiago gingerly opened the archive box. Inside, the yellowing papers were still at rest, still as untidy as the last time they had peered inside.

'Okay then,' Thiago said, taking a deep breath. 'Let's do this systematically, from the first reference you found.'

Helen turned to the relevant page in the diary, using the

notes she had taken to double-check it before reading it out to him. 'It says, *4a, third quarter, line 7. Revision to first, single line above.*'

'We will assume that the first numbers in a reference refer to pages?' Thiago asked. 'So this is the fourth page we are turning to now, yes?'

'I think that makes sense, certainly in the first instance – don't you? Although I don't know what the "a" in "4a" signifies, in that case.'

'Let's find out,' Thiago said, and he carefully moved aside the first three ancient leaves. They both leaned forward to peer at what they thought Cyril Gissing had meant by '4'. Neither of them said anything for a moment, though Thiago frowned. This sheet was not a page of playscript, that was clear. In fact, it was difficult to read the tiny lettering at all, but it looked more like notes or prose than dialogue. They both studied it in silence for a few minutes.

'The note seems to say that there should be a single line of revision above line seven,' Helen said, eventually. 'But I can't see anything that would match that description, can you?'

Thiago shook his head. 'No. This . . . seems to be a letter, perhaps?' He hovered his index finger over what could have been a sign-off line at the bottom, although there was no signature. 'But I cannot make out the name, if that is one. I think this page has suffered water damage – look at this blotching.'

They looked at it for a little longer, re-examining the note in the diary, trying to work out if they might have misconstrued its meaning. It was entirely possible.

'We should try another,' Thiago said.

And so Helen picked out another reference, and after that another, and another, but none matched up, or at least, never completely, without them finding more questions than definitive answers. In fact, the more they looked at the documents before them, sheafs and sheafs of yellowed pages and inked letters, the more both of them became convinced that Cyril Gissing had been deluding himself.

'Let's keep going, just a little longer,' Helen said, though she could see a black pall of melancholy beginning to settle over Thiago as he sat, increasingly hunched, over the manuscript pages before them. 'Try this one: *34, lines through 20. Second hand, original.*' That sounds as if Cyril thought all those lines were written by the hand he thought of as Shakespeare, doesn't it?'

Thiago turned page after page, scanning each before he placed it on the pile they had been through. 'This is not a script,' he murmured. 'It is not even foul papers. It is letters, notes – scenes perhaps, even, yes – but not a complete manuscript, not even close to one. It could have been assembled from anywhere, by anyone. Cyril, my friend, what were you thinking?'

Helen rested her hand on his forearm, squeezing slightly. She could feel the depth of his disappointment. 'We could still be reading this wrong,' she pointed out.

Thiago shook his head. 'No. I do not think so. Since—' he stopped, because he'd reached the page he was looking for. Page 34. It was indeed a page of playscript, and there were clearly two authors, for the handwriting that occupied the top two-thirds of the page was distinctly different from the one that filled the bottom third. It was the first time that the description in the diary had unequivocally matched the pages they were looking at, and it stopped them both dead. Thiago laid the page down again, and Helen leaned in as he read it to himself.

'Can you read it?' she asked, for the words were tightly packed, scrawled rather than neatly figured.

'A little,' Thiago said, his voice quiet. His expression had sharpened, as if through shock. 'I think – this might be it, Helen. This might really be—' he broke off, as if overcome. 'This, here,' he indicated a word to the left of the page: a name, designating a character, followed by the lines it had been given to speak. Helen could make out that it began with a 'C'. 'It says Cardenio. This page, these very words, could have been written by Shakespeare himself.'

He put down the yellowed sheet and clasped his hand over hers where it still rested on his forearm. It wasn't really *The History of Cardenio*. It wasn't even close to being a whole manuscript, and most of it wasn't in Shakespeare's hand. But even this, these twenty short lines, even if this was all Cyril ever actually had – it was everything.

They were still in the priest hole the following morning. Martha came to find them, having come to tell them that breakfast was ready and finding Helen's rooms empty.

'You haven't been in here all night?' she asked, peering in through the tiny door but refusing to step foot over the threshold. It wasn't as if she'd fit anyway, not with the two of them in there.

'We were engrossed,' Helen confessed, looking at her watch. They really had been poring over the manuscript all night, she realized.

'Does that mean you've found what you were looking for?' Martha asked.

Thiago looked up and then glanced at Helen. He was wearing a pair of glasses. Black, thick-rimmed, they made him look far less pirate, far more alternative university lecturer. Behind them, his eyes were rimmed with darkening circles, evidence of their sleepless night.

'It is certainly something,' Thiago said. 'What, we are not sure yet. But yes, I do think it's what we were looking for – what Cyril had been excited about all these years.'

Martha nodded. 'Well, that's good, I suppose. But you both really should come down for breakfast while it's still hot. There's another storm forecast for later: you might end up with stew again. Or soup. The stew stocks seem to be running low, and if that isn't an indication of how often we've had storms this season, I don't know what is.'

Helen and Thiago did as they were told, leaving their work behind and closing the priest hole up again. Thiago had found an empty notebook and had begun meticulously recording the contents of each mismatched leaf inside the archive box, or at least as far as he could make out, pairing them to Cyril's comments in his letters, recreating his map of the different handwriting in the manuscript. In most cases they didn't match, or at least didn't seem to, but it was clear to both of them that there was something fascinating contained within the mass of mismatched ephemera that Cyril had been guarding so closely. It might not be a complete playscript, or even a playscript at all, but if they had found even a single page of handwriting that could be definitively attributed to Shakespeare himself, that would be a seismic event in the world of Shakespearean academia. Particularly since it really did seem to come from the lost play.

'I think it was his version of *Double Falsehood*,' Thiago said, around a mouthful of bacon.

'The Lewis Theobald play?' Helen asked. 'The one that was "rediscovered" a hundred years after Shakespeare died?'

'*Sí*. But instead of rewriting the play himself, Cyril pieced it together from actual documents he'd found over the years. I think that the page that seems to be in Shakespeare's hand was the first one he had – maybe it really did come from Abington Park, if the bill of sale Rufus said he had is to be believed. That sparked a fascination, a determination. And after that, Cyril spent years collecting together an approximation of what *Cardenio* might have been, but instead of writing it himself, he used other ephemera he searched for and found, some of which could really be by Shakespeare. Not,' he added ruefully, 'that it would ever really be possible to prove it one way or another.'

'It'd help if we could find that bill of sale, wouldn't it?' Helen said. It was only as she'd started eating that she'd realized just how hungry she was – and how tired. But Thiago's excitement – Cyril's excitement – had caught hold of her now, too. 'That might actually detail for certain what in the Shakespeare Room came from Abington Park.'

Thiago looked at her, amused. 'The Shakespeare Room?'

Helen found herself smiling too. 'Sounds better than "priest hole", don't you think?'

'*Sí* – I do think,' he laughed. He continued watching her, and his eyes, though tired, were warm. 'I'm so glad that I found you here, Helen,' he said. 'I'm so glad that this thing we are doing, we are doing it together. I think Cyril would have liked it, too. I think he would have liked you nearly as much as I do.'

Helen's heart jumped. Perhaps it was how tired she was, or the excitement of this strange literary quest on which she had so unexpectedly found herself, or the distance she felt from her real life and the mess she had made of it so early on, but his words and his expression set up a thrum in her chest.

'I am glad I'm here, too,' she said, and despite what it was that had put her on Rathbrooke in the first place, it was true. 'I can't think of anywhere I'd rather be, to be honest.' *Or anyone I would rather be with*, she thought, but did not say.

Chapter Twenty

Cora remained convinced that her dad would come, right up until it was clear he wasn't going to, which was when the sun began to fade into the horizon, a sharp wind rose and all the shadows grew long enough to taunt her. At first, she had sat on the deck of the *Quick But Dirty*, because she wanted to impress him. She wanted him to see how responsible she was, how capable. *Look at me, Dad, I can sail a boat all by myself. Aren't you proud of me?* Later, she would curse herself for being so pathetic, so horribly *needy*.

What a sad sack, what a loser. That's probably why he didn't come, she would think to herself, bitter and angry at the hope she had let flourish. *Or maybe he did and he took one look at you, sitting there on this floating heap of junk like the hopeless loser you are, and he turned tail and went right back home again.*

In the moment, though, she hadn't thought this way. She had sunned herself on the deck, watching the tourists thronging the harbour walls, coming and going from the tour boats that would chug them out and around the Farnes on sightseeing trips. It was weird, she thought, that here were all these people paying good money as a treat to see what she saw every day. It made her feel a bit proud, actually. She was the girl who lived on the 'secret' island. And her dad did think that was cool, didn't he? He'd wanted to know everything about it in their letters.

It was a year since she'd been writing to her dad behind her mum's back. She'd found the address by accident: her mum had left out a piece of official-looking paperwork – a bill or something like that – with his name on. Cora wouldn't usually take any notice of that sort of grown-up detritus, except that this time there was an address beside it, or at least what she assumed was an address. It had what looked like a postcode and the name of a place: Erlestoke. She'd looked it up in the roadmap of the British Isles that Cy kept in the library, and had discovered it was a little village in Wiltshire, not far from Salisbury Plain. She had quickly scribbled the information onto a scrap of paper and kept it in her pocket like a piece of treasure too valuable to ever let out of her possession.

It had taken a month for her to write the first letter, because she'd needed to think carefully about what she wanted to say. It was so long since she'd seen her dad – she wasn't even sure that what she remembered of him was a real memory, and not something she'd made up for herself – and Cora had wanted to show how mature she was, how much of a person she was in her own right. She wanted to impress him and make him eager to reply. More than anything, what

Cora had really wanted to know was why he hadn't ever tried to visit her. Why, when he and her mum had divorced, he hadn't shown any interest in getting custody of her, or even visitation rights. But instinct told her that would be a bad idea. That kind of question was for later, when they knew each other better, when he had realized how much he wanted her in his life. Right then, all she'd needed was for her dad to write back. That would be enough of a start.

He did write back. It was one of the best days of Cora's life when the letter arrived. She'd given him the address of a friend in Seahouses, and every time Cora went over to the mainland the girl had brought the letters to her. That first letter had been short, friendly but distant, with a level of caution in it that even Cora could detect. He probably thought it was some sort of trick, Cora thought. Maybe he suspected her mother had put her up to writing to him to get him onside so that she could get more money out of him in child support, something like that. Her mother never talked to Cora about money, but that must be involved somehow, mustn't it? She was careful to make it clear in her reply that she was writing because she wanted to, that no one else had made her. That seemed to loosen the cogs. Little by little, they both opened up. There were six months of letters before Cora first asked about going to visit. The reply had taken longer this time, and she had spent the additional waiting in a fog of misery, thinking that she had pushed too hard. When the reply did come, a knot had settled in her stomach as she'd torn open the envelope – although it seemed to her as if someone might have already opened it and then closed it again with tape. Her eagerness to read what her dad had written overrode any caution she might have sustained on this score, and when she read his words and realized that he wasn't angry at her after all, relief washed away anything else she might have thought.

Maybe one day, had come the answer to her question. *But really, I'd prefer to come and visit you. I'd love to see the island.*

That's how the planning had begun and, eventually, the date had been set. But now, here Cora was, waiting, and her dad was nowhere to be seen. It was getting late. The sun was setting and there was yet another storm forecast; a bad one. If she didn't get back to Rathbrooke soon, her mum would notice that she was gone. Then Rufus would see that she'd taken the *Quick But Dirty* without either of them saying it was okay and it'd be game over.

'Say there, are you Cora?'

She turned to see a strange little man standing on the docks, looking at her. He had spoken in an American accent and he was wearing a three-piece-suit in muted blue pin-stripe wool that looked entirely too smart for the dockside. He had an actual bow-tie, red, around the crisp white collar of his crisp white shirt. There was a neat triangle of matching red handkerchief peeking out of his top pocket and he carried a tan leather briefcase in one hand, a hat that looked as if it belonged in a historical film in the other. His hair was short and parted in the middle, and he wore gold wire-rimmed glasses with round lenses that perched smartly on the bridge of his nose. Cora stared at him in much the same way as she would have if Mickey Mouse or Cinderella had appeared on the dock beside her.

'Only . . . ' – at her silence the little man looked around and nodded back towards the pleasure trip booking huts – ' . . . the lady back there said you were. She said you were from Rathbrooke Island?'

'Yeah,' Cora said, wondering if her dad had sent her some sort of representative to explain why he wasn't there himself. Maybe he'd had some big business emergency, and this was one of his 'people'. 'I'm Cora. Cora Darling. Did you want to tell me something?'

The little man flashed a warm smile. 'Actually, I was hoping you could help me. I need to get to the island. Could you maybe give me a lift?'

'The island's not open to the public,' Cora said. 'It's private.'

'I know that,' the man said, still smiling. 'That's why I need to get there. There's someone on it I need to see.'

'Oh.' Cora's heart jumped, but she played it cool as she tried to work him out. This funny little man had to be from her dad, didn't he? But she'd told him her name and he hadn't seemed to recognize it, so how would that make sense? Maybe it was her mum? Maybe now her dad knew where they lived, he was going to demand custody and this little man was a lawyer come to demand that Cora go with him, back to her dad? 'Who . . . who do you need to see?'

His next words crushed Cora's soul, and fury immediately ignited amid the ashes of her disappointment.

'Helen Thorne.'

'*Helen?* What do you want *her* for? Unless—' she stopped, a thought occurring to her. She scanned the little man again, eyes settling on his leather briefcase. A little frisson of spiteful excitement licked at her wounds. He didn't look like a pap, but then, it'd make sense that he'd disguise himself, wouldn't it? Go undercover, or whatever. They'd been looking for Helen for weeks now – she'd seen so, in the papers. If she'd had an iPhone, like any normal person, she would have taken a photo herself – it'd probably be worth a fortune. 'Is it . . . about all the stuff in the news?'

He regarded her for a moment, looking at her steadily from pale blue eyes. Then he smiled, conspiratorially, as if he and Cora shared a secret that no one else in the world knew. 'It might be.'

Cora grinned back, suddenly cheerful. Maybe even if nothing else had gone to plan, the day could still turn out well. She'd never wanted Helen here in the first place, poking around Cyril's things, camping out in the library as if she owned it. She'd even taken over Thiago's every waking moment so that he didn't have time for anyone else, even though *Cora* was the one who knew him as well as Cyril had. And now they'd even found the priest hole, one of Cyril's biggest secrets, one that only she had known about before now. Maybe if the newspapers found out where Helen was, she'd run and hide somewhere else and finally leave them all alone.

'Well, then,' she said, slowly, as if pretending to consider the matter with all due caution. 'Maybe I *can* help you. If you really, really *need* to see her. If it's really *urgent*.'

'It is,' he said. 'That would be fantastic, Cora. And perhaps there would be a little something in it for you, too. A reward, I mean,' the little man said, smiling again. Then he stuck out a hand. 'I'm Crawford Brooks.'

It was probably the most American-sounding name Cora had ever heard in real life. She shook his hand. 'Okay,' she said, indicating the skiff as she added, 'this is the *Quick But Dirty*.'

He laughed. 'That's quite a name. I like it.'

Cora grinned again. 'Mum doesn't. She says accurate isn't the same as good.'

Crawford Brooks laughed at that – a big, untidy guffaw that didn't match his Strict Professor cosplay at all. 'Ah well,' he said. 'Perhaps there's something in that for sure. Permission to come aboard, Captain?'

Cora hesitated for a moment. It would be the first time she'd ever broken Cy's cardinal rule: never bring anyone to the island without permission. But Cy wasn't around anymore, was he? And he'd never met Helen Thorne. He hadn't seen her rooting through the library, nosing through all of his most precious books and papers, finding the places he had thought were safe. If this was how they could get rid of her, if this was how they could send Helen packing off the island before she found the thing that Cy had been most worried about keeping secret, Cora thought, then he would surely have approved.

Then she glanced at the sky and frowned, realizing something.

'There's just one thing,' she said. 'There's a storm rolling in. If you come with me now, I won't be able to bring you back tonight. You'd have to stay on the island, at least until tomorrow. And no one can know you're there, not until the last minute. Like – you'd need to hide, pop out to take your pictures and then scarper. Because if Rufus or my mum found out you were on the island, they'd go *ballistic.* Like, proper full-on meltdown. They'd probably call the police and press charges for trespassing.'

Crawford Brooks looked past her into the middle distance, where Rathbrooke Island sat out at sea beyond the harbour. 'So – what, then? I'd have to hide? Where?'

Cora shrugged. 'I've got somewhere you can go. But you'd have to stay quiet.'

The little man looked at her steadily. 'Is it inside the house?'

'Oh, yeah,' she said. 'I wouldn't stick you in the barn or anything. There's an empty wing and I'm the only one with the keys to it. It's pretty bare but there are still a couple of beds in there. I can give you a sleeping bag. You'd be fine.' Even as she said this, Cora felt a frisson of doubt. But what damage could he do in the west wing? Nothing, as long as he stayed where she put him. He wouldn't be able to steal anything, because he'd need her to get off the island. Not that there was anything to steal from the west wing anyway. Still . . . 'But if you don't want to do that, it's fine. You can stay here, and I'll come back to get you when the weather clears.'

'No,' Brooks said, quickly. 'No, I'll come with you now. No time like the present, is there?'

Cora nodded. 'Well, in that case, you can help me load those,' she said, nodding at the three sealed black sacks. 'And then we'd better get off.'

He nodded and put the briefcase down before hefting the sacks and passing them to her. As he handed her the last one, the top flopped open, revealing what was inside.

'Kitty litter,' Brooks said. 'So you're a cat person, huh? Me too. Never did get on with dogs. Too *needy*, am I right?'

Cora pretended not to hear him. She sealed the sack again and stuck it under the bench alongside the others.

'Come on,' she said. 'We need to get going.'

Chapter Twenty-One

Neither of them wanted to handle the *Cardenio* papers more than necessary, and so Helen had begun to look through the rest of the ephemera in the room. She'd just finished yet another stack without locating what she'd been hoping to find. If Gissing's will wasn't here, in this most secure and secret of safe places, then, as inconceivable as it seemed, perhaps it really didn't exist at all.

She moved another stack of papers, which revealed a small, thin piece of brass, hammered flat and curved almost into a semi-circle, leaning against the ancient wall of the priest hole. It had been engraved with a florid, cursive script and had obviously at some point been attached by nails to hang from something, although one of the nail holes had split and broken, leaving a ragged edge. Helen picked it up, holding it to the light as she tried to make out the inscription.

'Thiago,' she said. 'Listen to this: *This tree was planted by David Garrick Esq. at the request of Anne Thursby, as a growing testimony of their friendship. February 1778.*'

He looked up at her, a frown settling on his face. 'David Garrick . . .'

'Yes,' Helen said. 'The great Georgian actor. He specialized in Shakespeare, didn't he?'

Thiago stood and took the plaque from her, studying it carefully. Then he nodded. 'He did,' he said, quietly. 'And, Helen – do you know what else he did?'

He looked up at her, and she could see the spark of excitement deep in his dark eyes. 'What?'

He looked at the plaque. 'Cyril spoke of this when he told me of the Shakespeare mulberry. It was Garrick who spread the saplings far and wide. In commemoration of the playwright that he saw as the greatest of all.'

They both looked at the plaque in his hands. 'Then the tree mentioned here . . . was probably a Shakespeare mulberry? Could it have been . . .' She looked up, her heart jumping at the implication of the plaque being here, surrounded by other precious Shakespeare artefacts. 'Could it be the one from Abington Park? The tree that was sold at the 1841 auction? The one that's now out there in Rathbrooke's orchard?'

Thiago stared at the inscription. 'Anne Thursby. Could she have been a lady of Abington Park after Elizabeth Barnard passed?'

'I don't know, but we have to find out.'

A look of frustration passed across Thiago's face. 'But how?'

Helen laughed. 'We're in a *library*,' she said. 'I know *exactly* how.'

She led the way, searching the stuffed stacks of Cyril

Gissing's shelves, convinced that he must have what she was looking for here somewhere. After all, he had spent his life chasing down rare books of literature, and where would they be housed except in the great libraries of great houses just like Rathbrooke Hall and Abington Park? Eventually she came across exactly the volume she was searching for and cast a triumphant look at Thiago as she pulled the heavy tome from where it sat.

'Here,' Helen said, showing him the gilt-embossed spine. 'I bet this will tell us everything we need to know.'

'*The History of Great Houses and Their People*,' Thiago read.

They sat at the desk on the ground floor. Helen flicked through the thin pages of the 'A' section until she came to Abington Park. Thiago leaned in close as they both looked at the potted history the encyclopaedia gave of the families that had lived there across centuries. Helen pressed the tip of one finger to the page beneath one particular name.

'*The manor was purchased in 1669 by William Thursby*,' Helen read aloud. She scanned down through further mentions until she reached what they had both hoped to find, her heart lurching into a heavy thump. Helen breathed out to steady herself. '*Anne Thursby (1742–1823)*,' the entry read, '*was a great patron of the arts and known as a particular admirer of the works of William Shakespeare*.'

'She died in 1823,' Thiago said. 'And less than two decades later, the house and everything in it and its grounds were auctioned off.'

'Including the tree Garrick gifted to her and the plaque

that had once hung on it,' Helen agreed. 'And who knows what else was still left in the house from earlier centuries? The plaque, the tree, the papers . . . If Anne Thursby really was a Shakespeare buff, imagine how pleased she would have been to look after whatever had been left there by his only granddaughter. This really is provenance.'

Thiago nodded, his hands on his hips. 'I think you're right. Especially if we can find that bill of sale and this plaque is listed on it with the tree.'

'What are we going to do with all this?' Helen asked, after a brief silence. 'Who do we talk to about it, outside these walls?'

'There are plenty of universities with departments specializing in Shakespeare studies,' Thiago murmured, attention still on what was in front of him. He looked up. 'Are you thinking of contacting somewhere straight away?'

She looked at him. He seemed reticent about this idea, and she wondered why. They were both tired, and yet didn't seem able to take a break for more than a few minutes. The puzzle was maddening. Sometimes it seemed as if Cyril's 'code' was entirely clear; at other times it seemed completely nonsensical, connecting to nothing. Helen had the idea that Thiago was being sucked into a labyrinth in the same way his friend Cyril had been – an endless path with high walls made of and supported by nothing but his own theories. Perhaps, after all, Gissing had been deluded. Perhaps this gathering of papers was simply random, put together to tell the story of nothing but the owner of Rathbrooke Hall's imagination.

All the time it remained here, unexamined by experts, it stayed that hallowed, lost text. Perhaps that was the real reason Cyril Gissing had never wanted to let any academic look at it. He could not bear to risk his perfect dream of paper being reduced to ashes.

'I think we have to,' she said. 'Don't we?'

Thiago nodded, but said nothing.

'Had enough of that hidey-hole, have you?'

It was Rufus, appearing in the doorway of the library.

'Not quite,' Helen said, with a cheerfulness that was a little forced. 'We just needed to do a little research.' She saw the shadow of anxiety on the old man's face. 'Rufus? What is it?'

'There's another storm coming in,' he said, as Thiago closed the book they had consulted and turned to look too. 'I wondered if I could beg some help. Got to get the sheep in, for starters. Young Cora's gone AWOL and poor Martha's out of her mind worrying about it.'

'Cora's missing?' Helen asked, getting up. 'But how is that even possible?'

'She took the *Quick But Dirty* out earlier without telling us,' Rufus said, unhappily. 'She's never done such a thing before – she's always asked permission and usually one of us is with her. She can handle the motor all right, I'm not worried about that, as long as she's not out when the storm hits. But I don't know what she's playing at. She's been right fractious the last few days, but won't say about what. And now this. Poor Martha's at her wits' end. They had another fight earlier and Cora went off in a huff. At first Martha assumed she'd have gone to her cousins in Bamburgh, but she called them and they haven't seen her.'

'But – what are we going to do?' Helen asked. 'Have you called the police?'

'Martha's taken the *Lady Jane* over to look for her,' Rufus said. 'I'd have gone too, but I need to get things squared away here or we'll be in real trouble.'

'Tell us what you need,' Thiago said. 'We'll help.'

In the hours that they had been working in the library, the world outside had changed. The sky had turned a roiling, inky black. Hard rain pelted from the heavy clouds, whipping like hail against the windows of the Hall. The wind was picking up, ruffling the petals of the roses as they followed Rufus beneath the arch of the terrace gate and towards the sheep pastures. The animals were already sheltering as best they could, standing close against the protective island wall. Helen squelched through the wet grass in her borrowed wellies, she and Thiago following Rufus's instructions as they herded the creatures towards the barn, the great open wooden doors of which were already rattling on their huge iron hinges. Several times Helen had to stop and wipe the rain from her eyes, it was so blinding. She thought of Cora out on the water. The girl wouldn't try to make it back through this, surely, especially not if it was set to worsen? Even if her mother found her, they'd both be better staying on the mainland until the storm blew over. Had she intended to run away from the island for good? Poor Martha must be frantic.

After the sheep were inside and fed, Helen and Thiago helped Rufus close the shutters on all the windows of the Hall that looked out over the North Sea, cranking shut the screens over the ancient diamonds of glass. Rathbrooke began to take on the aspect of a tomb. Helen felt enclosed despite the vastness of the rooms, as if the whole building had become a priest hole, hidden away from the world and anyone searching for it.

'When you first asked me to help you do this,' she said, as they sealed the last window covering shut, 'I wondered why you didn't just leave these all closed instead of having to do this for every storm, but now I get it. This is . . . beyond creepy. I feel as if I've been buried alive.'

Rufus patted her shoulder. 'We don't do this with every storm, only the really bad ones. We've had a lot this year.'

Helen looked at some of the empty candelabra around them. 'I suppose it's inevitable that we'll lose power?'

'Probably,' Rufus said. 'The storm lamps are all charged and there are plenty of candles.' He looked at Thiago. 'I don't suppose you're any good with generators, are you? Our ancient old beast only ever listens to Martha, as a rule. Maybe you could charm it if she needs coaxing into life.'

Thiago flashed a smile. 'Always willing to try.'

Rufus nodded, turning away. 'We'd better go and get some supplies out of the freezers. Won't want to open them once the power's out if we can't get the generator going. Martha's always got a few stews stashed away for emergencies. Whatever's there will heat over the gas stoves.'

They went with him to help carry, but once they were all leaning over the huge chest freezer in the pantry that abutted the main kitchen, Rufus looked puzzled.

'This in't right,' he said, looking into the abyss. It was stocked with neatly wrapped joints of meat, the island's supplies taken from their flock, but there was no sign of the promised ready-made meals that Rufus had been so confident about finding. 'There's nowt here. Maybe she's due to make a batch.'

'She said we'd eaten a lot. There are more of us on the island, after all! It doesn't matter,' Helen told him. 'There's plenty else to eat in the Hall kitchen.'

'Aye, same at the lighthouse,' the old man agreed. 'And in the cottage pantry too, no doubt.'

'Maybe you should stay with us in the big house tonight, Rufus,' Helen suggested. 'If the storm's really going to be that bad?'

But the gardener flashed a grin. 'Never stayed inside Rathbrooke in all the years I've been on the island, lass,' he said. 'Not planning to break the habit now.'

Helen helped to close the shutters on Martha and Cora's cottage, and then Rufus and Thiago went down to the harbour to make sure Thiago's boat was as secure as possible before doing the same at the lighthouse. Helen made her way back through the orchard, pausing at the mulberry tree. The island wall was doing its job here, with only the very highest branches of the tree affected by the gusts rolling over the great stone barrier. Here in the orchard, Helen felt protected, as if the storm couldn't reach her amid Rathbrooke's oldest living inhabitants. She hoped the wall lived up to its promise and that the Shakespeare mulberry would continue to stand, unsullied by the storm. It had, after all, survived for four hundred years, during which time it had traversed half the country. It must have seen some truly bad times, both natural and man-made. She thought for a moment about the peel tower. What attacks had it weathered, while this great tree had stood here as witness?

She lingered, unwilling to go back into the great house alone. Helen had quickly become so used to having Thiago there with her to fill the empty rooms. Without him, the true enormity of the place was hard to ignore. She would make herself tea, she decided, and go straight back to the library. Not to the priest hole – the idea of going in there alone made her shiver – but she could at least light the fire and stave off the darkness outside.

Helen was passing the path that led to the kitchen garden when a movement caught her eye. It was quick, fleeting, but still left her with the impression that a figure had passed by in her periphery. She stopped, wondering for a second if it was Thiago, but he did not appear, and neither did anyone else. Besides, whoever it was had been heading towards the greenhouse, not making their way back to her or the kitchen door that would take them into Rathbrooke Hall.

The hairs stood up on the back of Helen's neck. For a second, she stood frozen in indecision. Then she headed down the path and through the arch in the wall.

Beyond, the kitchen garden was as tranquil as ever despite the drops of rain that were beginning to fall, whipped by the invading gusts of wind. There was no one amid the immaculate neatness of the raised beds. She stopped for a moment, wondering if she'd imagined that quick movement. Could it have been a shadow cast by the rioting clouds? Then, through the old glass of the lean-to greenhouse, she caught sight of a familiar figure.

'Cora!'

The girl didn't hear her over the noise of the rain on the glass. She was focused on something and had her back to the greenhouse door, bent over at the waist. Helen moved closer, calling her again, and she turned, straightening up. An expression passed over her face, quick and furtive – surprise, was it? Or something slyer than that?

Helen went quickly to the greenhouse door and turned the handle, but it was locked. Cora came towards her, hauling a black plastic bin bag that was evidently weighty because it took both hands to carry it and the girl had to put it down in order to unlock the greenhouse door. Cora did this, blocking the entrance to the greenhouse and pushing her way out before Helen had a chance to even think about getting inside.

'Cora!' Helen exclaimed. 'Where have you been? You know your mother is worried sick? She's gone out looking for you.'

Cora looked up at her, puzzlement on her face, although Helen knew an unconvincing act when she saw one. 'Eh? What do you mean?'

'She's gone to the mainland with the *Lady Jane*,' Helen said. 'Rufus said you'd taken off in your boat.'

Cora guffawed. 'What are you talking about? I've been in the greenhouse all day, potting on. I've not been anywhere. Why would I go out in this, anyway? I'm not an idiot.' She gestured expansively to indicate the weather. The rain was getting worse, and so was the wind.

'You can't be serious,' Helen said. 'That's impossible, the greenhouse is the first place Martha would have looked for you.'

Cora shrugged and bent to pick up the bin bag again. 'I had my headphones on. I probably didn't hear her knocking on the door.'

Helen glanced at the glass behind the girl. 'I thought your mum was the one who had keys to everything?' she asked. 'Isn't that what you told me, that you use your mum's keys?'

Cora froze for a split-second, as if she'd been caught in a lie. Helen thought she probably had. She'd long suspected that the keys she'd seen the girl with were in fact her own. She wondered if Cora would confess the truth now, but it seemed not.

'I've got a key to the greenhouse, *obviously*,' Cora said, with a scathing note to her dismissive tone. 'Of course I do – I'm the one that looks after it. I borrow Mum's for everything else.'

'Why do you always keep it locked?' Helen asked, looking up at the greenhouse again. 'Why don't you want to let anyone in there?'

Cora frowned. 'Not that I need to explain myself to *you*,

but I keep it locked because the door blows open otherwise and if the glass gets smashed it'll be a nightmare to replace.'

Helen narrowed her eyes. 'You're lying. I know you are.'

The girl snorted, her jaw set hard. 'Yeah? Well, I guess you'd know exactly what that sounds like, wouldn't you?' Cora hefted up the bag again.

The rain had worsened during their brief exchange and Helen was drenched. Drops trickled from her hair down her back and soaked her shoulders.

'What's in the bag?' she asked, as the teenager shoved past her.

'Nothing you'd be able to sell,' was Cora's thrown answer, as she headed for the path that would take her to the garden's incinerator, soon disappearing from view.

Helen didn't follow. She turned back to the greenhouse instead, moving close enough to cup her hands against the glass in an attempt to see inside. She could see nothing that didn't belong there, and the rain was really falling now. It was dark, too, the sky heavy with night and the storm, and there were no lights on in the windows of the west wing. Why would there be? It was disused, and had been empty for a decade – that's what everyone who knew the place kept telling her. Helen gave up, retreating through the miserable weather towards the great house, wondering how they could get word to poor Martha that her daughter was safe on the island after all.

Chapter Twenty-Two

The storm made landfall proper against the island while Thiago was still out with Rufus. The rain lashed against the windows, the hard torrent forming a fractured arpeggio against the ancient panes. It seemed that this time the wind was too much even for the island wall. It made Helen wonder how strong that ancient barrier really was. Could it withstand a hurricane? It must have, more than once, but everything has a weakness in the end.

She was in the kitchen when there came the distant sound of something crashing through glass, followed by a shout rising over a blast of wind. She opened the kitchen door and it blew back out of her hand to hit the wall behind – the storm had indeed breached the island wall. She could barely breathe against the onslaught of the wind. It was pitch-dark now, the air a howling scream, whipping debris into projectiles that made her retreat. But she saw figures running towards her up the path, sticking close together, their arms up to shield their faces as from somewhere the sound of falling glass continued. The figures resolved into Rufus and, with him, Thiago. She stepped back to let them in and they stumbled over the threshold, gasping air to fill lungs blasted empty by the wind.

'What was that?' Helen asked. 'I heard breaking glass.'

'A branch has gone straight through one of the greenhouse panes,' Rufus said, still gasping and coughing. 'Cora will be so upset.'

'Did you see her?' Helen asked. 'She's here. I saw her coming out of the greenhouse on my way back. She says she never left the island.'

'*What?* Then we need to go and get her,' Rufus said, immediately. 'She can't stay in the cottage on her own, not in this. This night is going to be bad, worse even than I thought, and with Martha not here—'

'I will go,' Thiago said. 'Rufus, you stay here.'

'But—' Rufus began to protest, but Thiago had already started back down the path.

'Close the door,' he shouted over the storm, as he went. 'I will be back.'

Helen drew Rufus further into the kitchen and pushed the door closed again, battling against the wind.

'I need to get home,' Rufus said. 'I should be in my own place.'

'Not tonight,' Helen insisted. 'Stay here – we should *all* stay here, it'll be safer. And Cora's far more likely to stay put if you're here, too.'

Rufus shook his head, but didn't protest further. 'The

greenhouse,' he said, 'the poor girl will be upset. The plants . . . we should bring them in . . .'

'The greenhouse can be repaired,' Helen pointed out, firmly, 'and plants can be regrown, even if it takes a long time. No one should be out there in this, especially not in a glass room that's already been damaged once. Come on – let's go and light a fire. We'll find rooms for you and Cora later. It's not as if the Hall doesn't have enough to spare, is it?'

In the end, they all hunkered down in Helen's suite, bringing blankets and mattresses from elsewhere and arranging them on the floor rather than lighting fires in other rooms. Cora was sullen around Helen, but obviously anxious. When she heard about the greenhouse she wanted to go and see the damage for herself, but Rufus insisted she stay where she was. The girl was jumpy and restless, which Helen put down to the storm and worry about her mother.

'I can't believe she went to the mainland,' Cora muttered. 'Why did she do that?'

'She was worried about you,' Rufus said. 'You can't blame her. She thought you'd run off who knew where. Now she's stuck away from home, still wondering where you are, poor woman.' Rufus had used the phone in the cottage to call everyone he knew on the mainland, leaving messages to let Martha know Cora was home and safe, but Helen thought he probably wanted to drive the consequences of Cora's behaviour home.

The girl said nothing, staring morosely into the fire instead.

The storm grew worse. The power went out around 8 o'clock, as they were finishing the toast and soup that they'd carried upstairs to eat around the fire. They lit a couple of the storm lamps and played board games – Helen had remembered the store of them she had found during her early walk-through of the house, which seemed like months ago now, years. They started with Scrabble as the storm grew worse, screeching around Rathbrooke's ancient corners, whistling down the chimney and sending smoke back into the room to make them all cough. It didn't seem as if the island wall was offering much protection at all. Helen thought again about the mulberry tree.

'I feel for any poor bugger out and about in this,' Rufus muttered, pulling a blanket closer around his shoulders. 'And the state this'll leave behind . . . If the island wall holds, it'll be a miracle.'

Thiago reached out and patted the old man's shoulder, but had few words of comfort. 'It's survived this long,' he said. 'It'll survive this, too.' What else was there anyone could say?

It grew late, then later still, but despite their collective tiredness, none of them talked about sleep. It was after 11 o'clock when they heard it – a scream, very distinct, though muffled and distant. Helen froze, looking at the others, wondering whether she'd imagined it, or if she'd momentarily drifted off to sleep and dreamed it. But it was clear they had all heard it too.

'What was *that*?' Thiago asked, standing up.

'It's just the wind,' Cora said, unconvincingly. 'That's all. The storm—'

Then came another distant scream, followed by a crash and the sound of running feet pounding against wooden floorboards, clear despite the raging of the storm outside. This was different to anything Helen had ever heard in Rathbrooke before, and very definitely *in*side the house. Rufus shot to his feet, sending the gameboard board flying – they had moved on to Monopoly by then, and sheaves of paper banknotes and tiny houses scattered across the floor. Thiago went to the door and opened it onto the darkness of the rest of Rathbrooke Hall. There came the noise of more crashing and further running feet. It sounded as if someone was blindly charging around, knocking into furniture.

'It's coming from the west wing,' Helen realized. 'There's someone *in* there!'

'It's nothing,' Cora insisted, still standing beside the sofa. 'It's just the wind.'

Helen looked back at her. The girl looked nervous and pale. 'You know who it is, don't you?' she said.

'No,' Cora protested. 'How could I?'

'Cora,' Rufus said, his voice sounding a note of warning. 'I can tell when you're lying.'

'I'm not!' the girl protested, weakly. 'It's all locked up, Rufus, you *know* that.'

'But you've got a key. Haven't you?' Helen pushed. 'Like you've got one to the greenhouse and probably a lot more rooms you haven't told us about on that big keychain of yours.'

Cora crossed her arms, her chin jutting in defiance, just as another scream – though it was more like a bellow, really – echoed from the disused wing.

'Cora, if you've got a key, you need to give it to us,' Rufus said. 'Whatever's going on, the game's up. Whoever's in there needs help. There's no power! They're in there in the dark – you realize that, don't you?'

'He's got a storm lamp,' Cora said. 'He's fine. He should be fine. I told him to stay—'

'Cora,' Helen said, raising her voice in frustration, 'just give us the damn key!'

'Fine!' the girl yelled back, digging in her jeans pockets and dragging out the enormous mess of keys she carried around. 'But this is *your* fault! If you hadn't come here, if you hadn't been such a disgusting *cheat*—'

Helen grabbed the key the girl held up and ran to the massive wooden doors that closed off the disused wing. Thiago and Rufus held up their lamps as she wrestled the huge iron key into the old lock. It was heavy and stiff, difficult to work. She had to put all her weight against it to force it to turn. She could feel the mechanism protesting under her fingers, unoiled and disused as it was, but slowly it grated open. Thiago gripped the wrought-iron handle and pulled at the door, heavy and unwieldy with age. It squealed on its old hinges, but opened nonetheless. The three of them crowded into the empty doorway, holding up their lamps to illuminate the darkness. Cora hung back, silent and watchful.

'Hello?' Thiago called, leaning forward, but not stepping over the threshold. 'Is anyone there?'

Silence settled, so absolute that for a moment Helen thought they must all have been caught in some kind of collective delusion. Either that, or else the ghosts she had been living with since arriving at Rathbrooke – half-acknowledged, half-believed but actually, truly real – had melted away back into the ether once again. The air that wafted from the opened door was still and strange. It wasn't musty in the same way that the other rooms Helen had opened up in Rathbrooke Hall had been. This wasn't the stale air of a long-sealed room, but something else that she couldn't quite define. Something animal. Something *living.* Then there came another cry.

'Who's there?' Rufus called. 'Show yourself!'

'Hello?' came a man's quavering voice, echoing out of the darkness. American? Helen thought so. 'Are you – upstairs? I can't – I can't move. They'll attack if I move.'

Thiago glanced at Helen, frowning. 'What? What will attack?'

'Did you let them out?' Cora shouted, from behind them. 'I told you to stay in the room I gave you! I told you—'

'Cora?' Rufus asked, turning to her. 'What have you done?'

'Nothing,' she said, tears in her eyes. 'Nothing *bad*, anyway. And I told him – I told him not to leave his room! He shouldn't have opened any doors!'

'Lions!' the distant voice half-shouted, in a hoarse call. 'There are lions in here! Huge, slavering beasts!'

Thiago, Helen and Rufus all turned to the teenager behind them. '*What?*'

'They're not *lions*,' Cora cried. 'They're not attacking! They probably just want to play! Or they're just scared, because of the storm. But he shouldn't have let them out, I *told* him—'

There came the sound of running feet – someone charging up a wooden staircase some distance away, fast. Whoever it was stumbled over themselves, crashing to the floor with a cry. Something went skidding across the floor. It sounded like a book skimming across the wood. Thiago moved down the hallway towards the noise, Helen and Rufus behind him and Cora making up the rear. They could hear scrambling as their unknown guest found his way back to his feet. A figure stumbled towards them from a staircase that led from the lower floor, finally illuminated by the light from their storm lamps. It was a small man with dishevelled hair and a pale face, dressed in a white T-shirt that had come adrift from its moorings in the waistband of his trousers. His feet were bare. In one hand he clutched a leather briefcase, which was just one of the odd things about the scene. Then, from behind him, there was the sudden, fleeting notion of movement. Something large leapt up the stairs behind him – a creature, for sure, not a human – moving sinuously through the shadows before landing, feet pattering in a swift run across the floor.

Rufus held his lamp higher and there, fleetingly caught in the LED wash of his beam, was a large leonine face surrounded by a halo of thick orange fur. Then it was gone, vanishing before any of them got a proper look.

'Oh my God,' Helen exclaimed, electricity passing down her spine as she went cold with shock. 'Cora – what the hell is going on? What *is* that?'

'There's a whole pack of them,' their unexpected visitor moaned. 'They're *everywhere*. Get me out of here, get me—'

'Wait,' Thiago said, his voice changing as he peered more closely at the figure struggling to get up from where he'd collapsed at their feet, still holding on to his bag. The Spaniard reached out, grabbing the man by the shoulder and hauling him up, thrusting his lamp closer to the man's face. '*You*.'

'Thiago?' Helen said.

He flicked his gaze to her, and the pure, sudden fury in his dark eyes was so fierce that she took an involuntary step back.

'Crawford Brooks,' Thiago spat, letting go of the man's arm so suddenly that he fell back to the floor. 'What the hell are *you* doing here?'

'Cora!' Rufus called, more interested in the teenager, who was disappearing down the shadowy hallway in pursuit of the beast. 'Wait! What are you doing? It's not safe!'

'They're not lions,' Cora shouted back. 'They're just big cats, that's all. Like, really big. They're *mine*.'

Outside, the wind rose sharply into a gust of staggering strength. It blasted against the windows and ripped across the roof. Something rattled and clattered overhead, a long, rolling tumble that seemed to go on and on before plummeting over a precipice into nothing – a slate, tugging free and plunging to its death on the terrace below. This was accompanied by a strong gust of freezing-cold air that rushed at them inside the Hall, washing up the darkened stairs in the middle of the west wing as if there were no walls to protect them at all.

'The greenhouse,' Cora's diminishing voice cried from the dark ahead. 'It's smashed, isn't it? And if he opened the doors, they'll be able to get out!'

She went on down the stairs, the light of her storm lamp bobbing up and down until it disappeared around a corner.

'Cora! Wait!' shouted Rufus, going after her.

Thiago cursed and followed them both, looking back at Helen and the man still at her feet. 'Don't let him out of your sight,' he said. Then he ran to the stairs, and was gone.

Chapter Twenty-Three

'Thiago Montera,' muttered the man whom the librarian had identified as Crawford Brooks, as Helen helped him back to her suite. 'I should have known. I hope I'm not too late.'

'Too late?' Helen asked, seating him on the sofa opposite the fire, still roaring in the grate. She went to the door and shut it, wondering briefly how sensible it was to shut him in with her. But what else could she do? And he didn't look as if he could put up much of a fight. She eyed the poker beside the hearth, which reminded her of the night Thiago had arrived, a pirate navigating a storm to take her by surprise. 'What do you mean?'

Brooks finally put down his briefcase, eyeing the bottle of scotch that Thiago had purloined from the drinks cabinet in the dining room earlier in the evening. 'May I? I could do with a little nerve-settler, to tell the truth.'

Helen obliged, pouring and passing him a tumbler of amber liquid. Brooks took a slow sip and shut his eyes, letting go of a long breath.

'Mr Brooks?' Helen prompted. 'Is that your name?'

He opened his eyes and smiled, his eyes twinkling behind his gold-rimmed glasses. 'It is,' he said, and held out a hand. 'Crawford to you, of course, dear lady. You must be . . . Helen Thorne, am I right?'

'Yes,' she confirmed, uncomfortable. 'Now, please tell me why you're here and how you knew I'd be here. No one else does.'

He shrugged a little. 'Your mother does. I spoke to her as Cyril's solicitor, to tell her I needed to talk to whomever was dealing with the administration of Cyril's effects.'

'Right,' Helen said, mulling this over. She hadn't expected her mother to go around telling people where she was, but . . . 'You and Thiago obviously know each other.'

Brooks gave a long, painful sigh. 'We do indeed, more's the pity. But, then, everyone in the antiquarian book world knows Thiago. He's got quite the reputation. I was praying that he hadn't managed to reach the island yet and that poor Cyril's legacy would still be safe and intact. I suppose it's too much to hope that you have not let him have access to the library?'

Helen's stomach curled in on itself. 'He was Cyril's friend,' she said. 'They communicated for years, by letter. I've seen those letters. He knew Cyril probably better than anyone. Why shouldn't I let him see the library?'

Her guest laughed, though it was a small, sad sound. 'Ah, my dear,' he said. 'Many of us have sheafs of letters – correspondence with dear Cyril going back decades. He and I, for example, first met in 1979, at a book fair in London. I'm not sure Thiago had even been born by then. Even if so, he certainly would not have been haunting the antiquarian bookshelves. No, that's a far later occupation, which only arose after he found out how best to use his charm and skill at confidence trickery to divest unwitting owners of their most valuable volumes for next to nothing. He's been doing it since he was a teen.'

Helen stared at him, uncomprehending. '*What?*'

Brooks smiled sadly. 'I'm sorry,' he said. 'I'm sure he's been the perfect gentleman, and my words will seem like complete nonsense.'

She stood up, dread creeping down her spine. 'That's *exactly* how they seem.'

Her guest nodded. 'He's such an impressive young man, isn't he? Charming, friendly, helpful. And I'm guessing he's been here a while? Whereas I have only just arrived, and unannounced, too. As Chaucer would say, *Alwey the nye slye*, eh?' He looked around for a moment, and then his shoulders sank a little, as if realizing something. 'I could prove to you what I say, but what I need is in my briefcase. I dropped it back there, in those darkened rooms.' He stood. 'I should retrieve it, before Montera can steal it.'

Helen was struggling with an intense feeling of nausea, which swept over her as Brooks listed Thiago's appeal, which was almost exactly why she had been so reluctant to trust him when the Spaniard had first arrived. Spurious reasons. That's what she'd told herself, but . . . 'Why would Thiago steal your briefcase?'

Brooks replaced the empty whisky glass on the coffee table and spread his hands. 'Because a leopard does not change its spots.'

'I want you to stay here,' Helen said, tamping down on her growing panic. 'Until he and Rufus get back. I'm not comfortable with you roaming the Hall. You shouldn't even be here. You're trespassing.'

'Miss Thorne,' Brooks said, 'I know you are here to do a job, a very difficult task for one person. I know that, right now, *I* seem like the interloper. But there is something here that you do not know about, something more valuable than anything else Cyril possessed, and knowing that Thiago Montera is already here, I am anxious to make sure that it is safe.'

'If you mean the *Cardenio* manuscript that Mr Gissing was convinced he had,' Helen said, 'I do know about it. We found it.'

Brooks blanched, the blood draining from his face. He took his glasses from his nose and rubbed them against his shirt, an anxious, reflexive motion. Without them, his cropped hair still mussed from his ordeal, he looked far younger than he had a few moments previously.

'My God,' he said. 'Please tell me – I suppose that when you say "we", you mean you and . . . Montera found it?'

'He helped me locate it, yes. And now he's helping me work out what it is, exactly.'

'What it *is*?' Brooks scoffed, shoving his glasses back onto his nose. 'As if he has the skill to authenticate anything! He's a shyster, a charlatan.' He paused, narrowing his eyes. 'I suppose he told you he works for the Spanish National Library?'

'I—' Helen stopped. 'Yes, he did.'

Brooks put his hands on his hips, the large gold signet ring that he wore on his right index finger glinting in the light of the fire. 'That doesn't surprise me. It's one of his favourite grifts. And I don't suppose you verified that for yourself? You just . . . took his word for it?'

'I . . .' Helen raised a hand to her forehead. She hadn't, had she? She *had* just taken his word for it. She hadn't done even the basic due diligence – and sure, there wasn't any internet on the island, but there was a phone, wasn't there? Why hadn't she used it? Why had she been so willing to take Thiago Montera at his word? 'Why would he make that up?'

Brooks gave her a sympathetic look. 'It got you to trust him, didn't it? Despite all your best instincts, I suspect. Who doesn't trust a librarian?'

Helen felt sick, shaky. She wanted to sit down, but Brooks was pacing and she didn't want to give him the advantage. This was all nonsense, it had to be. She didn't know this man at all. He'd turned up here out of the blue, without permission or warning – *just like Thiago did*, her mind pointed out, helpfully – and he hadn't even really explained who he was. How could she trust him? *You trusted Thiago*, her mind pointed out again, still trying to be helpful, *even though your first instincts told you not to.*

For the first time in weeks, she wished she could access the internet.

'We'll wait here until the others get back,' she said, trying to stay calm. 'I want to see this proof of yours. And I want to talk to Thiago about this—'

'Oh, I wouldn't confront him, not directly,' Brooks said, a look of concern crossing his face. 'He's . . . volatile, to put it politely.'

'Thiago?' Helen said, genuinely shocked by this suggestion. 'Now I know you're lying.'

It was then that Thiago and Rufus appeared in the doorway, their clothes and hair wet and windswept by the storm. Thiago's face was dark with fury, and he glowered still further as Crawford Brooks stood up from where he had sat again on the sofa.

'Where's Cora?' Helen asked, because the teenager had not reappeared with them.

'Seeing to the cats,' Rufus said, shaking rain from his drenched beard. 'I can't believe it. Of all the idiotic things . . . Six of them, there are. Six! Great, brutish-looking beasts all as high as my knee, and she's got them roaming about as if they own the place. Thank goodness we rounded them up before they could get too far. She reckons they're just big lap cats, but I don't know – as a pack I wouldn't be surprised if they could take down a sheep, never mind the poor puffins!'

'They're Maine Coons, I think,' Thiago said, his voice dangerously quiet. He was looking past Helen, his forbidding stare fixed on their visitor. 'Cora says she brought the first over because the owner didn't want her anymore and the woman didn't know – or likely, just didn't bother to tell

Cora – that she was already pregnant. They've been in there the past year.'

'Explains where all the lamb stew has gone, not to mention why she was so keen on learning how to use the incinerator,' Rufus said, gruffly. 'She's been feeding the beasts our best scran and burning the cat litter, so we were none the wiser! I tell you, once her mother finds out, there'll be hell to pay.'

'It explains the ghostly noises, too,' Helen said. 'Doesn't it?'

'What it *does not* explain,' Thiago said, taking a step towards Brooks, 'is *you*, Crawford. What are you doing here?'

Brooks, for all his commentary on Thiago's nature, didn't seem inclined to back down from the Spaniard. 'I'm here to make sure that Cyril's last wishes are complied with,' he said. 'Because I very much doubt that will happen with you in the picture. Tell me, have you been completely honest with Ms Thorne here about your . . . how shall I put this? History?'

'Don't,' Thiago said, raising one hand, fingers outstretched in warning.

'But surely,' Brooks persisted, 'if there's nothing to hide, then there's no need for you to hold anything back, is there?'

The Spaniard smiled, but there was nothing happy in it – in fact, it seemed distinctly menacing. 'You know as well as I do that I'm not the one who needs to hold back, Brooks.' He'd taken another step closer to the newest inmate of Rathbrooke, but now he stopped. Thiago took a steadying breath, as if making a conscious effort to rein himself in. He turned away, looking to Helen instead. 'You can ask me anything you want,' he said. 'You know that.'

'Really?' Brooks asked. 'You mean you're even happy to tell her all about Alejandra?'

Thiago's face, which had lost a little of its fury, showed first abject shock and then a renewed anger that bordered on rage. He took two steps towards the little man and punched the American full in the face before Helen even realized what was happening.

The next moments were pure pandemonium. Rufus and Helen both shouted, both lunged for Thiago, who was readying himself to pummel Brooks again, even though he towered over the smaller man and the latter had already slumped sideways onto the sofa, blood pouring from his nose.

'Stop!' Helen screamed, grabbing hold of Thiago's arm and hanging onto it even as he tried to swing another punch.

'Thiago!' shouted Rufus, pinning his other arm.

Together they dragged the enraged man backwards, Rufus pulling and Helen pushing, until, with one last shove, Helen let him go.

'Get him out of here,' she said to Rufus.

'Wait,' Thiago said, though he let the gardener drag him away. 'Listen. You have to listen to me. You can't believe a thing he says.'

'No?' Helen said, angrily. 'Funny, he says exactly the same about you.'

'He's lying,' the Spaniard insisted. 'Whatever he told you, it wasn't true.'

'He told me you don't really work for the Spanish National Library,' Helen told him. 'What would they say, I wonder, if I called them tomorrow morning and asked if they had an employee called Thiago Montera? What would they tell me?'

Thiago's shoulders seemed to drop. He sagged a little, as if defeated, Rufus's grip lessening on him. His eyes lost their anger, and were filled instead with sadness. 'I can explain that—'

'No need,' Helen said, coldly. 'Rufus, we need to get hold of the police. There's been an assault.'

'Oh, it's fine,' Crawford Brooks said, weakly, from behind them. 'I'm fine, really.'

The sound of his voice caused a fresh spark of anger from Thiago. 'You—'

'Get *out*,' Helen said, the adrenaline of her fear now giving way to shock and disgust. She pushed Thiago out of the door before slamming it shut.

Chapter Twenty-Four

Rufus returned as Helen was cleaning up Crawford Brooks' face. He appeared with their visitor's briefcase in his hand.

'He can't stay on the island,' Helen said, her back to him as she wiped blood from Brooks' nose. Focusing on that was keeping her shock at Thiago's show of violence at bay. 'We should never have let him stay in the first place. We don't know the first thing about him, not really. We shouldn't have been taken in. As soon as the storm drops enough – he has to go.'

She was still shaken by the sheer, rank rage she'd seen explode on Thiago's face, the way he'd lashed out so quickly with that closed fist. She felt sick. Worse than that, she felt afraid, which was a lingering sickness all of its own. It was an old fear, one that she'd carried since the night Brett Pottinger had 'accidentally' knocked into her and she'd fallen down the stairs, breaking her nose and shattering the last of her confidence. She'd thought she'd finally outgrown it. In fact, she had. She was determined not to go back there. She'd stand up to it, instead.

The gardener said nothing. Helen glanced up to see that his face was grey with concern. It had been a troubled night, for sure. The fire around which they had all played board games just a short time before was dying in the grate. Rufus went to it, stoking it so that it flamed again.

'Rufus?' she said. 'Will you make sure he leaves?'

Rufus nodded, although to her mind he still looked doubtful. 'I'll send him on his way just as soon as the storm breaks up.'

There wasn't much more that he could do. 'All right. But stay with him until then, won't you? I don't want him coming back here, to the house. He's got everything he came with, anyway.'

It was true, she realized. Aside from the letters from Cyril, which she thought now should probably stay on the island anyway, Thiago Montera had brought little with him. Perhaps because he had always wanted to be able to leave quickly.

'I don't want to leave you alone with – with him,' Rufus said, nodding at Brooks.

'It's Thiago I'm worried about,' Helen told him, tersely. 'Go and deal with him, Rufus, please.'

Rufus looked as if he might say something else, but in the end he left without a word, pulling the door shut behind him. Helen went back to tending to their visitor's wound, wondering whether he would want the police to press charges.

'It's not broken,' she told Brooks. 'But it'll be swollen for a few days. You've got a nasty cut across the bridge of your nose, that's where all the blood came from, but I think it's stopped now. Try not to move too much – you don't want to reopen it. We should really get you to a hospital as soon as we can.'

'I'm fine.' Brooks seemed a little dazed, and had grown quiet under Helen's touch, resigned. 'It was my fault,' he wheezed, through the dressing she had pasted across his nose. 'I provoked him.'

'Of course it wasn't your fault,' Helen said, her heart burning a little at the words. How many times had Melanie said the same thing to her, when Helen herself had voiced similar sentiments? 'He punched you.'

'We used to be friends,' Brooks said, sounding a little lost. 'Or, at least, I thought we were. He and Alejandra and I – we used to—' He trailed off, staring into the fire.

'Who *is* Alejandra?' Helen asked.

Brooks looked at her, his blue eyes clouded with pain. 'His wife. He hasn't mentioned her?'

The burning in Helen's heart grew, became a familiar kind of destruction. She was shocked and yet also not. She should know how these things worked by now, shouldn't she? She should know. The inevitability of it was somehow the worse part. She swallowed, tamping it all down because, really, what was the use?

'No,' she admitted. 'But then I suppose he didn't really have a reason to.'

Brooks had opened his briefcase. Inside, everything was

meticulously organized, nothing like Thiago's haphazard cabinets aboard his boat – the *Alejandra*, Helen remembered. Named for his wife. She was still thinking about this when Brooks retrieved a business card and passed it to her before taking out more files and folders, laying them on the sofa beside him.

Crawford Brooks, it read. *MA, MSc, PhD. Emeritus Professor of Printed Antiquities, University of Pennsylvania. Antiquarian, Scholar of Shakespeare, Bookseller, Collector, Enthusiast-at-large.*

Helen read this as he said, 'You'll want to check my credentials, of course. I can give you a contact at the University of Pennsylvania for you to call. Or if you prefer, Google will give you a direct contact for their English department.' He paused. 'Although I suppose that will have to wait until the power is back up and the hours align.'

'You seem young to be retired.'

Brooks smiled a little awkwardly and then patted the leg she'd seen him limping on as he'd come towards them from the darkness of the west wing. 'Taken early, though not particularly voluntarily.' He paused, looking distant again for a moment. 'An old injury began to take a little too much of a toll. I still lecture occasionally. And I like to keep my hand in at the department, keep on top of all the latest developments – I help with them, in fact, quite a lot of the time. To whit, you may want to take a look at these.'

He passed her a file, inside which were sheets of meticulously kept letters. Helen's stomach turned as she recognized Cyril Gissing's handwriting. It didn't take much more scanning to realize that this correspondence went back years, and covered very similar ground to the conversations the island's owner had held with Thiago.

'Thiago did say that Cyril had been talking to a lot of different people in the antiquarian book world about his theories,' she murmured.

'Did he?' Brooks said. 'Interesting. And another untruth, I'm afraid. Cyril told the two of us about it, but no one else. And Thiago's knowledge of it was at first . . . incidental, shall we say? The two of us once worked together, back when I still thought of him as a friend – and a trustworthy pair of eyes.'

Helen drew in a painful breath, still looking at the letters held in her hands. 'When was it that you worked together?'

'A long time ago, when he was a student. He came to Pennsylvania to do an elective on Shakespeare when he was still an undergraduate.'

She looked up. 'He didn't tell me that.'

'No? No, well, I don't suppose he would have a reason to volunteer that information, any more than he would have had a reason to tell you about dear Alejandra,' Brooks said. 'His departure from America was . . . ignominious, shall we say.'

'What happened?'

Brooks shifted, as if uncomfortable. 'He was caught selling valuable volumes from the university's research library to private collectors. He had become quite adept at covering his tracks – not even I suspected. If I had, I would never have let it go on as long as it did. He persuaded Alejandra to flee with him back to Spain before he could be exposed.'

'He was married, even then?' she asked, her mind catching on the least important fact in the flow of information her tired mind was trying to absorb. 'He must have been very young.'

'Yes,' Brooks said with a sigh. 'Poor Alejandra. They met as students, when she was studying the restoration of old manuscripts. She was completely enamoured by him, of course. Utterly taken in, wouldn't hear a word against him. He is, as they say, a charmer. I've personally seen him warm the hearts of the coldest grand dame. A born confidence trickster.'

Helen swallowed. 'And what he told me about working for the National Library of Spain – that's a total lie?'

'Well, not completely,' Brooks said. 'He went back to Spain and the library welcomed Alejandra with open arms, which in turn gave Thiago a way to finagle his way into that institution. As far as I understand it, he worked as a clerk in the main library. But of course, his relationship with her gave him access to the rarest volumes the library possesses.'

'The university didn't try to extradite him?' Helen asked. 'For what he'd done in America?'

'There wasn't enough evidence to prove it was him who had been responsible for the theft,' Brooks said. 'He was good at misdirection and covering his tracks. In fact, it was his poor wife who bore the brunt of the suspicion at the time. I never believed that, of course. I spoke up on her behalf.'

'But Mr Gissing,' Helen said, 'that is – Cyril – obviously saw him as a friend. A very close one. I've read his diary. There's no sense that he has any reticence about trusting Thiago. None at all.'

'It doesn't surprise me,' Brooks said, simply. 'As I said – a charmer, through and through. I . . . imagine you have seen that for yourself.'

When Helen fell silent, wondering how she could have been so easily taken in again and also how far she could trust this new arrival. Brooks reached for another folder from his briefcase, rummaging through it as he spoke.

'Cyril confided much to me over the years. I found him to be a kindred spirit: we both wanted to save as much of the written word as we could. My specialism, though, has always been Shakespeare. I confess that when Cyril first approached me, I did not put much store in his beliefs about the manuscript he was convinced was *Cardenio*. Even his handwriting analysis of the samples he photographed and sent to me, while compelling, didn't—'

Helen looked up at this. 'He . . . he sent you photographs?'

'Oh yes. And this.' Finding what he was looking for, Brooks held it out to her.

Helen took it, unfolding the sheet of paper. It was a colour photograph, copied and printed at A4 size, of a very old handwritten document. The penmanship was in immaculate copperplate, processing with florid determination across the yellowed, slightly crumpled paper, the ink turning sepia with age.

At the very top of the page was a large legend declaring that this was a *Bill of Sale*. Below it, in smaller, printed letters, was written *Abington Park, Northampton, Grand Auction of Goods* and a date: *1841*. Beneath this, written in the style of a ledger, were the details of what had been bought and paid for as part of this purchase. '*Eight (8) quartos of Shakespeare's plays, being namely: Titus Andronicus; Henry IV Part II; The Taming of A Shrew; Henry IV Part III; Richard III; Richard II; Romeo and Juliet; Love's Labor's Lost; Misc papers; One First Folio of Shakespeare's Plays bound and in a red leather case; Several assorted cases of paper ephemera.*'

Helen stared at the words before her, trying to take them in. 'This is the bill of sale Cyril found . . . this is provenance,' she said, a little breathless. 'Isn't it? It proves where the contents of some of the Shakespeare Room came from.'

Brooks tipped his head to one side, interested. "The Shakespeare Room'?'

Helen shook her head. 'We found a hidden part of the library – an old priest hole, carved out of the peel wall. It's impossible to find it if you don't know it's there. It's full of . . . of these things, listed here. That's where we found the *Cardenio*.'

Helen didn't know what to do. Her instant thought was that she needed to show this to Thiago, but no, she couldn't. He wasn't the man she'd thought he was. Who, then? Who could she trust here on the island. Rufus, of course, but—

'You . . . haven't seen this before, then?' Brooks asked, reaching out to take the copied bill of sale from her.

'No,' Helen said. She wanted to take it back from him, to study it again. Did everything listed there match what they'd found? Something niggled at her but—

'You haven't found the original?' Brooks asked. 'The sheet that this photograph was taken from?'

'No, we've found nothing like that. And I've looked through a lot of paper, searching for Cyril Gissing's will.'

A flicker passed across Brooks' face. Helen read it as concern. 'You haven't found his *will*?'

'No,' Helen said. 'He told the solicitor that he was updating his wishes and to discard the old one. That was years ago and he must have made a new one, but—'

'He definitely did,' Brooks said, firmly. 'He told me about it and showed me at least part of its contents. That's one reason I'm here.'

'What do you mean?'

He turned away, leafing through more papers until he came to another that he pulled out and handed to her. It was a letter, but far more formal than the friendly correspondence that had passed between the literary friends over the course of years. It was not addressed to Crawford Brooks himself, but to the Folger Shakespeare Library in Washington DC. It was dated just a year previously, and read:

To Whom it May Concern,

This is to confirm that I, Cyril Hansard Gissing, intend to bequeath the full contents of my library as it pertains to

> *William Shakespeare into the care of the Folger Shakespeare Library on the event of my death. This includes the collected papers that I am convinced constitute the manuscript of* The History of Cardenio *and all my research and collected supporting documentation that has led to this conviction, on the condition that the Folger Shakespeare Library will both preserve and continue my research into this collection of papers after my death.*
>
> *The transport of these documents, in their entirety, is to be entrusted to Mr Crawford Brooks. Mr Brooks will make as many trips as necessary to personally safely transport every item listed below from my library directly to the Folger Shakespeare Library in Washington DC.*

Below this, Cyril Gissing had signed the letter, and thereafter followed a full list of what was, as far as Helen could make out at a glance, the entire contents of the priest hole.

'I'm going to need to verify this too,' Helen said, faintly, looking up at Brooks. Suddenly she felt extremely tired. 'And I don't know when I'll be able to do that. Certainly not immediately.'

The power was still out. Outside, the storm was still raging, although it was nothing compared to the turmoil rolling around inside Helen herself.

Brooks held up both hands, his stance full of understanding. 'Of course. It's important to make sure everything is above board. I agree, and wouldn't want to do anything until you can speak to the Folger personally. They will confirm that they had been in contact with Cyril about this and I am happy to be patient until then. I am glad, however, that I got here when I did. Perhaps no damage has yet been done.'

'Damage?'

The professor spread his hands. 'I have to assume that Montera came here with the express purpose of stealing from Cyril's collection,' he said.

'He hasn't done that,' Helen said. 'I would know. He's never even been alone in the library.'

'Really?' Brooks said. 'Never?'

A prickle of fear crept along her spine. 'No,' she said. 'Or at least, not for long enough to take anything.'

Brooks made a sound in his throat. 'Ma'am, he has been pilfering his entire life. I've been a personal witness to his sleight of hand, and I would have sworn blind he never even moved.'

Helen stood, agitated. 'I should go and check.'

Brooks put a reassuring hand on her arm. 'Don't panic, my dear,' he soothed. 'Listen to that terrible noise outside. The storm is still very much at full strength. Even if he has stolen something, not even he would be fool enough to try to escape in this storm.'

'But he came here in weather not much different from this,' Helen said, her panic growing. 'And it's the perfect cover, isn't it? I told Rufus to get him off the island as soon as possible.'

Her mind racing, Helen wondered when Thiago might have had time to steal from the library. Any time she'd been asleep, for one. Then there was that time he'd gone to make tea and had been so long that she'd gone to look for him. She'd found him in Cyril's rooms, just standing there. Helen had thought the sad look on his face had been because he'd been contemplating his friend's end. But what if he was simply a very good actor? She'd met those before, hadn't she? This wouldn't be the first time she'd been fooled. And Thiago had lied to her. He'd lied to her face about working at the National Library. And what about Alejandra, back home in Madrid? Alejandra, who had been so taken in that he'd been able to blame her for what he stole?

You're such a fool, she told herself. *When will you stop being so gullible and naive?*

Brooks stood. 'All right,' he said. 'Then perhaps we *should* check, just in case. I will come with you. But please, don't worry. I am sure he would not try anything so blatant, not when he knows I am here as witness and already know of his past crimes.'

Chapter Twenty-Five

They took a storm lamp each. Outside Helen's suite, the Hall creaked and groaned under the onslaught of the storm. The huge double doors to the west wing were still open – another nightmare that needed sorting out. Where was Cora now, she wondered? She hoped that Rufus had had the presence of mind to keep the girl close. Or perhaps she was in the empty wing now, with her pets. *What a mess*, Helen thought. *What a terrible mess.*

She led the way downstairs, the wind pressing against the windows as if it might force its way in. Aside from the storm's assault, the house was silent, and so were Helen and Brooks. She unlocked the library doors and stepped over the threshold, Brooks close behind her. He paused once they were inside, awestruck in much the same way she had been the first time she'd seen it.

'Oh my,' Brooks said, in wonder. 'Oh my, my.'

Helen was in no mood to defer to his first moment of communion with Gissing's books. She went straight to the stairs that led to the mezzanine, her light illuminating the spines of the volumes around her, glancing off the gilt embossing like sparks from a fire as she passed. Brooks hurried after her, and when she stopped on the second floor he looked around, raising his lamp.

'It's marvellous,' he muttered to himself. 'Not even I could have imagined—'

'There's a hidden entrance here,' Helen interrupted, setting her lamp down so that she could find the correct place to engage the mechanism of the hinged bookcase. The volume that Thiago habitually turned inwards to mark it was still there. The thought of him doing that turned her heart inside out. Of course he'd wanted an easy way to find it.

Brooks helped her pull the bookcase from the wall. It swung as smoothly and silently away from the hidden door as ever. Helen pulled the key from her pocket and turned it in the lock, her heart hammering so hard the pounding of it echoed through every vein she had.

Inside, the priest hole looked untouched, exactly the same as the last time she'd seen it. The box containing the *Cardenio* papers was still on the table. She ducked to pass inside the tiny space and went straight to it as Brooks followed behind her. Helen opened the cover of the archive box, half expecting it to be empty – but no. Her relief was so acute that she could have fainted clean away when she saw that this little storm of paper, this haphazard, untidy, priceless collection of scrawl from four hundred years ago was still intact.

'He hasn't taken it,' Helen said, her voice quavering as it navigated the pounding of her heart. 'It's still here.'

Brooks stepped up beside her, his eyes fixed on the box. 'Good,' he said with a smile, patting her on the arm. 'That's wonderful to know. Although—'

He stopped with a small shake of his head, surveying the rest of the room, his sharp blue eyes scanning the bookcase full of Gissing's other Shakespeare treasures.

'What?' Helen asked, turning to follow his gaze. 'What do you think—'

She stopped, her relief curtailed by a sudden, freezing wash of abject fear.

'Miss Thorne?' Brooks prompted. 'What have you seen?'

There was a gap on the second shelf of the bookcase. It would not have been obvious to Crawford Brooks, but to Helen it was a glaring void. The last time she had been in here, the shelf containing the set of quartos had been full. Now, some of them were missing. At a glance she couldn't tell which titles were gone, but there was now a considerable space at the very end of the shelf, where before it had been full.

'Is something missing?' His voice was tense.

'Yes,' she said, her voice hoarse. She scanned the table again, realizing with a sinking heart that she had been so fixated on the box containing the fragmented manuscript of *Cardenio* that she had not fully taken in the rest of the scene. She should have catalogued it herself, immediately. What else had gone? Was the stack of papers she'd been working her way through thinner, too? 'Yes. At least, I think so. Perhaps. Some of the quartos have gone. And . . .' she swallowed, nausea rising as she realized that there was something easily identifiable as missing. 'A book of poetry.'

'Well,' Brooks said, his face pale and grave. His eyes flicked across the bookshelf, clearly as perturbed as Helen herself. 'Well, that is indeed a shock. Although perhaps we should look on the bright side. At least you know for sure who the perpetrator is, and that he is still here, on the island. And I clearly arrived before he managed to take his biggest target.'

'I can't believe I didn't notice those things going missing,' Helen said. He must have been taking them too gradually for her to see the gaps until she looked for them. And he'd been charming her more with each day, lulling her into a false sense of security, to do exactly that.

Brooks was agitated too. 'He has probably been purloining individual pieces for as long as he's been here at Rathbrooke.'

Helen's fear grew worse. Here in the peel tower, even inside this hollowed-out cell and its thick walls, where they must be so much closer to the elements outside, all was silent. There was no hint of the storm. Was it simply that they were cut off from the fury of the elements? Or had it blown itself out? Was the weather lessening? Because if it was . . .

'You did say he had his own boat,' Brooks said, as if he could read her mind, a flash of concern passing across his face. 'Presumably that's where he's hidden everything he's stolen. And with him being such a proficient sailor—'

'We have to stop him leaving,' Helen said. 'I told Rufus to

make him leave the island just as soon as he could! He arrived here in a full-on maelstrom, I'm sure he could . . . oh, *God*!'

She turned for the door expecting Brooks to follow, but he didn't.

'Perhaps I should stay,' he suggested. 'I've got the list of the full contents of the Shakespeare Room here, after all. I can conduct an inventory to work out exactly what has been taken.'

'No,' Helen said, pausing at the door, looking back towards the scholar, so prim even at this late – or should that be early – hour and despite his ordeal. 'Please, I may need your help. Thiago's far stronger than me. And Rufus . . . well. Please.'

Brooks put down his briefcase and followed her out. 'Absolutely,' he said. 'Of course.'

Helen locked the door to the priest hole behind them, the bookcase sliding seamlessly back into place. Their storm lamps swelled light into the cavernous darkness of the peel tower, which was otherwise silent. Helen rushed ahead, down the stairs to the ground floor. She was almost at the threshold when she heard a commotion behind her – the sound of someone stumbling with a curse. She turned in time to see Crawford Brooks tumbling down the stairs, trying to grab hold of the banister as he almost pitched head-first down the narrow steps. For a split-second Helen thought he was going to lose the battle and crash right the way down the steep flight. She cried out, launching herself towards him as if she might be able to break his fall. He finally found purchase on the handrail, but his legs kept going, until he eventually landed at the bottom in an ungainly pile.

'Professor!'

Brooks groaned, trying to pull himself upright. He reached out for Helen's help, but as she tried to get him to his feet, her arm around his shoulders and him hanging on to her waist, he cried out, sharper this time. His leg gave way so that she had to lower him to the bottom step of the stairs.

'What is it?' she asked.

'My ankle,' he said, sucking in a sharp breath as he hoiked up his pant leg. His foot was turned in at an odd ankle. 'Damn and blast it – a sprain, or a twist, at least. Don't wait for me, Helen, go after Thiago. We can't risk him getting off the island. Go! I'll be all right.'

Helen barely hesitated. A sprained ankle would heal, but what Thiago was doing . . . Once he was off the island, she knew that at least some of Cyril Gissing's most precious possessions would be gone for ever.

'I'll be back,' she said. 'As soon as I can.'

'Go,' he shouted after her, urging her on. 'Stop him, for goodness's sake!'

Chapter Twenty-Six

She met Rufus on the path to the lighthouse. His white hair was wildly vivid in the dark, a puff of smoke sent up as a warning.

'Rufus,' she shouted, as they met. She was breathless from the run, from the constant assault of the wind. The old man gripped her forearms. 'Where is he? Where's Thiago? He hasn't gone, has he? He hasn't got off the island?'

'No, lass,' the gardener shouted back. 'He's at the lighthouse.'

'Where are you going?'

'To check the boats. Where's that Brooks gone?' He looked worried. 'You didn't leave him in the library?'

'I had to,' she said. 'He fell down the stairs, twisted his ankle.'

'You need to talk to Thiago, Helen,' Rufus said, still holding on to her, leaning in close that his voice might make it to her beneath the rage of the wind. 'He's not what you think he is. And neither is Crawford Brooks.'

'He lied to me, Rufus. Thiago lied to *us*. He doesn't work where he said he does. He's not who he says he is. And Brooks has shown me evidence – papers Cyril sent him. He's a Professor at Penn State. There are things already missing from the Shakespeare Room – Thiago's the only other person who's been in there since Cyril died, isn't he, aside from me? Rufus, I'm sorry. I know you like him. But he's not what *you* think he is.'

Rufus shook his head. This was an impossible conversation to have, here of all places, in a garden being torn apart by an almighty storm. 'Talk to him,' he begged. 'I have to check on the boats.'

'We've got to make sure Thiago can't leave,' Helen said. 'That's what I came to tell you. Forget what I said. He's got to stay here until we can search the boat. I've got to find what he's stolen.'

'Don't you think, if he had any intention of leaving, he'd be the one going to check on the boats?' Rufus squeezed her one last time. 'He said he's going nowhere until he's spoken to you. Talk to him, lass,' he shouted again. 'And remember this – I'd never let you go to him alone if I thought there was one ounce of danger in the man.'

They parted ways, Helen turning back as she made her way along the path, but Rufus had already been swallowed by the storm. Ahead of her, the square, squat form of the lighthouse crouched beneath the roiling sky. It was dark, no power now, although as she neared Helen could see an uncertain glow emanating through one of the windows from the single downstairs room. As she reached the door it opened, and Thiago stood there holding a storm lamp. His face was ashen in the LED shine, his eyes worried beneath his heavy brow.

'Helen!' He reached out, grabbing her arm to draw her inside, out of the storm.

Helen yanked herself free of him. 'I know what you've done,' she said. 'Where is it all, Thiago? Everything you've taken from the Shakespeare Room?'

'What?' Thiago backed away as if she'd burned him, somehow. He looked shocked. She suspected that, had they had proper light, his face would look bloodless, drained. 'What are you talking about?'

'Were you planning to take it all a bit at a time? Did you assume I wouldn't notice? Have you been taking bits of the *Cardenio* page by page, even as you played me for a total fool? Is that why not all the page references from the diary meet up – had you already started stealing them? Were you going to substitute it for something else? Or were you just going to make a run for it with whatever you could get your hands on?'

Thiago dumped the storm lamp on the table, rubbing both hands over his face and through his hair. 'I haven't taken anything! How could I? You were with me, the whole time. I've never had the *key*.'

'Who else could it be?' she demanded. 'Who else has come here like the thief he so clearly is, to steal what he couldn't get Cyril to give up willingly?'

Thiago stared at her, his eyes dark and fathomless. 'You know I'm not a thief,' he said. 'You know Cyril and I were friends.'

'Do I? Do I really?' she asked. 'You picked the lock right in front of me, Thiago!'

He shook his head. 'What has Crawford Brooks said?' he wanted to know. 'What lies has he been telling you?'

'A truth that makes far more sense than you ever have,' she said. 'And unlike you, he came with proof of who he is and who he works for.'

'Who he *works* for?' Thiago spat, the anger she'd seen an hour or so earlier back on display. 'Brooks works only for himself. He's a thief, Helen, a conman, plain and simple. He steals to order for the highest bidder, and he will say anything, do *anything* to get what he wants. Yes, Cyril knew him. Brooks had been trying to get an invitation to Rathbrooke for years before he died.'

'He got more than that,' Helen said. 'He's got a copy of the bill of sale listing the contents of the Shakespeare Room and a letter, which certainly looks genuine, from Cyril to the Folger Shakespeare Library. It proves that Cyril wanted all of his Shakespeare collection to go to them, and that Brooks is to transport it. If you really were the close friend of Cyril Gissing's that you pretend to be, how did you not know that?'

Thiago appeared to be speechless. His mouth fell open, but he formed no words.

'Obviously, he's not taking a thing until I've verified the contents of the letter and his credentials,' Helen said. 'Which

I'll do as soon as we've got power back. By which time, I want the missing artefacts returned. You're not winning this one, Thiago. You're not getting off this island with what you've stolen.'

Thiago was shaking his head now. 'This is insane,' he murmured. 'Brooks isn't who you think he is. He's a conman, a trickster. He's known for it in the industry. Whatever he's shown you will be fake.'

'Funny,' Helen said. 'He told me almost exactly the same thing about you.'

'Anything he's said about me will be a lie,' Thiago told her.

'Oh, really? Then he's wrong when he said you do not, in fact, work for the National Library of Spain?'

Thiago dropped his hands down and dipped his head. 'I did,' he said.

'But you don't anymore?'

'I don't at the moment,' he corrected her. 'I took a sabbatical last year. To look after my mother. She was sick,' he said, quietly. 'She died a few months ago. I'm going back to work soon.'

Helen almost laughed at that. 'Right. Of course.'

Thiago looked away, his eyes finding the darkness of the lighthouse's windows. 'It's another reason I did not contact Cyril for too long when he went silent. There has been much to organize in the wake of her death, and only me to do it.'

'Only you?' Helen asked. 'You mean you couldn't ask your wife back in Madrid to help with any of the arrangements?'

Thiago's gaze snapped back to her face, a look of total confusion in his eyes. 'My *wife*?'

'Yes,' Helen said, swallowing an unexpected, uneven and unhappy judder of her heart. 'Alejandra, isn't it? You named your beloved boat after her, didn't you?'

Thiago drew in a sharp breath. For a moment he seemed not to be breathing. His lips drew into a thin line. But his eyes held not the rage she might have expected. Instead they seemed full of pain. He seemed to be trying to say something, but his first attempts were thwarted, as if his mouth had gone dry and his throat had closed up.

'I have no wife,' he managed, finally. 'I have never had a *wife*. I didn't have the chance. Alejandra died before I could even ask her. It was the worst and yet perhaps the deepest aspect of life that Cyril and I shared – that we had both lost the woman we loved.'

Helen studied him. If he was acting, she thought, he was phenomenal at it – so good that he should be on screen. But . . .

'Why would Brooks lie about that?' she asked. 'Something that could be so easily disproved? It makes no sense.'

'Because he only needs you to believe it long enough for him to get what he wants and then he'll be gone,' Thiago said. 'And because it was his fault she died. He used her. He made her trust him, believe him, and then he stole from right under her nose and let her take the fall for it. She . . . ' his voice cracked and he turned away. 'She was a librarian, too. That's how we all met. He was posing as a restorer of manuscripts. And she trusted too easily. She trusted *me*, and

I couldn't keep her safe. She trusted *him*, and it ruined her. She never recovered. She never worked again. She spiralled and I couldn't pull her back. All because of *his* lies.'

Helen watched him, saw the genuine tears he was trying to blink back. What was true? How could she *know*? This looked like the Thiago she had come to know over the past weeks – open and warm. But how could she be sure? How could she trust him?

'Brooks just wanted the reaction,' Thiago said. 'He knew I'd lose it if he – he of all people – brought her up. And let me guess – right before Rufus and I walked back in, he'd been telling you how violent I was. Or, no – that's not a word he'd use. He would be more subtle. He always was good with words, that one. Unstable. Is that what he said? That I am *unstable*?'

Helen swallowed. 'No,' she said. 'Volatile was the word he used.'

Thiago gave an ugly laugh at that. 'Ah yes, that's much more his vocabulary. Much more polished. Far more than me, anyway, yes? He wanted a reaction, and it needed to be big. I was already shocked and angry at him turning up here. And he needed you to be convinced that what he was saying – and the worst of what you'd suspected about me when I arrived – was true. I am not a violent man, Helen. It is not in my nature. He used the only thing he knew would work. He used my Alejandra, and I lost it, right on cue.' He laughed again, a bitter sound. 'I'm an idiot. But there you go. He's a master manipulator. He always was, and—'

Thiago stopped, mid-flow. Helen was still trying to process his words, trying to pick out what truth may be within them, trying to work out how to tell what was the truth and what was rank lies. He looked at her, his expression different suddenly – stricken, fearful.

'Wait,' he said. 'Where is he? Where is he *right now*?'

'I left him in the library,' Helen said. 'He fell in the dark as we were coming to check you hadn't escaped. He twisted his ankle.'

Thiago made a strangled sound in his throat. 'Did you show him the Shakespeare Room?' His voice was urgent, perhaps even edged with desperation, and she still couldn't see the edges of the act. 'Please, Helen, please, tell me you didn't.'

'I locked it again,' she said. 'I've got the key, you know that. Besides, he couldn't walk.'

Thiago's gaze flashed over her from head to toe. 'Then where is the key?'

'It's right here,' she said, her hand going to her jeans pocket. 'I just used it to lock—'

But her pocket was empty. There was nothing there.

'I . . . It was here, just a minute ago,' Helen said, frantic, turning the scrap of fabric inside out as if it might somehow be hiding the large iron key from her in its corners. Then she searched her other pockets, just in case she'd put it in a different one in her panic to chase after the man standing before her. 'I must have dropped it on the path. I stopped to talk to Rufus, perhaps—'

'Helen,' Thiago said. 'You didn't. Brooks took it. We have to go, now. Right now.'

'No,' she said, on the verge of tears and hating herself for it. Who could she believe? She didn't know either of these men, and they were both lying, they were both . . . 'What was missing from the room was already gone before I showed it to Brooks. He couldn't have taken anything; he didn't even know where to find the priest hole until I showed him. You *had* to have taken it.'

'Helen,' Thiago said. 'I think you know that's not true. I think you know I didn't take anything. I'm not that good a liar. I have *never* been a good liar.'

'Then who else?' she demanded. 'Who else could it be?'

Thiago spread his hands. 'Either someone else must have a key, or someone else has broken into the priest hole.'

Cora. The answer came to her in a flash. Cora, with that huge bunch of keys she didn't want anyone to know she had. Cora, sneaking in and out of the west wing. Cora, with her own boat. Cora, smuggling over a massive cat and hiding it in plain sight, and then a strange man despite it expressly being against the rules. Cora, with her *it's just the wind, it's just the creaking of an old house, the priest hole probably doesn't even exist anyway.* Cora, who had known about Cyril's diary, who had written all his letters for him, who had loved the old man and loved the island just the way it was and hated, *hated* Helen being in the library.

'Cora,' Thiago breathed, reading her mind. He reached out, taking both of Helen's hands, drawing her closer, but he did it almost absently, looking over her head into the middle distance, thinking of this revelation and not the way he had reached for her. He realized when she did not respond, did not let herself be pulled towards him. Thiago stopped, looking down at her, blinking himself back into the moment. He looked down at her, a flash of sadness in his eyes, and then raised both of her hands to his lips, kissing the backs of her hands quickly, one after another before letting her go. 'I will make you trust me again,' he said, softly. 'I promise I am everything I have told you and nothing I have not, and I will prove it just as much as you need me to. But right now, we have to stop Brooks. I swear, Helen, I swear on every year that the mulberry in the orchard has been alive, that he is here to steal and nothing more.'

At that moment, Helen realized what had been niggling her about Brooks' copy of the bill of sale. There was something missing from it, something that would have been on there had it been genuine.

One strong tree of Shakespeare's mulberry.

'The tree,' she whispered.

Thiago frowned. 'What?'

'The bill of sale he showed me,' Helen said. 'There was no mention of the mulberry. Oh, God – run,' she said to Thiago, turning for the house. '*Run.*'

Chapter Twenty-Seven

Cora's day was growing progressively worse. First her dad, and now the cats. At least they were all back inside and safe now, but her mother was going to kill her. It was all that stupid professor's fault. He'd lied to her, just like everyone else. He'd said he was a pap, that he was here for Helen. Or, at least, that's what she'd assumed, and he hadn't told her any different. That was a lie of omission, and as she'd been told enough times by her mother, that sort of lying counted just as much as the outright kind. If he hadn't lied, if he'd been who he said he was, she was pretty sure she could have got away with it – Helen would have been done for, and she could have got him off the island after the storm with no one the wiser. But no, he had to snoop. What had he been looking for, anyway? What did he think he was going to find, that he was willing to pick open a locked door?

What kind of professor knew how to pick a lock anyway?

Cora didn't care, as long as she never had to see him again. He was as bad as all of them – as bad as her dad, who should have been here instead of him, as bad as her mum, who didn't understand anything about her own daughter. As bad as Helen – lying, cheating home-wrecking cow that she was. As bad, even, as Cyril, for dying and leaving her with all these secrets to deal with on her own.

At least she'd got the cats to settle. They didn't like being confined to one room, but she couldn't let them roam further, not with the greenhouse smashed and Rufus on the warpath. She'd never seen him so angry – he looked like a right old salty sea devil. It had been quite funny. Except it wasn't, really, because now she wouldn't get to keep her cats. Not that the cats had been entirely intentional. There was another liar, the woman who had given her Ophelia. If she'd just had one cat to hide, however big, it probably wouldn't have been a problem. But before Cora had known what was happening, Ophelia was very obviously pregnant, and there wasn't anything she could do about it. She couldn't tell her mum. She couldn't tell Cyril – he wasn't well enough to take it in by then anyway. She couldn't take Ophelia back to the mainland and just dump her, could she? Anyway, even with five kittens, there was plenty of room in the disused wing. It was the feeding and the cleaning that was the hard work. Bags and bags of litter they went through – thank goodness she knew how to use the incinerator. And they were all very happy to eat the stew out of the freezer. It was probably why they all had such healthy coats.

She just hadn't expected them all to be quite so *big*. To be fair, it was also one of her favourite things about them.

Brooks hadn't been completely over-exaggerating when he'd described them as lions. They were massive. She thought Faustus, one of the boy kittens, might get big enough that his head was as high as her hip. At the moment, when he put his front paws up against her for strokes, he could reach her chest! Perhaps when he was fully grown, he'd be able to put them on her shoulders. Perhaps he'd break some sort of world record. Perhaps he was the biggest housecat in the world. Not that her mum would care, or Rufus. They'd just want him gone. They'd want all of them gone, even though there was so much space on the island, even if they weren't allowed out of the bit of the house that they called home right now.

Cora knew that her mum was worried about them having to move and find somewhere else to live. She had no idea why. For a start, she'd heard Cyril tell her that they would always have a home here as long as they wanted it. He'd *said* that, to her mum's face. Was her mum so used to being lied to that she couldn't believe anything anyone else said?

Then she thought of her dad, and Cora's ire dipped towards misery. He hadn't come. He'd said he was going to, and he hadn't. He hadn't even written to tell her he'd changed his mind. He'd just . . . stood her up.

One of the cats, sensing her mood, rubbed its big head against her knee. It was Orlando, a big orange and white ball of fluff with zero sense but all the love. Cora smiled through blurred eyes and stroked him as he purred, the sound rumbling like the outboard motor on the *Quick But Dirty.* She picked him up, pulling him against her chest as he let her wrap him up in her arms. He was as heavy as a bag of shopping and it made her want to cry more. She didn't want to give Orlando up. She didn't want to give any of them up. Not Orlando, not Faustus, not Ophelia, not Wooster, not Hero, and definitely not soft-as-feathers Antigone. She had named them all after characters from the books and plays that she had read with Cyril, except that Wooster was a girl, not a boy, like Bertie Wooster. It fitted the daft black-and-white idiot that was cat-Wooster, which was all that mattered.

If there was one thing Cora had learned from all the reading she had done in Cy's library, it was that to get anywhere in life, one – that was the right way of saying it back in the old days when you were talking about yourself, 'one', not 'you' or 'I' – one had to take what one wanted no matter how against one the world was. And that went double for women and girls. Otherwise one just ended up doing as one was told, and as far as women went, that usually meant taking up as little space as possible and putting everyone else's wants first until there was no room for what you – what *one* – wanted, even when that wasn't really asking for much. Even when you were just being *one*.

Never trust anyone who wants to keep you small, Cy had told her once. *Who really benefits from you taking up less space? Whose voice is it that fills that space you leave empty when you're being quiet? Always ask yourself that, Cora. Always. Don't whisper just so other people can shout.*

Cora hugged Orlando to her, feeling his giant purr rumble right through her ribcage. She missed Cy. He was the only adult she knew who had been straight with her about the world. Although not even he'd been willing to tell her about her dad. He'd always said that was something that her mum would have to tell her when she was ready to hear it, even though it was clear Cy knew everything.

Fine. If everyone else was allowed to keep secrets, Cora had decided that she should have some of her own.

Orlando got tired of being cuddled and squirmed free, wandering off to examine the shadows cast by the storm lamp. Outside, the weather was still blasting at the house. Cora had never known it so bad – usually they were well protected by the island wall, but tonight this weather seemed to have found its way right to their door. She thought about her mum, still on the mainland. Guilt tickled at her gut.

As Cora got up from where she'd been sitting with the cat on the floor, a noise came to her, not from outside the house, but inside. She stopped, listening, and for the first time since the cats had escaped, she wondered what the rest of the adults on the island were doing. Rufus had demanded that Thiago go with him to the lighthouse, but Cora had been more worried about the cats than in hearing whatever was going on with Professor Brooks and Helen.

She went to the door and listened for another minute. There was definite movement in the room on the other side, but there were no voices. Cora opened the door and stepped through, quick to shut the door behind her – she didn't want to risk any more unplanned feline escapades.

Professor Brooks was in there, alone. There was no sign of

Helen, Thiago or Rufus. He was fiddling with the door of the old steel safe that stood in the corner of the room, which had probably once been an office – or whatever the equivalent of an office had been back in the olden-timey days.

'What are you doing?' Cora demanded.

'Oh,' he said, turning to glance at her. He did it almost as if he could barely be bothered to look in her direction. He had a bandage on his nose. Had someone hit him? It couldn't have been Helen; she was too much of a wet blanket. '*Cora.* You again.'

'What are you doing?' Cora asked, again, though she remained where she was, her back against the door. She was picking up a different vibe from him now. He didn't look like the slightly hapless geek he'd seemed on the harbour at Seahouses.

'Miss Thorne has asked me to help her with the task of sorting this place out,' Professor Brooks said, his voice cool and level.

'But Thiago's already doing that,' Cora said, thrown.

He looked at her again, but only briefly. She could see that he was trying to open the combination safe. Had he known it was there? How? It could only be from his snooping earlier, she thought. No one else knew about it except her. His briefcase was propped up beside the sealed safe.

'Yes, well,' he said. 'I'm afraid you've all been rather taken in by Thiago Montera. It's a good job I came along when I did, or he'd have stolen even more than he surely already has.'

For a second, Cora's mind shorted out. 'Thiago's not a thief,' she said then. 'He was Cy's friend.'

Brooks snorted a short laugh. 'I know that's what he told you,' he said. 'And I know that's what you want to believe, both you and Helen Thorne. It's so easy to be taken in by someone so very dashing, isn't it? But it's not true. I knew Cyril Gissing far better than Thiago Montera.'

'It *is* true,' Cora retorted. 'Thiago was a friend of Cy's. His *best* friend. I should know, I wrote all of Cy's letters for him! I read his letters to Cy, too, in the end, when his eyesight was too bad to read them himself. You're the one I've never heard of. He never mentioned you once. Anyway, you didn't say you were here for Cy. You said you were here for Helen, so who's the real liar?'

The professor stopped.

'Where's everyone else?' Cora wanted to know. 'Why are you here on your own?'

Her suspicion was growing stronger by the second. She looked again at his briefcase. It looked as if it had something in it – it was bulkier than before, and the top looked as if it wouldn't do up properly. The catch hung undone because it was too full to close.

When she looked back up at Professor Brooks, his eyes were fixed on her, narrowed, like he was trying to work something out. For the first time, Cora felt a frisson of fear.

'You know this place pretty well, don't you?' Brooks said, quietly.

'Obviously. I do *live* here,' Cora said, a knot of anxiety

pulling tighter in her gut. She reached behind her, to the door handle, not that it would do her much good. There was no way out of the room behind her, it was right at the end of the wing, and the windows had all been locked fast years ago. To escape, she'd need to get through one of the two doors on the other side of the room, which were both closer to Brooks than her. She couldn't get out without having to go through him.

'It's more than that though, isn't it?' the American said, his voice low but his eyes hard, assessing. 'The cats. Your little boat. This empty wing that only you come into. You can get in and out of places that no one else even knows about. How?'

The hand that Cora had twisted behind her back instinct-ively went to her pocket of her jeans. The bunch of keys Cy had given her was still there, but checking for them was a mistake. Brooks saw her move.

'Have you got a key to the library?' he asked, watching her intently.

'No,' Cora said, too quickly. 'Cy gave the only key to mum and now Helen's got it.'

Brooks gave a smile that made Cora's anxiety turn into outright fear. 'What about what's *in* the library?' he asked, his voice very soft, very quiet. 'Did you know about the priest hole? I bet you did.'

'I didn't,' Cora said, her breath coming in short bursts now, like they might be sobs if she had to raise her voice much more. She wanted to run, but Brooks stepped in front of her, blocking her escape.

'I think you've got something I need, Cora,' Brooks said, softly. 'In fact, I think you might be the answer to all my problems. The question is, are you going to help me? Or are you going to be difficult?'

Chapter Twenty-Eight

Out they went together, back into the storm. Helen kept feeling in her pocket, in case she'd somehow missed the key and it was still there, safe and sound. This was, of course, a foolish hope and one that was destined to remain forlorn. But she still couldn't believe she had been quite so gullible, quite so easily taken in. *Again.* Was she really that stupid? Worse, she now had no idea what to think of Thiago. It had taken her such a lot to begin to trust him. Or, rather, it had taken a lot to begin to trust *herself.* Because she'd been drawn to him immediately, hadn't she? But she knew how misleading that could be – knew with the kind of certainty learned only by bitter experience. She'd been burned by this before – so badly, in fact, that the flames seemed as if they would never die, but simply banked and guttered, waiting for a time she was least prepared for them before flaring up again to consume what little good she had made from her life in the wake of their first kindling. Woe betide she let herself be burned again.

Brooks was the opposite of Montera in every physical sense. She was not attracted to him in the slightest, and so she had immediately trusted him in a way she had not Thiago. He too had arrived in the middle of a storm, but he didn't look like a pirate. He looked as he confessed himself to be: a bookish man, a scholar. And thus, he had taken her in, far more quickly than she had allowed herself to trust the man beside her now, running in the wet dark back towards a house that she was beginning to wish she had never used as an attempted escape hatch from the disaster that was her life. All she'd done was bring the chaos with her, it seemed.

Why couldn't she know – oh, so many things. What was right for her? What was right full stop? Helen kept thinking that at some point she would reach a stage in her life where the path ahead would become clear, where she would *know*. But it never seemed to happen. *Did it ever?* she wondered now. She wasn't sure she could bear an existence where there was never any certainty, where she was never *sure* of anything and couldn't trust anyone, least of all herself.

Instead of cutting through the kitchen garden, she led the way past the dolphin fountain, its white marble glowing in the dark, heading for the terrace entrance. They were soaked again by the time they reached the glass doors, their dark reflections rearing up inside the bubbles of light they carried with the storm lamps. Helen wondered how much life they both had left in them – surely the batteries must be nearly spent? What if they both gave out at a crucial juncture? How could either she or Thiago function in the near darkness that was the labyrinthine interior of Rathbrooke Hall?

'Let me go first,' Thiago said, once they were inside. He wiped rain from his face, slicked back his hair with one hand, looking like that night he'd first arrived, a stranger wet through from the storm. 'I don't want him coming at you out of the dark.'

He didn't wait for her to answer, already heading out into the hallway, his footsteps falling heavily on the old parquet as they echoed into the dark. Helen followed, their lights bobbing, the empty house feeling huge around them, cavernous. Before they had even reached the entrance foyer, however, she heard a sound from somewhere behind them, lost in the unlit folds of the house. Helen stumbled to a halt, half-turning back the way she had come, though Thiago went on ahead without her, not having heard a thing.

'Thiago!' she shouted. 'Wait! Listen!'

He stopped and turned towards her. She put her fingers to her lips to silence him before he could ask what was going on. They stood there for a moment inside the bell jar of Rathbrooke Hall, the storm rumbling overhead. The moment stretched and Helen was beginning to think that she had imagined the noise, or else that there were other ghosts not of feline origin at large. But then it came again – a shriek, a shout, the sound of scuffling, all followed by an almighty crash. The cacophony echoed to them from the other end of the house. Thiago immediately charged back towards Helen, who had already turned to run back the way they had come.

At first Helen thought the sound was coming from the dining room, but then she realized that, no, it was emanating from the open doors of the west wing. She didn't know her way around this part of the house – she had not been present when Thiago and Rufus had been trying to round up Cora's huge cats. Still, she followed the commotion, anxiety growing as she realized there were two voices.

'Open it!' Brooks was shouting, words accompanied by a ruthless and furious thumping noise.

'I don't know *how*!' came the answering howl – Cora, her voice high, full of fury too, but also fear. 'I told you!'

'You know the combination! I know you do, you little—'

He must have heard the sound of them coming closer at that point, because the shouting broke off, but was followed by the more worrying noise of a scuffle and what sounded like a strangled sob from Cora. Helen and Thiago reached the source of the noise at the same time, crashing through the open door to find Crawford Brooks with his forearm bent tightly around Cora's neck, pulling her back against him as he stood with his back to a large and very old combination safe that stood in the corner of the room. Thiago immediately threw both hands up, breathing hard.

'Let her go,' he said. 'For God's sake, Brooks, she's just a child.'

Brooks curled his lip in a smile that made Helen's skin crawl. He looked dishevelled – pink-cheeked, his hair mussed. There was no sign of his glasses. Helen wondered if they had been as much of an artifice as the rest of his persona.

'This brat knows how to open this safe,' Brooks said. 'I'll let her go when she gives me the combination, not before.'

Cora put her hands up to the arm around her neck, trying to tug herself free, but in a surprising display of strength, Brooks lifted her of the ground, choking her until she coughed.

'Don't,' Helen said, horrified. 'You'll kill her!'

Brooks relented and Cora gasped for air, but quieted. The girl looked at Helen miserably.

'He's got a load of stuff out of the Shakespeare Room,' she said, tearfully. 'Cyril's collection – he's stealing it.'

'Shut up,' Brooks said, curtly, shaking Cora a little so that she fell silent again, afraid. 'The next thing I want to hear out of your mouth is the combination to this safe.'

'I don't *know* it,' Cora whispered, tears trickling down her cheeks.

'Then who does?' Brooks demanded. 'Someone must. The old gardener – what about him? What was his name? Rufus?'

'He doesn't know either,' Cora said, between sobs. 'No one did! No one came in here except me, for years.'

'She's not lying about that, Brooks,' Thiago insisted, his hands still raised. 'Look at this place. You've probably spent more time in here than anyone else but Cora in the last decade. It was empty. Abandoned. She does not know what you think she does.'

Helen saw Brooks' leather briefcase at his feet. The top

had flipped open, and she could see a red archive box stuffed tightly inside it. Her stomach churned. He had the *Cardenio.*

'Look,' she said, quietly, indicating the bag. 'You already have a fortune in there. That's what you came for, isn't it? Take it. Just take it and leave. We won't stop you, I promise. As long as you let her go, right now.'

Brooks' lips twisted again. He shook Cora slightly, as if she were an extension of his fist and he was expressing mild frustration. 'I want the bill of sale.'

For a second, Helen drew a blank. 'The . . . what?'

Brooks made a sound, scornful, in his throat. 'The bill of sale. From Abington Park.'

'I don't have it,' Helen said. 'I told you. We haven't found it.'

Brooks clenched his jaw, as if he was on the verge of losing his final iota of patience. 'I know that,' he hissed. 'But it's here somewhere. It has to be. There's no way Cyril Gissing misplaced it. There's *no way*! And I think it's in this safe. Probably with a lot of other very valuable items. Which is why I want this dumb kid to *OPEN IT*.'

'And I keep telling him,' Cora sobbed, her voice rising, 'that I don't know *how*!'

Helen glanced at Thiago and realized that he'd moved a little during the last exchange. He was edging away from her, and she realized he was aiming to circle Brooks, to split the thief's focus between himself and her. Helen's stomach churned again, because she realized he was intending for the two of them to take Brooks on. They had to, didn't they?

They were two against one – three, if Cora could see past her shock. She glanced around, looking for something she could use as a weapon. The room was almost empty, no sign of the dusty antiques that filled the rest of Rathbrooke Hall. But there was still a sword mounted on the wall to her right, probably blunt but heavy enough to deliver a good blow if she could get to it. Brooks saw what Thiago was trying to do and tightened his grip on the girl again, choking her until her eyes rolled back in her head.

'All right,' Thiago said, backing off. 'All right, all right. Stop. Please!'

'Cora? Is that you? What's going on in there?'

The voice took them all by surprise, including Brooks, who jerked around towards Rufus, who had appeared in the second doorway behind him. The old man was drenched, his old wax jacket shiny with rain, his white hair slicked back against his head. His eyes widened as he took in the scene before him.

'What—'

Helen used the momentary distraction to lunge for the wall. She leapt at it, grabbing the sword mounted there while Brooks was still in a state of confusion. At the same time, Thiago ran at him, charging at Brooks and his captive with all the fury of a bull running at a matador. Helen swung around with the weapon just as Brooks saw his nemesis coming. The thief used Cora as a battering ram, shoving the girl straight into the Spaniard's path. They collided, both of them going down with a massive, reverberating *THUMP*.

Cora screamed and then kept screaming, Thiago's full weight landing across her as one arm bent awkwardly beneath her against the floor. In the chaos, Brooks grabbed up his briefcase and swung it around at head height, aiming for Rufus, catching the old man on the underside of his jaw so that his head snapped back against the window behind him. It smashed on impact, glass shards raining down on him as he slumped to the floor, the storm rushing into the now-open space. Cora's cries of pain and fear grew louder, though Thiago was back on his feet now, trying to help the girl up, trying to get to Rufus. Brooks was already out of the door, taking the route that the gardener had used, down the stairs to the ground floor, heading for the open through the broken greenhouse, the briefcase clutched in his hand.

'Rufus!' Cora was screaming, trying to get to the old man, who was by some miracle still conscious despite the blood pouring from the back of his head.

'Get after him,' the gardener cried, shaking Helen off as she threw down the sword and ran to him. 'I'm fine, lassie. Get after him, both of you! Don't let him leave the island! Don't let him get away!'

Helen went after Brooks, not even pausing to see if Thiago was behind her. Outside, it was raining hard. The wind was still blowing, though with less ferocity than before. There was light in the sky, too, just a tiny tint, but it was there: the thin bright smudge of early dawn signalling a new day. The mulberry tree was still standing, leaves torn and branches askew, but it had lived through another storm. Helen heard

Brooks, the receding sound of his feet crunching hard and fast on the gravel of the kitchen garden path. No doubt about where he was headed. It was the only way off the island. He was running for the harbour.

Chapter Twenty-Nine

'Helen! Wait!'

Thiago's voice carried to her as she ran through the tattered rose garden, but she didn't stop. She'd already heard the harbour gate clang on its hinges and wondered if Crawford Brooks knew how to handle a motorboat. If he did, there was no time to spare, and she couldn't risk waiting for Thiago to catch up. By the time she herself had made it through the wrought-iron gate, there was enough light in the sky to make faintly recognizable shapes out of the harbour below her. She could see the figure of Brooks already at the bottom. The stone steps were slick beneath her feet, drenched in rain and treacherous – one slip and she'd be over the edge, plunging down into the dark water beneath. Brooks had made it in one piece – he didn't even pause to look back; he just threw himself into Cora's little motorboat, untying it with frantic pace.

The gate clanged again: Thiago, only steps behind her. Still, they were too late. Helen got to the bottom of the steps just as the outboard motor roared to life under Brooks' hand. A second later he was pulling away, the little boat's prow plunging from the dock towards the gap in the harbour wall, too fast by any sensible margin.

'Come on!' Thiago reached Helen and passed her without pause, heading for his own boat. 'We can still catch him!'

By the time the *Alejandra* was free of her moorings, Brooks and the motorboat had cleared the island. Outside the shelter of the harbour, the weather was still wild. The wind hit Helen in the face as soon as they left the lee of the harbour inlet. She had to grip the gunwale just to stop herself being blown over the side. Rain cut across the narrow deck in torrents, slicing into her exposed fingers and face like sharp splinters of ice. She was numb in seconds. Thiago fought the boat, trying to turn it against the waves, against the driving rain. Even with the trace of dawn in the sky, the night was still on them, the harbour lights of Seahouses ahead of them indistinct. Helen kept having to gasp to fill her lungs, she was so exposed on the *Alejandra*'s deck.

Ahead of them she could see the motorboat, ploughing through the choppy mess of roiling waves. It wasn't, she realized, making for Seahouses. Instead it had drifted to port, turning south as if towards Beadnell. Had Brooks missed the harbour entrance, or did he seriously think he could outrun Thiago's more powerful boat on the open water, in this weather? Hope surged in her chest as she saw they were gaining on the smaller boat. Thiago stared through the boat's drenched windshield with a black, determined look on his face. His hands gripped the wheel so tightly his knuckles had turned white in the darkness.

'What's the plan?' Helen shouted, over the roar of the engine and the cacophony of the wind and waves. 'What do we do, when we catch him?'

Thiago set his jaw, still staring out at the watery landscape beyond, at the fleeing boat in front of them. 'We get that bag back. We stop a thief.'

Helen didn't have time to ask how he was actually going to accomplish these things. Thiago gunned the engine and wrenched the boat's wheel. In another second they would be abreast of Cora's tiny, struggling boat. Despite the rain-streaked glass, she could see Crawford Brooks looking back at them, his white face grim. Beyond him Beadnell beach was a dark rim of land beneath crashing waves. Weren't there rocks here? Big striating lines of them, stumbling down into the water from the beach. If they hit them—

'Get ready to take the wheel,' Thiago shouted, standing up, already turning away from the cabin.

'What?' Helen shouted, shocked. 'I can't handle a boat!'

'You can,' he told her, and they were alongside the motor-boat now. 'You have to. Now! Ram him if you need to!'

I don't know how, she would have shouted, but Thiago had already surged past her out of the cabin so that she had no choice but to take his place, grabbing at the wheel before it could veer off course. The *Alejandra* bucked beneath her grip like a furious creature desperate to escape. She grappled with it, doing her best to keep it steady. She felt their hull connect with the *Quick But Dirty*, saw Brooks' white, angry face as the bigger boat scraped against Cora's little skiff.

She heard a shout and turned to see Thiago disappear over the side of the *Alejandra*. The motorboat's engine stuttered and then cut out, but the *Alejandra*'s engine was still running. The *Quick But Dirty* turned on the waves, powerless, in danger of being ploughed under the churning waves by the bigger boat. Through the windshield Helen saw that Thiago had made it on board and was scuffling with Brooks. The rain still lashed down even as the smaller boat rocked against the *Alejandra*'s prow, tipping, dangerously close to capsizing. Helen, panicked, stared down at the controls with no idea of what to do. She wrenched at the boat's wheel, trying at least to turn it away from the motorboat, but that just succeeded in ramming it further. She was terrified it would break apart, splinter like jetsam on the tide. Frantic, she saw the ignition key and twisted it – killing the engine was all she could do. The *Alejandra*'s power died as Thiago and Brooks continued to struggle, stumbling about on the precarious, rocking boat.

She realized that the two boats were drifting apart on the waves even as the men continued to grapple with each other. She hadn't brought her phone – hadn't even bothered to charge it for the past week. There was no way for her to call for help. She couldn't even see properly, it was still too dark, and when she'd killed the power to the *Alejandra*'s engine the electrics had all gone too. Out of the semi-shelter of the cabin, she could barely see, the rain just kept coming.

There was a shout and a sudden thump, followed by a

crashing sound and a splash, which was immediately swallowed by the noise of the waves against the prow. Helen wiped rain from her eyes and saw that there was now only one figure on Cora's boat.

Time slowed between one breath and the next. The figure on the smaller boat was in darkness, just a shape, nothing more. She thought it was facing her, staring at her, but she couldn't see features.

Then a huge beam of yellow light cut through the lifting darkness: a flashlight, but a thousand times bigger and more powerful. It glared through the storm and Helen squinted against it, blinded again, but only for a second. She blinked, her vision cleared, and she saw the person standing in Cora's boat.

It wasn't Thiago. It was Crawford Brooks. His face was white against the glare, eyes wide, hair wild.

'Thiago?' Helen screamed over the waves, still black around them. She lunged for the gunwale and leaned over it, trying to see him below them. 'Crawford! Where is he?'

She couldn't see a thing. Helen worked her way along the railing, the bright beam above them turning everything to glare and deep shadow.

'Where is he?' she screamed again, but her words were lost beneath the growling stutter of an outboard motor. She looked up to see Brooks yanking at the chain, drenched but whole. Then the growl became a roar as the engine took. Brooks cast her one last baleful look and turned away.

The light changed, cutting out for a second, then coming

back on for a brief blip before cutting out again and then blasting back full on. *Blip, blip, blip, pause. Longer blip, blip, blip, pause. Blip, blip, blip.* Helen jerked towards the source of the light. It was coming from the island: it was the old lighthouse, decommissioned but still functional. It was Rufus, or maybe even Cora, signalling the mainland in the only way they could. *SOS*, they were shouting into the first lit embers of dawn. *SOS, SOS, SOS.* Then the beam returned full blast, falling right across Helen and the dead boat; on the empty, churning waves around her; on the endless *slash-slash-slash* of the rain.

Helen sobbed into the wind, leaning over the gunwale, searching the water. How long had Thiago been down there? Was he dead already, drowned and sinking into the silt of the North Sea? Had Brooks run him over with Cora's boat? Time was an impossible creature, elusive, unfathomable.

Then she saw him – a shape, rounded against the waves, too far away for her to reach, but he was bobbing, not sinking. Helen screamed into the wind, leaning as far over the rail as she dared. Thiago raised an arm, his strength stretched thin and fading against the waves. She saw him disappear from view until just his hand was showing. He struggled back to the surface, gasping, and she knew he was almost lost. The next time he went down he wouldn't come back up. She turned to search for anything she could throw to him and saw the orange life ring fastened against the rear of the boat. She stumbled for it, fingers so icy cold that she struggled to undo the quick-release clasps. Pulling it free, she went back to the rail and shouted to him, no idea whether he could hear her or even see her.

He raised his arm again and she threw the buoy, but the wind caught it, blowing it out of easy grasp. Thiago struggled to swim towards it, the waves buffeting him back, sending the life ring further out of his reach, threatening to drag him away. Helen looked around, but there wasn't another; there was nothing.

In desperation, she went back to the cabin. She didn't know how to operate a boat, but she'd turned it off: surely she could turn it back on, and she knew how a wheel worked. She stumbled, the cold and shock threatening to stop her legs from working altogether, and collapsed against the console. She fumbled for the ignition and prayed that turning the key would start it up, that it really was as simple as that. The engine took, roaring into life, and her shout might just have been loud enough to be heard over the still-raging wind.

Helen wrenched at the wheel to turn the boat but had no idea how to accelerate – was too afraid anyway, in case she ran straight over the man struggling to survive beneath her in the freezing North Sea. Instead she swung the boat around, hoping that this would at least bring him close enough for her to reach without smashing into him with the prow.

She scrambled out again onto the deck, and now it really was dawn, the wind easing and the rain lessening under a blush of pink at the horizon. But there was no sign of Thiago. She screamed his name, searching the water, but she couldn't see him. Had she run him over? Had she crushed him with the hull of his own boat?

'*Helen.*'

The cry was weak, from the starboard side. Helen turned to see a pale fist clenched around a rail support. She rushed over and saw Thiago splayed against the hull, holding on for dear life as he bobbed with the motion of the boat, drenched and ghostly white, exhausted, but alive. Helen tried to drag him up and over the gunwale, but he was a dead weight, too heavy for her to lift, too tired to help himself. She knelt beside the rail, instead, wrapping her hands around his cold fingers. There must be a rope, but what if she let him go and he couldn't hold on? He'd sink and be gone for good. She'd never find him again; he'd be lost beneath the waves.

'Thiago,' she said. 'Thiago—'

It was then that she saw the pages. They floated in a halo all around them, a storm tide of paper, spreading out like a blast wave, moving inexorably away from them, scattered and lost for ever, drowned. She turned to look towards the coast, but Cora's boat and Crawford Brooks had vanished into the dawn light.

There came a loud, honking wail, the sound of an engine purring closer, fast. Helen looked up, and there was one of the tourist catamarans from Seahouses harbour, answering the island's SOS.

Chapter Thirty

The police found Cora's boat down the coast, dragged up on the low sandy beach at Football Hole, but Crawford Brooks was nowhere to be seen. They thought he'd probably had a car parked up waiting there, and they knew he'd flown out of Newcastle airport the same day. He'd been headed for Geneva, but from there, who knew where he'd gone. He'd not taken another flight, at least not on the same passport with which he had landed, and so the search would be ongoing. Wherever Brooks was, he did not have the *Cardenio*, or that page that had most probably been written by William Shakespeare himself four hundred years hence. That had tumbled into the North Sea and been separated by the waves, lost for ever. There was part of Helen – a not inconsiderable part – that thought it would have been better for Brooks to get away with the archive box and its precious contents intact. Better that it be stolen than destroyed, though it was too late now.

The storm blew itself out while Thiago was being treated

at the hospital for hypothermia and a mild concussion. He and Helen spoke to the police, but by that evening were back on Rathbrooke Island, hitching a lift with Martha and Rufus on the *Lady Jane*, because Thiago was in no condition to pilot the *Alejandra*, which would remain in Seahouses harbour until he was well enough to collect it. Poor Martha, her anxiety already stretched to breaking point, had seen the SOS signal from the mainland and sailed over as soon as she could. She'd found her errant daughter in the lighthouse with a still-bleeding Rufus. She had brought them both back to the mainland, where both Cora and Rufus had been treated at the hospital and had added their statements to the police investigation. Now here the five of them were, subdued and tired, returned to the scene of the crime. Cora was the quietest of all, her broken arm in a cast and sling, guilty and silent because she was the one who had brought Brooks into their midst. No one was of a mind to make an issue of this, least of all her mother, who was more than anything relieved and grateful that her daughter was in one piece, given the horrifying story of events she'd been given by Thiago and Helen.

Helen was also willing to cut the girl some slack, even knowing the spiteful reason she had brought Brooks to the island in the first place. This was partly because Cora's motives had been revealed in a tearful admission, followed by what seemed to her to be a heartfelt apology, and partly because Martha had filled Helen in on the rest soon after. As a result, Helen knew that Cora would be dealing with a lot more upset and trauma than what she'd endured that night.

Cora's father couldn't come and visit her because he was currently in prison for the domestic abuse of his then wife and young daughter – Martha and Cora herself. He was not allowed to have contact with either of them, but Cora had somehow got wind of his address and written to him, not realizing that what she'd thought was a postcode was in fact a prison number for HMP Erlestoke in Wiltshire. He'd called her a nickname when he'd written back, and the prison service was stretched too thin to see through this small disguise, and thus had not intercepted or stopped the correspondence. The arrangement to come and visit her had never been going to happen the way Cora had thought it would, and was likely a ruse merely to find out where the wife he still held a grudge against was now living. The information would not go down well with the parole board, which was the only upside to the whole debacle that Martha could see. Cora now knew exactly what kind of man her father was, and also why they had sought safe haven on Rathbrooke all those years ago. The processing of this information was likely to be lengthy and painful.

Helen didn't tell either Martha or Cora that Cora's original wish regarding the press had been granted anyway by Brooks' exploits. When she and Thiago had left the police station, there had been a wall of photographers waiting. By now, the pieces would have fallen into place. Everyone would know where she was and how she had managed to avoid them for so long. Helen didn't have the energy to care. She'd been taken in – again, and now the most valuable part of Cyril Gissing's precious collection was gone, lost to the waves thanks to a conman she should have seen coming. At some point Helen thought she would have to address this part of her past with her new friends, but now was not the time. They were all too tired, still trying to process what had happened the night before.

The island was a mess, the storm having done a number on both the gardens and the house. In some places the island wall had crumbled, and the work to rebuild it was clearly more than Rufus would be able to handle himself. Tiles had become dislodged from the Hall's roof and now lay smashed on the courtyard terrace below. The kitchen garden was battered quite beyond the shattered glasshouse and the window that Rufus had cracked with his poor head. Martha, Helen and Cora, as the three most able-bodied in the wake of the storm, patched these holes with timber and plywood and swept up the glass inside and out.

The sheep were fine, at least, their stone barn sturdy enough to withstand the onslaught, the animals well fed and sheltered together within. The mulberry had lost a branch or two, and plenty of its torn leaves and fruit lay scattered about the orchard, but otherwise it seemed unharmed. Clearing that all up could wait, Martha decreed, wearily, once they had checked on and completed the most urgent tasks, and they all agreed that right now, what both they and the island itself needed was rest.

Rufus went back to the lighthouse, guided by Martha, who was fussing over him like a mother hen. Thiago put his feet up in the parlour downstairs, content with a blanket, too tired even to make it upstairs. Helen wasn't sure she would sleep, despite being exhausted to her very bones. But she went upstairs anyway. Perhaps if she lay down, the whirring guilt of her thoughts might abate a little. When she went into the suite that had become her own, however, she immediately saw what Brooks had left behind. It was on the table, the 'evidence' he had provided and that she had fallen for so easily: the letter supposedly detailing part of Cyril's will, lying beside what she assumed was a fake business card. Her mother had confirmed that she'd been the one to tell Brooks that it was Helen he needed to speak to, as thoroughly convinced by the faked letter as Helen had so nearly been herself. She contemplated the Folger letter for a moment and knew that she was not going to sleep. She had too much to think about, too much to blame herself for.

'Helen?'

The voice was small and hesitant and came from Cora, standing behind her in the doorway. The girl looked as exhausted as Helen felt, with dark circles beneath eyes puffy and red from weeping. Helen didn't have the heart to maintain any anger towards her. After all, she was neither the first nor would she be the last young woman to mistakenly put her trust in the wrong man. Helen's entire adult life was a testament to that.

'Hey, Cora,' Helen said, softly. 'Aren't you going to get some sleep? You look as if you could use some. Everything else can wait until we've all had some rest, don't you think?'

Cora shook her head. 'I need to go and check on the cats,' she said. 'They've been shut up for too long. And I thought – I wondered . . . ' she faltered, picking at the old wood of the doorjamb, and then shrugged, before starting again. 'I thought you might like to come and meet them. They're really good company,' the girl added. 'When you're feeling down or lonely. And I can't play with them properly at the moment . . .' she indicated her poor broken arm.

Despite herself, Helen managed a genuine smile at this offered olive branch. 'We can probably let them out into the rest of the wing now, can't we,' she suggested. 'Now that we've boarded up the broken window and swept up the glass.'

A flash of surprise passed over Cora's tired face, followed by relief. She nodded. 'I was hoping we could do that, yeah.'

Helen glanced down at the fake letter that Brooks had brought for another second, before picking it up and folding it in two and dropping it back onto the table. There was something else she needed to do as a matter of urgency, but she couldn't bring herself to face that at this precise moment.

'I'd love to meet the cats, Cora,' Helen said, instead. 'Let's go and let them out.'

Helen hadn't had a cat since she'd moved out of her parents' house to go to university. Being surrounded by a whole pack of them, especially the size that the Maine Coons were, was a little overwhelming. As she stood back, watching the animals all rush to greet the girl as soon as she walked in, Helen could see why, in the dark, in the storm, Crawford

Brooks had been so spooked by his encounter. They really did look like miniature lions, with slightly devilish scrunched-up faces and big tufted ears. In the case of the big orange one, whom Cora introduced as Orlando, it even had a lion's mane, albeit in miniature. Collectively, their purring resembled distant, growling thunder. But they clearly loved Cora, crowding around her, vying for love and attention. The teenager struggled to pick one of them up in her one good arm – a beautiful silver-grey tabby, who immediately rubbed her head beneath Cora's chin.

'This is the mum,' Cora said, looking at Helen over the milling creatures. 'Ophelia. She's really cuddly. I can't believe the owner was going to dump her.'

'Well,' Helen said, looking around. 'There are a lot of big mouths to feed, right here.'

Cora grimaced. 'Yeah. I think Mum's going to go mental when she finds out how much of her lamb stew they've eaten.'

Helen suspected the same, although she couldn't deny that the cats were all in superb condition, with shining coats and bright eyes. She felt sorry for them though, cooped up as they had been in this room for the past forty-eight hours.

'Can we let them into the rest of the wing now?' Cora asked, as if reading her mind. 'They really need a run around. They've got toys and things dotted around to play with.'

'Sure,' Helen said. 'Although, Cora, you do know you're probably going to have to find another solution, don't you? They can't stay here indefinitely.'

In answer, Cora buried her face in Ophelia's purring throat and nodded. 'I know. Mum's already been on the phone to the vet in Seahouses. She's worried that they haven't been spayed. She's asked them about rehoming already, too. I don't want any of them to go, though. I love all of them.'

Helen squeezed the girl's shoulder in silent solidarity. Cora gave a wan smile. Then she put the cat back on the ground and went to open the second door in the room, one that would allow the animals to roam more freely around the disused wing. At first the cats stayed with her, milling around her ankles, looking up at their mistress with quizzical trust. Then the big black boy – the rather appropriately named Faustus – scampered through the open door, and was quickly followed by the rest of the tribe. Helen listened to the sound of their running footsteps. It was definitely what she'd been hearing as 'ghost children' ever since her arrival.

She looked around the room in which she stood. A few bits of furniture, draped with old white sheets grey with dust – and, in some cases, cat hair. The paintings had all been taken down, and seemed to be propped up against the walls they had once graced.

'Do you want me to show you around?' Cora asked, watching as her attention wandered around the room. 'I promise the cats haven't done any damage. I made sure of that.'

It would be so easy for her to say yes, to linger here among these disused, harmless rooms. To follow the cats, maybe pick one or two of them up for a cuddle and a stroke. Hear Cora's story of how she managed to smuggle a pregnant cat onto Rathbrooke and into this hallowed hall, how she worked out a way to keep them fed and clean.

'I'd love to,' Helen said, 'but that's going to have to wait. There's something much more important I need to look at.'

Cora drew a breath. 'The priest hole.'

Helen nodded. 'Yes. I think there might be something we need to talk about, isn't there? But we can do it tomorrow, Cora.'

The girl squared her shoulders. 'No,' she said. 'No, let's do it now.'

Chapter Thirty-One

Helen had to steel herself to duck her way into the hidden library. Brooks had left the priest hole open, of course – no need to shut the barn door after the horse has already bolted. Cora came in immediately behind her and together they stood there quietly. Helen had harboured a faint hope that it wasn't the *Cardenio* that had been taken, but the First Folio instead. That would still have been a loss, but not a completely immeasurable one. But no – the Folio was still there, resplendent in its red case. It was Cyril's meticulously pieced-together almost-manuscript that had been taken and lost to the waves. Unexpectedly, Helen felt her eyes fill with tears, which she quickly wiped away. There was no sense in feeling sorry for herself. Only – it wasn't for herself, not really. What had been lost here, there was no getting back.

To her surprise, Cora took her hand and squeezed it. Helen squeezed back, and then let go to look through some of the mess that Brooks had left behind. It seemed as if he'd been searching for something – the loose papers that had been on the table were scattered on the floor. Other volumes had been disturbed, including the First Folio, the cover of which was open, as if the thief had looked through it in a hurry before deciding not to take it. Helen wondered why – it was worth a fortune on its own – but decided it had probably been too big. It was the same with the quartos. If he could only take one thing, he knew what he wanted. He'd likely already had a buyer lined up for it, a shadowy figure they would never be able to pinpoint, as Thiago had said.

'I suppose Brooks did all of this looking for the bill of sale from Abington Park,' she mused aloud, looking around the turned-over room. She glanced at the girl standing silently beside her. 'Although I don't think it was ever in here, was it?'

Cora took a breath. 'It was,' she said. 'But I took it.'

Helen nodded, but stayed quiet.

'It . . . wasn't the only thing I took, either,' Cora admitted. 'And now I need to show you something else.'

Cora led her back out of the priest hole and down to the ground floor, to reveal another hidden safe, within reaching distance of Cyril's crowded desk. There was no room this time – the locked steel cabinet had been fitted perfectly into the hewn stone so that only its front wall was revealed when a discreet portion of the bookcase was swung outwards. It was older than the one Brooks had tried to get Cora to open in the west wing, with no combination lock – just a keyhole, into which fitted a key that Cora carried on a long leather strap around her neck, always hidden beneath her clothes.

'No one else ever knew about it, except Cyril,' Cora said,

as she pulled the chain from around her neck and fitted the key to the lock. 'He found it even before he found the priest hole. This is what gave him the idea for the reading nook, back in the day. He told me about it last year. Just in case.'

The key turned easily, the lock mechanism well-oiled despite its age. The door was heavy – Cora could not move it herself with only one arm and Helen had to heave with all her weight on the ancient handle to get it to open. It swung back on its hinges, revealing a small selection of steel shelves housing a short line of small, slim volumes that Helen immediately saw were the missing quartos and the book of poetry from the Shakespeare Room. Lying beside them was a single piece of yellowing paper. Cora reached out and picked this up. It was folded in half but in reverse, so that it was clear to see what had been written at the top in elaborate, copperplate handwriting: *Bill of Sale*.

'I feel bad about this now,' Cora said. 'But when you came, I thought you were the one that was going to steal everything from Rathbrooke. And I knew Cyril would hate that. So when you found the hidden library, I started taking these.'

Helen frowned. 'But – why these ones? Why not all of them?'

Cora shrugged. 'These are the books that had come from Abington Park. Some of the others Cyril had collected since. But these – these were the ones that had come from the auction, along with the tree. Brooks obviously knew Cyril had them, and he also knew what that meant, especially alongside the bill of sale.' Cora gave Helen a searching look. 'Do you see? How important these ones are? Like, even more than the others?'

Helen felt a prickle course along her spine as she looked at the small volumes before her. 'These were published during Shakespeare's lifetime. And they came from the library of the house where the last surviving direct relative in Shakespeare's line lived until she died.'

'Right.' Cora nodded. 'And with the bill of sale along with everything else listed on it—'

'Oh my . . . ' Helen began, as what Cora was trying to get her to see hit her. 'Oh my *God*. Did Cyril think these actually came from Shakespeare's own library? Did he . . . Are these Shakespeare's own copies of his plays?'

Cora shrugged a little. 'Maybe. No one will ever be able to prove it for sure, that's what Cyril said. But they also can't prove they weren't, especially with the bill of sale as provenance. It's the closest we'd ever get, that's what he used to say. That's what you and Thiago didn't figure out about the Shakespeare Room. All the books and papers that came from Abington Park – Cyril thought they might have come from Shakespeare's own library. That they had been passed down to Elizabeth Barnard and then left there after she died.'

Helen actually felt a little faint. She reached out to touch her fingertips, featherlight and reverent, to the spines of the fragile quartos, her head spinning. Then she spotted something on the lower shelf. It was an archive box, leather, not unlike the one that stored the First Folio in the Shakespeare Room and that had once held the precious papers now lost to the North Sea.

'Wait,' Helen said, resting her fingers on Cora's shoulder. 'What's in there?'

'Oh,' Cora said, looking at the archive box. 'I don't know. I've never seen inside it. That's the only thing in the library I was never allowed to touch. It's the only thing Cyril always kept in this safe, even before I got here. But I suppose you probably need to see it now, too.'

Helen took out the box and opened the lid. Inside she found several sheets of clean white paper, far more modern than anything else she'd come across since her time in the library. They were neatly stapled together, and the heading at the top of the first untidily handwritten sheet gave Helen her first genuine smile in twenty-four hours.

'It's Cyril's will,' she said. 'Finally!'

She lifted out the stapled sheets and then froze as she saw what had been hidden beneath the last will and testament of Cyril Gissing.

It was a mess of fragile paper fragments, all scrawled with copperplate handwriting. They formed an uneven stack that had slipped and moved over time. Yellowed and dog-eared, the handwriting was dense and in some cases little more than a scrawl over, between and around other scrawls. There were crossings-out and additions, as if the writer – or perhaps writers, she thought, since there was clearly more than one hand at work – had been writing and revising, writing and revising.

Reading every word on the top page would be impossible without a concerted effort and a magnifying glass. But there were a few words written in large, florid lettering that Helen could read without too much difficulty, and what it said made her suck in a breath. There, amid the scrawl, figured in elaborate copperplate, was a title.

The History of Cardenio.

Helen drew a slow, shaky breath. *This* was the manuscript that Cyril Gissing had obsessed over for so long. It wasn't lost to the North Sea. It was here. It had always been here, she realized. In his precious, hidden library.

Alice Marsh
c/o Penny Trevellyn
The William Croker Agency
Fourth Floor
158 Fleet Street
London
EC4 BB8

Dear Helen,

I know this letter is probably going to come out of the blue, and I am sorry for the shock that receiving it will cause. Actually I have wanted to write to you long before now, but have always talked myself out of it. But I felt it important that I contact you directly before the open letter I intend to post online and send to most of the papers who have been hounding you is published, and eventually your agent agreed to pass this on.

I want you – and the world – to know that I do not blame you for my soon-to-be ex-husband's – for Brett's – behaviour. Most of all, it is my very sincere hope that you do not blame yourself, because I know how good he always was at making me feel as if every bad thing in our marriage was my fault alone. And while I suspect that our upbringings were distinctly different, and perhaps, by all objective standpoints, I had more to survive than you, I also know what showbusiness is. Especially for a young woman, even now: how precarious, how easily sent off track or truncated a career can be. I also know how charming, how disarming, how very focused *Brett is until he has hold of whatever it is he wants at the time. Perhaps more than all of that, I know how very young you were when you crossed his path. Barely older than our eldest child is now. Someone needs to point that out to the papers, I think.*

This, though, more than anything, is what I need you to know and what I will tell both the papers and the cesspit of online influence: he did it to me, too. The flattery, the charm, the lies, the guilt, the threats and, eventually, the violence that could be so easily explained away as 'accidental'. I think, perhaps, that the only difference between us – and whatever other women come forward as a result of me finally speaking up, because I am sure you and I are not the only ones – was that he married me and we had children. After that I felt I could not leave and he had a much easier way to manipulate me into silence. I had sworn to myself, when I was very young, that I would not do to any children of mine what had been done to me. I did not account for the fact that in so many ways I was still a child myself, and it was already too late. Back then, life was different, even more so than it was when you started out. I was seen as lucky. I thought of myself as lucky, too, right up until I realized I was anything but. But hindsight is 20/20, and there is no reason why it should only be we women who bear the brunt of bringing something into focus so long after the point when seeing clearly would have made a difference.

We are divorcing, though in truth we have been separated

for years. This will become public, at the same time as my letter. I think you might understand what I mean when I say it never goes away and there is little justice, and so the best we can hope for is distance.

I have also spoken to Perle Anders, who, as I suspected, had been talked into her stance on dropping All of the Above *by voices with no interest in truth, only money. It is my hope that this, at least, can reach a better resolution, because I have read your book and think it will make a fine film.*

With the wish that the future holds better things for us all,

Alice Marsh

Chapter Thirty-Two

THREE MONTHS LATER

'Noah?' Martha called, from where she was standing in the doorway of the bedroom she had just finished making up. 'How are you getting on with the Blue Room?'

The erstwhile Noah stuck his head out of the room two doors down from where Martha stood. 'Nearly there. What's next?'

Rathbrooke's housekeeper thought for a minute, frowning slightly. 'I had planned for us to use the Yellow Room,' she said, nodding at the door of another disused suite on the opposite side of the landing. 'But I had another look this morning and it really is a bit dingy. I'm worried the moths have got to the rug in there, too – I'll have a look later; it might have to go in the deep freeze for a bit. All that said, we'll be better off using the Pink Room, instead. That's the one opposite you, there.'

'Right-o,' said Noah. 'Give me five minutes and I'll be with you.'

'Martha,' Helen said, stopping in the door of her suite, her suitcase at her feet. 'Aren't you going to use this room?'

'Of course not,' Martha said, pulling the door of the bedroom she'd just finished preparing for visitors shut behind her before coming towards Helen, passing through the shaft of warm early autumn light falling in diamonds through the stairwell windows. 'That's your room, I'm not putting anyone in there.'

'Don't be daft,' Helen laughed, waving at the packed case at her feet. 'I'm leaving – and the room's already been opened up. It makes sense to use it instead of giving yourself even more work to do. I won't even be here. I won't need it.'

The other woman made a sound in her throat. 'Yes, well,' she said. 'I live in hope that you will see that this whole leaving the island thing is a terrible idea, and you'll be back before we know it. In which case, you *will* need it.'

Helen watched the young man called Noah appear from the room he'd just finished preparing. He had an armful of cleaning products and was wielding a feather duster. He was the son of one of Rufus's drinking buddies in the Schooner. Rufus had brought him over from Seahouses that very morning to help get Rathbrooke ready for its imminent influx of visitors.

'You don't need me anymore,' Helen pointed out. 'You're about to be so busy you'll have forgotten my name by tomorrow!'

'Nonsense,' Martha said. 'They're just visitors. You, though, Helen – from now on, you'll always be family here at Rathbrooke. Remember that, won't you?'

Helen smiled, although there was a sudden lump in her throat. 'I will,' she said. 'I promise.'

The past three months since finding Cyril's will had been a whirlwind. The document – signed, sealed, clear and irrefutable – had left the island and almost everything on it to Martha, with a proviso that Rufus be allowed to live in the lighthouse and work on the island for as long as he was bodily able and wanted to do so. If or when Rufus wanted to move back to the mainland or needed more help with his living arrangements, a lump sum had been allocated that would allow Rathbrooke's faithful gardener to rest easy about how he would be looked after in his sunset years.

The contents of the library – every single item within the library walls – had been left in the care of, and in most cases the ownership of, Thiago Montera. In fact, the details of what Cyril had wished for his collection was far more comprehensive and specific than for anything else that had been in his possession. This didn't surprise anyone who had known Cyril Gissing, or Helen for that matter. It also clarified the depths of Crawford Brooks' deception – the Folger Shakespeare Library confirmed it had never discussed taking on the contents of the Shakespeare Room, and that Brooks most definitely had not been in their employ.

Even after they had found the will and discovered the clarity of Cyril's wishes, there had been a lot to sort out – death duties, for one thing, which after consultation had been cleared by selling the island's flock of rare sheep. This sale had upset Cora, who really hadn't wanted anything about the island to change at all, but even she agreed that between that and having to sell anything else out of the house – or indeed the house itself – this was preferrable.

'Maybe I can build the flock up again,' she had said, in the end. 'You know, in the future.' Because the future was where she was looking to now, however distant it seemed at the moment: a future where Rathbrooke was hers, and her responsibility to preserve.

Helen had wondered privately whether the girl would think this was a burden, but in fact the opposite seemed to be true. She was excited, engaged – hopeful, in perhaps a way she hadn't been for a while. It was good to see.

Thiago, meanwhile, had learned the news of his inheritance with a level of shock that surprised Helen. It made complete sense to her – as it had to Martha, Rufus and Cora – that Thiago was the one Cyril trusted with his immense collection. Martha had seemed, in fact, incredibly relieved that the responsibility of what to do with what they had found inside the library had been laid at someone else's door.

The discovery of the *Cardenio* manuscript had been seismic and was still causing tremors near and far. When Helen had first shown Thiago what was in the archive box, she'd genuinely feared he was going to have a heart attack. This was partly because of what they had found, but equally because of what they had lost. Up until that point, they had both been convinced that what had gone into the North Sea, while not being an actual manuscript, had held an invaluable scholarly importance of its own. They each felt guilt over its loss, each blaming themselves for failing to look after the sum of all Cyril Gissing's work before anyone had even had a chance to examine it properly. Now, they realized that the true treasure of the Rathbrooke Library was still there – safe, undiminished and whole. For the first few days after Cora's revelation, Thiago and Helen had been scared to even touch what was in the box, it was surely too fragile for their clumsy fingers. In the end they did remove it, spreading it leaf by leaf across a table that had been laid with velvet, which would be kind to the ancient, brittle pages. It had not taken Thiago long to posit the theory that what they had here were the real 'foul papers' to the complete original script – a working draft, with writings and revisions from more than one playwright. Was one of those playwrights Shakespeare himself? Cyril had obviously thought so. The notebook they had tried to use as a key to the papers from the priest hole yielded far more accurate references when tried against this manuscript. Clearly it referred to this text, not the one lost to the storm. Still, it had not taken long for Thiago to declare himself out of his depth. He needed help – he was not, after all, a Shakespeare specialist. There were far more qualified scholars than him out there.

Which was why, three months after they had realized what Cyril's library had truly been hiding, Rathbrooke was preparing for visitors. A select group of academics, carefully chosen, vetted and sworn to secrecy (and having signed a carefully worded Non-Disclosure Agreement) by Thiago himself, were due to arrive to begin an initial month-long examination of the pages Cyril had kept secure and under wraps for so long. They would stay on the island for the duration, immersing themselves in the study of the *Cardenio* in the hope of reaching a conclusion as to its provenance.

They were arriving today, just as Helen was finally leaving. Her job here was done – it was time for her to return to the real world. For the first time in months, she felt ready for that. There was a part of her – a big part, really – that would like to stay, to follow the journey that Thiago was about to continue without her to its conclusion, or at least to its next step. But just as things on the island had changed, so had things on the mainland, and that was where her life was. Rathbrooke wasn't hers, though she loved the thought of being able to return at some point in the future to see how they were all getting on. Especially Martha. Four months ago they had been strangers, but Helen knew that she and Martha would now be friends for life. A few nights after the climactic events of Brooks' visit, the two women had shared a bottle of wine and Helen had told Martha the twisted, unhappy story of her connection to Brett Pottinger. There had been a strange catharsis in the telling that Helen had not expected. Recounting the story, in her own words and at her own pace, to someone who wasn't there at the time and didn't know anything of what had been said online since, had allowed her to reframe it to herself. It had also bonded the two women, a unity that came from shared understanding.

'Just think of poor Thiago,' Martha said now, as they finally let each other go from the hug. 'He'll be lost without you.'

Helen shook her head. 'He'll be no such thing. His head will be all taken up with his colleagues.'

'It won't,' Martha countered, with conviction. 'At least half of that mind of his is always thinking about you.'

Helen knew better. She'd believed the wrong person too easily, even though Thiago had done nothing to warrant her mistrust. Since that night, even despite their discovery of the real *Cardenio*, their relationship had been hesitant. There was a barrier between them that was her fault. She didn't know how to get over it, and wasn't sure she should even try. She had proven herself to be terrible at relationships and thought that she'd probably be better off leaving them alone for good.

'Helen? Are you up there?' His voice floated to them then, as if she had conjured him out of the shimmering sunshine, accompanied by the sound of footsteps as he ran up the stairs. Thiago stopped when he saw Martha and Helen standing together. His gaze fell to Helen's suitcase standing patiently at her feet, and he smiled. 'Ready to go?'

'I think so,' she said, though suddenly her chest felt tight.

Another figure appeared at Thiago's feet – Ophelia, Cora's huge mother cat, the only feline still on the island. The others had all been adopted and were settling well into their new homes, which were spread far and wide over the north-east. Cora had declared that as soon as 'the internet was sorted' – another future plan for Rathbrooke – she would be setting up a WhatsApp group so that she could keep track of all former residents of the west wing.

Helen went to the Maine Coon and scooped up the giant cat. She'd miss this massive walking hearthrug, who since being allowed the run of the entire house had frequently taken to curling up with Helen at night, perhaps missing the noise and bustle of being surrounded by her offspring.

'Bye, puss,' she said, rubbing her cheek against Ophelia's soft head. 'Maybe I'll see you again some time.'

'She'd better,' Martha retorted. 'Or you'll have me to deal with!'

Helen put down the cat and glanced up in time to see Thiago picking up her case. When he turned back to her, his face was downcast, but he smiled as he met her eye.

'All right,' he said. 'Let's get going. Better not keep the Shakespeare boffins waiting.'

Helen gave Martha one last hug and then followed Thiago down those old stairs for the last time. She stepped out of the patio doors through which she – and Thiago, too – had first entered Rathbrooke, which felt so very long ago now. It was close to midday, and though the mornings had turned frosty, the sun was clear overhead. The fountain was running, the beautiful dolphin sculptures seeming almost alive as the water flowed over them, tinkling a merry tune as it shimmered across their leaping flanks.

They made their way down to the harbour, neither speaking as they went. Helen wondered where Rufus and Cora were – they had already all said their goodbyes, over an emotional breakfast that they had shared together one last time in Rathbrooke's dining room, but still, Helen had thought they might come to see her off. She had, she realized, with a jolt and despite what she'd just said to Martha, begun to see them as family, and to feel as if she was somehow part of the island. But she wasn't, was she? She'd never even met Cyril Gissing. He had never known she existed at all. She'd come here to hide until the messy dust of her own life had settled, and to do a job while it did. She'd done that and now it was time for her life to resume, far away from here.

Thiago was ahead of her, making his way down the stone steps to the dock, when a sound echoed to them – the engine of a motorboat, roaring closer. They both looked up to see Cora and Rufus in the girl's little skiff, on their way back into the island's harbour. When Cora saw them, she shouted, and waved the arm that wasn't controlling the boat. Helen smiled as the *Quick But Dirty* slowed and slewed around to dock, Rufus tying up as Cora killed the engine.

'We were afraid we'd miss you!' Cora shouted, scrambling out of the boat with a parcel wedged under her arm, leaving poor Rufus to balance on the precariously bobbing boat.

The teenager ran to Helen and threw both arms around her, hugging tightly.

'I didn't know you'd gone to the mainland,' Thiago said.

'Aye well,' Rufus said. 'We had something to collect.'

'We weren't sure it was going to turn up on time,' Cora said, a little breathlessly, pulling away from Helen far enough to thrust the parcel she was carrying into her hands. 'But it did!'

Helen looked at the parcel, then at Cora, Rufus and Thiago. 'What is this?'

'Open it!' Cora said, excited.

Helen did as she was told as Rufus and Thiago stepped nearer. Thiago looked as puzzled as she felt, but Rufus had a beaming grin on his face big enough to rival Cora's.

Inside was a hardback of *All of the Above.* Helen held the copy of her novel between both her hands.

'It's a first edition!' Cora said. 'Rufus and I realized that it was wrong that the library didn't have a copy, so I got a friend to find one online for me and we ordered it the other day. This way you'll always be part of the library. For ever.'

Helen felt her throat closing up as her eyes pricked with tears that she tried to blink away. Did her work really deserve to be in such august company as the books she had seen within the old peel walls? 'I don't know what to say.'

'Say you'll sign it,' Thiago said, smiling, his dark eyes as warm as the summer day around them.

'You really want my book in your library?' she asked, with a laugh.

Thiago reached out and caught her fingers in his. 'Of course I want it there,' he told her. 'It belongs there. I should have thought of it myself. I'm just glad Cora had the presence of mind to find a copy while you were still here to sign it.'

'That's me,' Cora said, producing a rollerball ink pen from her pocket with a flourish. 'Always full of good ideas.'

*

Their journey to Seahouses was a smooth one, the calm sea a stark contrast to that night three months before when Thiago had gone overboard in the middle of a storm. Helen sat on deck, watching as they left Rathbrooke Island behind. She remembered the first night she had arrived with Rufus, how unsettled she had been by the forbidding face of the rearing island wall. She couldn't imagine feeling that way now. Now she wasn't sure she'd find anywhere she felt as safe, as protected from all the vagaries of the world, as behind that wall.

'You okay?' Thiago asked, from the wheel, as she settled beside him, finally turning her back on the island as they slowed to enter Seahouses harbour.

'Yes,' she said, although in truth she wasn't sure. She hadn't expected to feel this sense of dislocation, of loss. 'I just . . . I'm going to miss it.' *I'm going to miss you*, she thought, but did not say.

Thiago was concentrating on bringing the boat in, but smiled even as he kept his eyes on the harbour wall, and reached out with one hand to grip hers in a brief, hard squeeze.

'It will miss you, too.'

In the end, there was no time for a prolonged goodbye between them, because Thiago's group of academics were already waiting for him, standing in a slightly forlorn huddle on the docks, a mass of multicoloured suitcases at their feet. Helen was reminded of the time she had visited the puffins with Cora, and had to stifle a laugh even as Thiago introduced them both.

'Let's start getting you loaded,' he said, to the group, and then they were all in a flurry of movement, eager to get to the promised land of Rathbrooke Library. Helen saw with a jolt that the journey was already continuing, and that she had stepped onto a different path. She wanted to say goodbye to Thiago, but he was busy and, perhaps, after all, it was better this way, for her to slip away and say nothing at all. She separated herself from the little crowd and wrenched herself free by turning her back, hefting her case, and beginning to walk away.

Her phone rang before she'd gone very far at all: she had remembered to charge it the night before, ready for her return to the land of modern day, but still the half-forgotten sound made her jump. Helen pulled it from her pocket and had pressed answer before she had fully registered the number.

'Helen?' said the strident American voice on the other end of the line. 'I've been calling you for hours. Your agent said that you were going to be back in contact today. Where have you been?'

Helen glanced at her watch. It was only just 10am. She supposed, to a career American, 'today' meant that she should have been chained to a desk, fully made-up and totally engaged, from the crack of dawn. 'Claude?'

'Listen,' said the executive producer who had so brutally cut short her career just a few months before. 'We've got to get back on track ASAP, or the money men are going to lose it. I've sent you a conference link, be ready to go in ten.'

'I . . . what?' Helen asked. 'What are you talking about?'

There was a brief silence, then a sigh. 'You haven't checked your email.'

'Not for the past four months, no.'

There came a brief, muffled curse. 'The film's back on. We need you here in LA like, *yesterday*. I'm going to book you a flight—'

'Wait,' Helen interrupted. 'What do you mean, it's back on?'

'You'd be up to speed if you'd checked your email,' Claude said, testily. 'Perle Anders spoke to Alice again after her open letter went, like, totally viral. It's all sorted. More than that, the PR people have found a way to spin the whole thing in the film's favour. Now all we need is an actual film. We have to get the ball rolling, and sharpish.'

Helen turned back to look at the *Alejandra*. Thiago was still loading the academics' luggage – there was a lot, since they had all come prepared for a month. A month of immersing themselves in a single text, away from the noise of everything – everyone – else.

'Sorry,' she said, still trying to get her head around what was happening. 'You've found a way to spin *what* whole thing?'

'The story of you and that actor,' Claude said, in a tone that suggested there was an unspoken 'obviously' at the end of that sentence, even though this was anything but obvious to Helen.

'You're spinning it . . . in the *film*'s favour?' Helen repeated.

'Exactly,' said the producer. 'It's going to be great. Perle came up with a genius idea. Alice will play the lead role.'

'Right,' Helen said. She was still watching Thiago, almost through with his task. Soon he'd untie the boat and head back to Rathbrooke, leaving her . . . where, exactly?'

'And with you writing the screenplay, it'll be the perfect triumvirate. I can already see the Oscar campaign. Women united. Women for women, all that.'

Helen's attention snapped back in. 'What?'

'It's a shoo-in for a nomination, I can tell you that much already.'

'No,' Helen said. 'I meant, you think I'm going to write the screenplay?'

'Of course you are,' said Claude.

'But I'm not a screenwriter,' Helen said.

Claude gave an impatient sigh. 'Helen, look. Alice won't do it without you. She says it's your story, and no one should write it but you. If you're really worried, we can get someone in to help with the scripting side of it, but—'

'That's not what I meant,' Helen said. Thiago had finished loading now, but he was still on the dock. He was looking around, searching the middle distance, as if looking for something. Or someone. *Me*, Helen thought, her heart lifting. *He's looking for me*. 'I don't want to write scripts. I'm a novelist. I want to write another novel.'

The voice on the end of the phone made a noise that was almost as dismissive as its tone. 'Trust me, there's more money in this than writing a book. And besides, it'll rehabilitate you. In the eyes of the public.'

Thiago found her from across the dock, where she stood in

the harbour breeze with a phone clamped to her ear, whorls of holidaymakers eddying around her.

'I'm sorry,' Helen said, returning Thiago's smile across the distance that separated them. 'Really, I am. But I'm not interested.'

'What?' Claude said, obviously flabbergasted. 'But . . . you can't turn it down.'

'I haven't signed a contract.'

'No, but—'

'Claude,' she said, beginning to walk back towards Thiago. 'Have you ever thought that you might owe me an apology?'

'Look—' he said, still spluttering.

'Maybe you – and the rest of the production company – can work out how to say sorry, and I'll think about how I might be able to fit the film around my schedule. My agent will be able to get hold of me,' she told him, and hung up.

Thiago started towards her and they met a few feet from where the *Alejandra* and its little flock of academics waited.

'For a moment there I thought you were going to leave without saying goodbye,' Thiago said, once they were close enough to hear each other over the hubbub of the dock around them.

'Yes,' Helen said. 'Well, for a moment . . . I thought I was going to *say* goodbye.'

His eyebrows rose in surprise for a second, and then he smiled. 'You mean . . . you're *not* going to say goodbye?'

She looked past him at Rathbrooke's waiting visitors, offering a brief wave accompanied by a smile.

'Well,' she said, 'it just occurred to me that the island is the perfect place for a writing retreat.'

Thiago nodded, the smile still warm in his eyes. 'That is very true.'

'And I think I might have an idea for a new book.'

His smile widened. 'A novel?'

'Yes,' Helen said, her heart beating a little faster at the notion. 'A novel.'

'That is very good news,' he said. 'And you're right, Rathbrooke would be the perfect place to write it.'

'Especially,' Helen agreed, 'since Rathbrooke is my inspiration. At least, it is, among . . . other things.'

Thiago had a little flash of mischief in his dark eyes now as he said, 'What other things?'

Helen grimaced, laughing at herself, although only a little. 'I think there might be a pirate in it.'

'Ah. A good pirate?'

She looked up at him. They were standing toe to toe. 'Is there such a thing?'

He grinned down at her. 'I think you're the one who needs to answer that question.' He glanced over her head, then reached out to take her suitcase and put it down by her feet so that her hands were empty. Then her hands were in his, both of them, clasped firmly in his rough fingers.

'Has it got a title?'

'Not yet.'

'I've got a suggestion.'

'Oh?'

'Yes. How about *All's Well That Ends Well*?'

She squinted up at him, aware that the academics were listening as well as watching. 'I think you'll find that's already taken.'

Thiago shrugged. 'Ah well. Plenty of time to work that out, I suppose.'

'I hope so,' she said, and then stood on tiptoe, and pressed her lips to his in a lingering kiss, before saying, 'Although I'd like to get to work on it as soon as possible.'

If he was surprised by the kiss, he didn't show it. Thiago threaded an arm around her instead, pulling her in for another.

Thiago looked down at her as they finally parted, his dark eyes even darker in the shadow of the sun. 'I have wanted to do that,' he said, quietly, 'since the night you first brandished a poker at me, Helen Thorne.'

She laughed. 'Hmm. Me too. I thought it was against my better judgement.'

He tipped his head to one side, studying her, earrings glinting gold in his ears. *Pirate*. 'And now?'

'Now,' she said, 'I think my judgement might be pretty good, actually.'

'Come on,' Thiago said, picking up her suitcase for the second time that day, although this time he kept an arm around her, too, drawing her back towards the boat. 'Let's get home. We've both got work to do.'

Helen's phone rang again twice as they made their way out of Seahouses harbour, but she didn't look at it. She was already listening to the academics introduce themselves. She let it ring until the signal dropped out. The ringing stopped and then there was only the peace of the North Sea waves, the birds in the sky and the people around her, each telling their own stories in their own words, in their own way.

Acknowledgements

The idea for *The Hidden Library* had been bouncing around in my mind for a while but only really started to take shape properly a couple of years ago, after a chat over dinner with Doctor Matthew Wagner, senior lecturer in theatre studies at the University of Surrey. One of his many specialisms is Shakespeare in performance. I had originally thought that the manuscript at the centre of this story could be the fabled *Love's Labour's Won*, which is thought to have existed as a companion piece to the still extant *Love's Labour's Lost* and seemed like a fitting element for a romance novel. Thanks are due to Matt and also to my husband Adam Newell, who knows so much about so many different subjects (and has shelves of books on most of them just ready for me to raid before I even know I need them), that listening to the two of them talk about the history of Shakespeare in print and performance made me realise that *The History of Cardenio* would work far better. Returning home and looking at our 'Shakespeare shelf' gave me almost everything I needed. I've since added several volumes to that shelf specifically about *Cardenio* and also Shakespeare's mulberry (about which I could have written a whole book on its own), so we're all winners here. I loved the connections with *Don Quixote*, too. Why are we readers if not to disappear into another world? I've often wanted never to come back from the escape offered by a particularly well-written printed page, and despite the complications of four centuries' distance from the 'in-jokes' in Cervantes' story, it's hard not to feel sympathy for the want-to-be knight's tragi-comic adventures. Also, as a former writer of fanfiction, the idea that 400 years ago Shakespeare was essentially writing his own fanfic of Cervantes' smash hit novel makes me smile.

I live in Cumbria, so getting over to Northumberland was not difficult. It is such a beautiful coast, and I enjoyed exploring it more while I worked out the exact setting for the book. This research included walking the pilgrim's route to Lindisfarne at low tide, with Patrick Norris of Footsteps in Northumberland as a guide. Patrick is a true font of knowledge of both the human and natural history of the area and I highly recommend walking with him – either to Lindisfarne or on any of his other guided hikes. It was November when we made the crossing, and the only people we met on the way there or back was another guide Patrick knew with a party of librarians from Wooler, who shocked me by naming *The Lighthouse Bookshop* as soon as Patrick introduced us. If that's not a spiritual experience for an author I don't know what is! I was so shocked, in fact, that I didn't write down your names. But thank you, it meant a lot. Libraries forever.

Rathbrooke island is fictional, as is Rathbrooke Hall. The latter is based partly on Levens Hall in Cumbria, which is of a similar age and from where I borrowed the beautifully warped lead windows and the tooled leather wallcovering. It is well worth a visit, especially in summer – the gardens are stunning. The walled garden was partly inspired by Gertrude Jekyll's walled garden on Lindisfarne. The peel (or pele) tower is a combination of the one in the village where I live (thank you to Candi Hetherington for showing me around) and the home of The Pele pub in Corbridge. It's right opposite Forum Books, which makes for at least two good reasons to visit this beautiful town in Northumbria.

The team at Simon & Schuster have always been so good to work with, especially my editor Louise Davies. Thank you to Clare Hey for believing in my stories, and thank you both for your encouragement, guidance and keen eye. Thank you to Pip Watkins for the beautiful cover, I love it. Lastly but far from least, huge thanks to my agent Ella Kahn, for putting me in the right place at the right time in a world where there increasingly seems to be neither.